To Keep You Near

TESS BARNETT

ISBN: 0997861517
ISBN-13: 978-0997861518

ACKNOWLEDGMENTS

Thank you to Christa and Emily for all the encouragement, enthusiasm, and dirty pictures.

1

For the first time in a long while, things had actually been looking up. Trent had Ciaran back—actually Ciaran, and not a shell of a person—and they were on their way to a new life together. Sure, he hadn't imagined that life would ever involve the hunter who'd once held him hostage or the witch who'd nearly killed Ciaran in the first place, but he could adjust. That part was only temporary. He had Ciaran. That's what mattered.

And then their carriage had come to a sudden halt in the iridescent dark of Tír na nÓg. Ciaran had leaned out of the window to call to the driver and been forcibly dragged from his seat by two sets of muscular arms. Trent called out to him, and he heard Julien moving immediately, but a biting cold washed over the carriage, and Trent's vision blurred. Every muscle in his body stung from the chill, holding him in place until he lost consciousness completely.

He had woken up in an empty room made of the same slick black stone that made up the rest of Tír na nÓg, his hands bound behind his back with a smooth cord. His body still ached from whatever had chilled him to the bone. Julien and Noah were already awake, and the witch's hands gave a violent spark with every hasty phrase he muttered, but his wrists remained bound. The hunter stood by the door, leaning his shoulder against the wall to listen through the gap between wood and stone.

"What the hell happened?" Trent asked, shifting himself up onto his knees with some difficulty.

"They took Ciaran," Noah answered. A bead of sweat rolled down his temple, and he wiped it away on his shoulder as it reached his cheek.

"They? They who?"

"I think we're about to find out," Julien murmured from across the room. He looked ready to spring when the door creaked open, but though Trent could see his shoulders tensing, something kept him in place. A man in a simple tunic appeared in the doorway, and he walked by Julien and Noah without even a glance.

"Tar liom," he said, gesturing to Trent with a casual wave of his hand. When Trent only stared at him, the fairy gripped him by the shoulder and hauled him to his feet, letting him stumble as he was dragged from the room.

Trent was pulled down a long corridor and pushed back to his knees in a room draped with tall tapestries and lit by a single low fire in a brazier near the door. Three men stood in front of him, and when they turned to him, he spotted Ciaran at the far wall, bound to the stone by thick cuffs at his wrists and ankles. The fairy instantly jerked against the dull metal chain, but he couldn't budge. The skin on his arms already looked torn and red.

"Tá sé seo an ceann," one of the men rumbled, amusement in his voice. He looked down at Trent with folded arms and tilted his head. His dark hair hung down to his shoulders, kept out of his face by a pair of thin braids fastened at the back of his head, but his pointed ears poked through. He had a rough face half hidden by a thick beard that he idly scratched as he looked Trent up and down.

"I remembered men being bigger than this," he chuckled.

Ciaran lurched forward, his movement clanking the single link of chain keeping him against the wall. "You lay a hand on him, Gaibhne, and your brother will have to make you a new one," he growled, but the man only clicked his tongue like he was dealing with a child.

"Such threats from someone who should already be dead." The larger man turned back to face Ciaran with a dark smile in his eyes. "You owe a debt, Scal Balb. Our brothers were killed by your son's cruel game, and we lost our father from grief. Because you hid."

"It doesn't occur to you that the whole issue might have been avoided had your brothers not tried to murder me in the first place?"

"Blood was shed in your name!" Gaibhne snapped, taking a step forward and prodding Ciaran roughly in the chest. "Blood unjustly taken. You will repay us in kind, or those dear to you will suffer in your place."

"You can't touch him," Ciaran objected, but Trent could see the hint of fear in his eyes. "He's human. He isn't subject to our laws—you've no right to him."

"Ah, but is he the only one dear to you?" The man's voice dropped to a low, dangerous rumble as he leaned in, an inch from Ciaran's nose. "That sister of yours is looking very lonely lately, all by herself in that unguarded estate."

Every muscle in Ciaran's body tensed, but the chains binding him only dug into his skin as he pulled against them. "You wouldn't dare."

"Dare to take what's owed to us?"

"I'll pay you," Ciaran countered. "Let the Court decide an amount."

"You want to go before the High King?" Gaibhne snorted. "To bring this shame on your family and face the Court after all this time?" He shook his head. "For a crime such as this—the High King may just decide you deserve to die. All *we're* asking is a favor."

Ciaran paused, his lip curling into a suspicious sneer. "A favor."

"This all began because you wanted to leave Tír na nÓg, didn't it? You wanted to be detached from your people? You do what we ask—clear your debt—and we'll keep your secret. If not, all of Tír na nÓg will know what you've done. You'll be hunted. So will your pets," he added, tilting his head in Trent's direction.

"If I cooperate, you threaten my sister, and if I don't, you threaten my lover? Your negotiation skills are lacking."

"Consider dear Airmed collateral," Gaibhne said. "Do as you're told, and no harm will come to her. You have my word. I can't say the same for your human friends, should you decide to run." He let out a chuckle that sounded like grinding gravel. "Not that running is an option for you."

Ciaran hesitated, keeping his eyes locked on the other man as though studying him for signs of a lie. Finally, he glanced over

Gaibhne's shoulder at Trent, who could only stare at him from the floor with a helpless look on his face. He had no advice to offer; he didn't even dare move for fear of drawing the wrath of the two men standing guard beside him. They both looked like they could have broken him in half with one hand even without the supernatural strength Trent knew they had.

Ciaran turned his gaze back to the larger man's smirking face. "What is it you want?"

"Appropriate recompense," Gaibhne drawled. "We decided it's only fitting for you to go on a quest. Don't you think?" He smiled at Ciaran's scowl. "We want you to fetch us a prize, just as our brothers were made to do for your vengeful son."

"What sort of prize? The world above isn't so ripe with treasure these days."

"There is at least one place yet where one may find magic. The item you seek is in Lochlann."

The color drained from Ciaran's face, and Trent risked shifting on his knees to try to get a look at the fairy over Gaibhne's broad back.

"Lochlann," Ciaran repeated, his voice soft. His arms went slack in their restraints, and he let out a silent breath before looking back up at Gaibhne. "If you want me dead, I'd rather you just kill me. Even if I could make the trip—even if there were still anyone there to meet me—what makes you think I'll be able to get what you want?"

"I'm certain you'll find a way or die trying," Gaibhne answered with a chortle.

A servant stepped through the doorway looking meek and apologetic, and the man pulled away from Ciaran just enough to snap at him.

"I told you we weren't to be disturbed."

"Mo Thiarna, I beg forgiveness," the servant answered with a slight bow. "You have a visitor."

"Then send them away," Gaibhne said, a patronizing tone in his voice.

"I didn't dare. The Lonnbéimnech awaits you."

Ciaran's eyebrows lifted in surprise, but Trent could only look between the men in front of him in confusion. There was entirely too much Gaelic being thrown around. He guessed he should feel grateful there was any English happening at all, even if it was most likely only to keep him intimidated.

Gaibhne seemed pleased by the news. "I wondered if he might show himself," he muttered, and then he nodded to the servant. "Bring him." He turned to Ciaran with a renewed smirk on his lips, and a moment later, Lugh's hulking form appeared in the room.

"Athair," Lugh said dryly, not seeming concerned in the slightest by the sight of Ciaran bound to the wall.

"Mo mhac," Ciaran answered in kind.

"You're just in time, Samildánach," Gaibhne said, and he showed his hands in welcome. Trent huffed out a short sigh. How many names did Lugh have?

"A servant in my grandfather's house confessed to me that she had told you about my father's unfortunate survival." Lugh barely spared a glance at Ciaran. "His debt is his own, but the blood of your brothers stains my hands because of his crime. I would ask your intentions."

"Only to find justice. Cian has been given a quest."

Lugh lifted one eyebrow and finally looked at his father. "And you expect him to complete it?"

"We have things he considers valuable well within our reach," Gaibhne answered with a pointed glance in Trent's direction.

"You put too much stock in his affections," Lugh said dryly. "He will vanish the moment you set him free." Trent scowled up at him, but he didn't seem to notice. Lugh watched Ciaran's frowning face for a moment, considering. "I will be his escort. Whatever task you have set him, I will ensure he carries it out."

Gaibhne shifted his weight, looking less than convinced. "We're to believe you won't help your father, your own blood, to escape?"

Lugh's expression visibly darkened, and he took a single step forward. Gaibhne stood his ground, allowing the other man to close the distance between them, but he didn't seem thrilled about it.

"If you question my honor, perhaps you would prefer to challenge me on the proving grounds and claim your satisfaction there?"

Now it was Gaibhne's turn to grow pale. He shook his head and lifted his hands, glancing toward his brothers as though confirming their agreement. Trent suspected he just didn't want to look Lugh in the eye.

5

"It is an acceptable arrangement," Gaibhne admitted after his brothers each gave him a brief nod. He gestured to the servant still lurking near the doorway, who moved forward to release Ciaran from the shackles binding his wrists and ankles.

Ciaran crossed the room as soon as he was free, placing himself between Trent and the other burly brothers, but he didn't try to run. He jutted out his chin at Gaibhne with one guarding hand on his lover's shoulder.

"What is it you'd have me die fetching, then?"

"The Gambanteinn," the other fairy answered, carefully alternating his attention between father and son. "It is a staff that is rumored to be able to remove all impurities from any metal it touches. With it, my brothers and I would be able to create treasures such as the Tuath Dé have never seen. Tools, jewelry, weapons, all of unparalleled quality. We could renew the pride of our people."

"For all that's worth," Ciaran snorted. He gave a weary sigh through his nose. "Fine," he said after a moment. "I agree to your terms. As if I had any choice."

"I'm glad you understand your situation," Gaibhne said with a smile that made Trent want to punch him. They couldn't even have a day, not a single day, where things went right.

He looked up when he felt Ciaran squeeze his shoulder.

"On your feet, lad," the fairy said gently. "We've a little side trip to take."

Gaibhne's servant led them back to the room where Trent had been held, keeping one eye behind him as they walked the long hallway. As soon as the door was open, Julien rushed forward to slam his shoulder into their captor's chest. The servant gave a startled grunt as his back hit the far wall, and Julien pinned him there with the weight of his body. Ciaran put a protective hand against Trent's chest to keep his lover behind him, fully prepared to shout at Julien not to be an idiot, but the hunter froze the instant Lugh appeared over Ciaran's shoulder.

"What is this?" he asked, his shoulder still pressing the fairy to the wall. The servant stayed obediently still, but Ciaran gave a silent sigh. Even a Tuath Dé servant could overcome a man if politeness hadn't stayed his hand. He was already regretting agreeing to travel with the hunter.

"Peace, an duine," Lugh answered. "Come."

Julien hesitated, but then he stepped back from the servant, who dusted off the front of his tunic with an air of disdain. Ciaran looked between Julien and Lugh, squinting skeptically at them. Since when did the hunter take orders—especially from a fairy?

The servant cleared his throat as Noah peeked through the doorway. "Your belongings have been kept for you," he said, "and you are to be escorted back to the world above. From there your concerns are your own until you return."

"What the hell is going on?" Julien demanded, twisting his arms against the cords binding his wrists.

"I'll explain on the way," Ciaran said with a sigh. "Let's not linger."

The servant freed Trent, Julien, and Noah, easily loosing the knots that even the witch's magic couldn't undo. He led them through the estate and to a small storage room. He gestured for them to enter, and they gathered their things in tense silence. Noah rushed for the silver-edged box on the table and held it to his chest like a treasure, tracing the spiral carvings with his fingers as though testing them for damage. Relief flooded his face as he found it unharmed. He couldn't lose his link to Sabin—not when he'd finally gotten the chance to make contact again.

Ciaran took up the duffel bag he shared with Trent and carried it over his shoulder, feeling his lover's eyes on him but not quite wanting to meet them. He knew Trent would have a hundred questions, but he also knew the boy wouldn't thank him for bringing up the more personal ones in front of Julien and Noah.

When they were fully outfitted, the servant tilted his head for them to follow and showed them to a narrow road at the back of the garden, where a fresh carriage awaited them. They settled inside, Trent and Ciaran sitting across from Julien and Noah as before, with the addition of Lugh sitting stoically on Trent's other side, causing him to press uncomfortably close against Ciaran. The wheels began to move at the pull of the heavy beetle strapped to the lead, urged on by the driver's clicking tongue, and they all rocked with the movement on the uneven streets.

"Well this feels a lot like being back at square one," Noah said.

"You're gonna share what all that was about, right?"

"I've been given a quest," Ciaran answered. "I owe a blood debt, and it's time for me to pay it. I'm to retrieve a magical artifact from a very dangerous place. Obviously, it's nothing to do with either of you, so you're more than welcome to piss off as soon as we're above."

"What about the spell?" Noah said, leaning forward slightly in his seat. "If we leave, you two will still have the whole mismatched-immortality problem."

"That is their problem," Julien pointed out. "I agreed to stay while you worked this spell for them, not to go on another fairy quest." He tilted his head at Lugh with a skeptical frown. "And I thought you didn't want anything to do with him?" he added, poking a thumb in Ciaran's direction.

"I am the insurance," Lugh answered simply. "His debt is partly mine. So I will come."

"I said I'd help," Noah interjected, squeezing the box in his lap. "We made a deal, right?"

"Not to help a fairy pay off blood debts," Julien countered. He frowned across at Ciaran. "Why agree anyway? What do you care if you have a debt? Your boyfriend is right here; they can't get to him with you watching him, can they?"

Ciaran paused as he looked at him, but then he sighed. "They threatened Airmed. If I don't bring back what they want, they'll kill her. Or worse."

Julien seemed to tense in his seat, and Noah looked up at him with renewed determination. The hunter glanced down at his companion and nodded, neither of them needing to exchange words.

"Then I guess we're on board," the hunter said. "For her sake," he clarified with a pointed scowl, "not yours."

"I'm so glad," Ciaran answered, not a shred of sincerity in his voice.

Trent turned in his seat to look up at Ciaran. "What is Lochlann?" he asked. "Why is it so dangerous to go there?"

Ciaran hesitated before answering. "Lochlann is—unsurprisingly—the home of the Lochlannan. They're a timeless, magical people, brutal and secretive. But no one has heard from them in thousands of years. We assume they've simply vanished, the way magic things do sometimes. There's likely nothing left in Lochlann at all, after all this time. But the journey is still dangerous."

"A nine-day voyage by sea, so they say," Lugh cut in, drawing the eyes of the other men in the carriage. "Through storms and monster-infested waters."

"By sea?" Trent echoed with a faint grimace. "Great." He could already feel his stomach churning along with the waves.

A few beats of silence passed in the carriage, and then Noah gave his box a decisive pat and offered his companions a cheerful smile. "Well, if we're going to go on a dangerous fairy quest, I'm going to need to make a pit stop. I had to leave all my stuff behind in Vancouver, and I'm pretty useless without supplies. Unless you think I can offer these timeless beings some yoga lessons in exchange for whatever we're looking for."

"What sort of supplies?" Ciaran asked.

"Some herbs, incense, eye of newt, toe of frog, wool of bat, tongue of dog—you know, witch stuff."

Trent eyed him uncertainly. "Are you serious?"

"No. Well, yes. Herbs and incense, yes. Some gross stuff, yes. But I don't think I could pick a newt out of a lineup of salamanders, and that's the sort of accuracy that really matters, so I usually skip that part." He smiled at Trent, then let out a small huff when the younger man only stared at him. "Would it kill you guys to let a guy lighten the mood?"

"We are nearing the borders of Tír na nÓg," Lugh interrupted. The carriage rolled to a stop, and they started the long trek back up the winding stone stairs toward the strange glowing portal hidden in the ruin above.

Trent peered over the edge of the steps at the gently lapping black water, and he grudgingly allowed Ciaran to hold his hand as they made their way toward the surface. He'd had enough of underground and darkness.

2

At the top of the long, narrow stairway, the portal snapped open as soon as Ciaran approached it, and he led the way through into the stone tunnel of Newgrange, which was even darker than the cave they left. The light of the moon barely reached inside the low tunnel.

Trent took a single step over the barrier and into the circular room, and then he crumpled, slipping free of Ciaran's hand as he tumbled to the ground. A wringing pain twisted its way through his stomach and his brain, and he clutched helplessly at his belly. He distantly heard two others hit the ground behind him, and when he turned his head, he saw Julien and Noah on their knees, doubled over as he was.

"Shite, forgot that part," Ciaran sighed. He crouched beside Trent and put a comforting hand on his back, stroking the younger man's skin through his shirt. "Just breathe, a mhuirnín. It'll pass soon."

Trent did his best to do as he was told, but the tightening in his stomach was torture. He squeezed his eyes shut and focused on his breath and the gentle heat of Ciaran's hand, and after an eternity, the pain eased to a dull, manageable throb. When he opened his eyes, Julien and Noah were already on their feet, looking pale but steady.

"What...?" was all Trent could get out as Ciaran helped him to his feet.

"Airmed said that time passes differently in Tír na nÓg," Noah spoke up, his voice a little rough. "Humans don't age when we're inside, but as soon as we leave, time catches up with us all at once."

"Are you fucking kidding me?" Trent scoffed. He wished he didn't have to lean on Ciaran for support. "You couldn't have mentioned? How long were we down there, really?"

"Well, *really* is a matter of perspective, I think," Ciaran said, but he cleared of his throat at the glare in his lover's eyes. "Well, we were there for a few days, maybe a week or so…?" He shrugged. "I'd guess about a month has passed out here, most likely."

"A month?" Noah squeaked. His lips pressed into a thin line as he looked down at the box in his arms, but he didn't offer an explanation.

"Come along then, you lot," Ciaran said, urging Trent gently along with him as they headed down the dark tunnel. "We'll get something in your bellies, and you'll be just fine."

"Why don't they look like they're dying, and I feel like I'm dying?" Trent muttered, tilting his chin toward Noah and Julien as he clutched at his stomach like a child.

"Well, one of them's a witch, so that probably helps, and the other's a big important hunter of some sort, apparently." Ciaran glanced sidelong at Julien, but the other man ignored his barbs.

Outside the stone mound, Ciaran took a deep breath of fresh air and let it out in a long sigh. Lugh whistled, and his mottled grey horse came immediately to his call, trotting to a stop a few feet from his master.

"We'll need to get to Carnalridge," Ciaran said as his son settled himself in the saddle. "But these ones will want rest first."

"Nearest village is called Donore," Lugh offered. "Food and shelter there. We can make for Carnalridge at first light."

"Don't suppose you have any spare horses," Noah piped up. "Not that I know how to ride one anyway, I guess."

"Donore is less than three kilometers. Even a man can walk that far." Lugh clicked his tongue at his horse and set it off down the hill at an amble, leaving the others to follow him on foot with bags in hand.

"What a gentleman," Noah sighed. He exchanged a small smile with Julien as the hunter shifted the bag on his shoulder and started after the rest of their little convoy.

Trent pushed away from Ciaran to walk on his own after a few minutes, the pain in his stomach finally dwindling to a thin ache. He still felt lightheaded and exhausted, but he could at least walk without leaning against the fairy.

They walked down the dark road, the asphalt cutting through the fields and hills around them, until they finally came upon the village of Donore. The streetlights were yellowed and dim, matching the faded paint and the worn bricks of the houses they passed. The town didn't seem to have much to it other than small homes and a single low-slung shop labeled "Drew's Stores," and even that was shut tight by rolling metal doors. Lugh waited for them outside a pale yellow building with a sign for "Daly's Inn" and a carved wooden marker above the door that read "Brú na Bóinne."

"I will collect you here at dawn," Lugh said, gesturing toward the door with his chin. He looked strange in the middle of the village street, his heavy cloak only half-hiding the assorted weaponry weighing down his horse's saddle. Trent wondered if anyone could see him, or if he cared.

"You aren't staying?" Ciaran asked. "Not much of a guard, are you?"

"I will be nearby," Lugh promised. "But Milesian comforts are of no interest to me. Make sure you are ready to leave when I arrive," he added, and he turned his horse and continued down the street without waiting for an answer.

Ciaran huffed and watched his back as he rode, but his glaring was interrupted by Noah's curious voice.

"What's a Milesian?"

"He means Irish," Ciaran grumped. "Humans. He's just being a ponce." He shifted the bag on his shoulder and led the way through the creaking door. Trent moved to fumble in their shared bag for his wallet, hoping he still had enough Euros left to pay for a room, but by the time he found it, Ciaran was already smiling and thanking the girl at the desk for her help. He took Trent by the arm to guide him up the stairs, glancing over his shoulder to make sure Julien and Noah were still following.

The room was small and warm, with a matching pair of standard beds. Trent happily collapsed onto the nearest one, not even flinching when he felt Ciaran's gentle hand in his hair.

"I'll fetch us some food," Ciaran said, and he paused to stare across the room at Julien and Noah. "I can trust you to behave yourselves with him, can't I?"

"What do you think we're going to do?" Julien argued. "We agreed to help."

"Aye," Ciaran agreed, but he seemed skeptical as he straightened. "But that doesn't mean I trust you. You have a history of getting young boys into trouble."

"Are you afraid one of us is going to get him pregnant while you go on a food run?" Noah let out a soft laugh.

"Please stop talking," Trent rumbled, his face half buried in the duvet. "We've been together for an hour and I'm already sick of this shit."

Ciaran lingered just a moment more so that he could squint suspiciously at Julien as he passed, but then he made his way back out of the room and down the stairs.

Noah dropped down onto the empty bed while Julien set down his bag and rubbed at the red mark his new eyepatch had pressed into his forehead.

"Can I still borrow your laptop?" the witch asked, leaning over on the bed until he was almost laying down in an attempt to catch Trent's eye. Trent gestured vaguely toward the duffel bag on the floor, so Noah took the wave as agreement and slid to the floor to dig through it. He crawled back up onto the bed and plugged the cord in with the laptop on his knees.

"What is it you're looking for?" Julien asked as he shrugged off his jacket. He sat beside Noah on the bed, but a wary glance in Trent's direction kept him from leaning too close.

"Somebody on the way to wherever Carnalridge is, hopefully," Noah answered. "I can ask around on some groups I'm in. I just need some basics; I need to know where to shop, at least." He paused. "Not that I have any money to shop with. Guess I'll cross that bridge when I come to it."

They waited in silence while Noah tapped out a few messages. When he was finished, he set the laptop aside to wait for replies and began to dig through the nightstand drawers in search of stationary. He leaned over the little corner table and hesitated with the pen just

13

over the paper. He needed to write to Sabin, but what could he possibly say? There were a million things to explain, and every one of them would make his young friend worry for him. What he really wanted was to see him, to squeeze him and ruffle his hair and remind each other that they were all right—but that was impossible. He let out a silent sigh as he stared down at the blank page. Simple was best.

Sabin,

I'm sorry I haven't written. A lot of stuff has happened. I'm not sure you'd believe all of it if I told you. For now, I'm safe. I'm in Ireland with Julien and some friends that we've agreed to help. One of them is a fairy. A real one. I met a lot of fairies, actually. They're very strange people. A kind one sent this box to you. I have an identical one. He said that anything I put in mine will appear in yours, and anything you put in yours will reach me. Maybe keep that a secret from your keepers for as long as you can.

I'll be able to send you anything you need now. And I'll write a lot more. In the meantime, see what you can do with this mushroom. I picked it from underground, where the fairies live. If you come up with any good uses for it, drop me a line—I have a whole bagful.

I hope to hear from you soon. Take care of yourself.

Love from,
Noah

The witch leaned back on the bed, carefully folded his note in half, and plucked one of the less-damaged mushrooms from Julien's satchel. He tugged the box toward him and lifted the lid, peeking inside and half expecting to find a void, or a portal, or even something sparkling and fairy-like—but it was just the inside of the box, empty and lined with dark velvet. He was grateful to Cu for the gift, but he wasn't sure how the magic was supposed to work. Noah tucked the note and the dimly glowing mushroom into the box, and when he shut the lid, there was a small snap from within. The carved silver dogs shifted on the front of the chest, dropping from rearing on their hind legs into a relaxed position lying near the base of the box. He hesitated and glanced back at Julien, who was watching over his shoulder with intent curiosity. When he opened the box again, only the soft velvet lining remained.

"Well, I guess that worked. The dogs are a nice touch. Some sort of 'message received' notice, I guess? Neat."

He smiled at Julien despite the hunter's skeptical frown. Maybe someday he would learn to trust that not all magic in the world was dangerous.

"That's for your young friend?" Julien asked.

Noah nodded. "I hope he hasn't worried too much. I don't like not hearing from him for this long, either."

"I'm sure he's all right," the hunter said softly, and Noah smiled and touched his knee. It was cute seeing him try to be comforting. He knew it didn't come naturally.

Noah returned to the laptop and sat with it open, taking notes on the remaining stationary. He'd promised Trent and Ciaran that he would help bind them together to solve their immortality problem, but first he needed to know exactly what he was doing. It was going to be difficult even with the few resources he found. But he was determined to try.

Ciaran returned with his arms full of bags and Styrofoam carry-out boxes, which he dumped unceremoniously onto the bed beside Trent's dozing face.

"There wasn't much this late at night, but I made do," he said. He didn't even look too surly as he handed Noah and Julien their share.

Noah could smell the oil before he even lifted the lid. When he looked inside, he found exactly what he expected—battered fish laying on a bed of thick fries. The smell made his stomach slightly sick, but he didn't want to complain. It was very late, and some food was better than none. He waited until Julien had his own box open on his lap before picking up the fish with two fingers and adding it wordlessly to his lover's portion.

Julien frowned in understanding and set his food aside to bend over his bag. He retrieved a slightly broken granola bar from a side pocket and offered it to Noah, who took it with a grateful smile. He nudged the hunter with his shoulder in thanks.

The movement didn't go unnoticed. "What," Ciaran said as Trent slowly lifted himself up into sitting, "are you on a diet?"

"I'm a vegetarian, actually. But it's fine," Noah assured him with a smile. "Thanks for getting it."

Ciaran stared at him with his lip slightly curled. "Why?" he asked, as though a vegetarian was a strange and unusual creature.

"Because farmed animals have next to no legal protection from industrialized cruelty?" Noah frowned at the skeptical lift of the fairy's eyebrow. "Also, it's *sattva*." He gestured vaguely at his head. "Good for the mind. It's a Hindu thing. Being clear-headed is important for working magic. The non-fairy kind, anyway."

"Nonsense," Ciaran scoffed. He tucked his legs underneath him on the bed and dug out the contents of his own bag—a sealed bowl, a bottle of milk, and a box containing a large serving of what looked like some sort of fruit crumble. "Are you the sort what throws paint on fur coats?"

"No."

"You look like the sort what throws paint on fur coats."

"Jesus Christ," Trent spoke up, pausing to swallow his mouthful of fish before continuing. "You're about to eat nothing but pastry and fudge for dinner, and you're giving him shit about not liking meat?"

Ciaran threw the younger man a petulant frown and took a pointed bite of his berry crumble. Trent barely glanced in Noah's direction, seeming to want to avoid his gaze, but the witch caught his eye for just long enough to show him a faint smile.

"Ah, here's something," Noah spoke up when Trent's laptop gave a soft ping. He set down his box of fries and wiped his hands on his jeans before touching the keyboard. He tapped out a reply bent over the laptop and then looked up at Ciaran. "Friend of a friend says he can set me up if we can meet him. He's in Belfast. Is that on the way to where we're going from wherever we are?"

"It could be," Ciaran answered, "if you promise not to try any more soul-sucking spells with whatever you get."

Noah snorted. "Believe me, one trip inside that brain was more than enough."

"Weren't you the one who asked for Noah's help?" Julien cut in, watching the fairy with one accusing eye. "You've got a funny way of being gracious."

"Didn't I just bring you both some supper? And it's me who's being ungracious."

"Shut up," Trent begged, groaning in frustration. Ciaran offered him a smile that almost passed as apologetic and mimed zipping his mouth closed, so Julien backed down and settled for maintaining his grumpy frown.

Julien had laid down early, his carved leather eyepatch abandoned on the nightstand, and Noah had kept to himself, staring at Trent's laptop screen and scrolling through pages until well into the night. But it was quiet now that everyone had gone to bed. Once he had eaten, Trent had begun to feel more human and less corpse. He didn't care in the slightest that Noah and Julien were in the room with them, no matter how often Ciaran glared over at them, as long as it was quiet. He was with Ciaran again. He was able to lie in bed with him, the fairy's feather-light arm around his waist, and feel his lover's heat pressed against his back. Even the warm puffs of breath on the back of his ear were comforting to him.

The room was quiet and dark, disturbed only by the occasional shifting on the bed across from them. Trent knew that he should sleep—it had already been late when they arrived, and Lugh had promised to come for them at dawn. But despite the lingering ache in his bones from the accelerated passing of time, he couldn't shut his eyes. He was on a crazy fairy mission again. There weren't going to be any relaxing evenings or trips to Greece. Not for a while, anyway. All he had in front of him for now was a week-long boat ride to a place that may or may not be extremely dangerous, depending on whether or not the mystical people that even fairies are wary of were still there. He felt remarkably out of place.

Trent took a slow, deep breath and let it out in a sigh, trying to will himself into sleep. He settled back against Ciaran's chest, but as soon as his eyes slipped closed, he tensed at the subtle movement of the fairy's hand drifting under his t-shirt. Ciaran's fingers brushed the skin of his stomach, tracing slow circles of heat that instantly ignited his blood. Trent sucked in a breath and kept it there. Ciaran was sleeping. He was just being touchy in his sleep, as he tended to do. In a minute, he'd doze off again and roll over, taking some of the blanket with him.

Ciaran's hand moved beneath the waistband of Trent's sleep pants, fingers slithering through soft black hair on the way to their goal. Trent seized the fairy's wrist and squeezed it tight in warning, but even the faintest brush of his lover's fingertips was enough to make him jump. Ciaran slid through his grip, undeterred, and took hold of his swiftly awakening prick. Trent dug his nails into Ciaran's skin even as his head fell back against the fairy's shoulder. He had to wake him up. No matter how easily Ciaran stroked him into almost painful arousal, he couldn't let him—

Trent bit the inside of his cheek to keep any noise from escaping him as Ciaran gave a firm squeeze, running his thumb over the tender slit at the head of his cock. He gave another insistent shove to the fairy's hand, but when he felt the wet heat of Ciaran's tongue tracing the shell of his ear, his efforts weakened, and a faint whine slipped past his gritted teeth.

"Hush now, a mhuirnín," Ciaran barely breathed against his neck. "They'll hear you."

Trent gave in, turning his head to hide his panting breath in the pillow. His hands balled into fists around the blanket, and he tried to keep still and silent as Ciaran's teeth fastened on the tender skin at the back of his neck. His lover drew shudders from him with each slow, teasing stroke, and soon Trent was half suffocating himself in an attempt to muffle his breathless whimpers, his bottom lip caught tightly in his teeth. He could feel the shameful heat in his cheeks at the thought of their companions overhearing him, but he couldn't bring himself to push the other man away.

When he let out a soft moan, Ciaran slid an arm under his head and tugged him close, covering his mouth with one slender hand. He kept Trent in place with a firm hold as the boy arched against him and twitched his hips into his caress.

The tension in Trent's stomach grew unbearable as Ciaran's expert touch pushed him to the edge, every heated kiss on his neck edging him closer. Just when he thought he couldn't take any more, Ciaran disappeared beneath the blanket in one fluid, silent motion, and Trent hastily clamped both hands over his own mouth to keep in the groan that threatened to escape as the fairy's lips closed around him. His hips jerked upwards instantly, his body curling away from the pillow as he spilled his release into his lover's eager mouth. Ciaran's hand on his stomach kept him steady until he relaxed against the mattress, and the fairy placed a single, soft kiss on Trent's hip before returning to his side.

Trent lay still, hands still hiding his mouth as he caught his breath in the darkness. As soon as his heart began to slow, he elbowed Ciaran sharply in the chest and turned away from him, tucking the blanket around his shoulders with a grumpy huff. He shut his eyes with a frown on his lips, but he softened just slightly at the low chuckle from the man behind him.

3

True to his word, Lugh came banging on the door to their room just as the sun was beginning to peek over the horizon. It was only a cursory gesture, as he opened the door and let himself in a moment later. Only Julien was awake, quietly gathering what belongings had made their way out of his bag the night before. Ciaran sat up obediently when Lugh barked at him, but he still made the others wait while he had a long shower.

"We're making a pit stop in Belfast," Noah said, looking up at the surly fairy by the door. "Do you have any recommendation for how to get there?"

"By rail, I suspect."

"Are you kidding? You can't give us a lift, like before?"

Lugh raised an eyebrow at him. "You want I should carry you all from here to Carnalridge, one by one?"

"I mean, maybe we could slap together some sort of chariot situation. That would be cool, right?"

Julien shook his head. "I wouldn't trust anything lashed to a beast like that horse. Even if it would let you."

"You show good judgment," Lugh said.

"So this guy," Trent spoke up, spitting toothpaste into the sink, "the one you want to meet. He's just going to give you what you need?"

Noah shrugged one shoulder. "I'll have to pay him. Not that I have any—what do they use here? Is it the Euro?"

"Belfast is in Northern Ireland," Julien said. "It'll be Pounds."

"Great," Trent sighed as he wiped his mouth and stuffed his toothbrush back into his bag. "Losing even more money to conversion rates."

"I thought you were crazy rich? People with apartments like that don't worry about losing two percent at the change bureau."

Trent scowled at the witch and zipped up his duffel bag. "Things change," he said. He wasn't willing to get into any more detail than that. Not with them.

Noah watched him with a soft frown and didn't press. "Well, maybe he'll take an exchange," he offered.

When Ciaran finally emerged from the bathroom, he picked up the duffel and headed for the door with a casual step, as though the other men hadn't been standing around for the last twenty minutes.

"Come along," he said. "We'll miss the bus to Drogheda."

Julien sighed through his nose and slung his bag over his shoulder. "For Airmed," he reminded himself as he followed the fairy down the stairs. Noah gave his arm a reassuring pat, and he smiled faintly.

Lugh watched carefully over Ciaran's shoulder while his father charmed his way into free bus tickets at the station, seeming satisfied with the chosen destination. Ciaran passed out the tickets as they made their way to the waiting buses.

"Is this how you always get around?" Trent asked, glancing down at his ticket. "Just fairy bullshit your way into free stuff all the time?"

"This is for your benefit, I'll have you know. When I was by myself, I didn't bother. Since no one could see me, I simply got on the bus, or the train, or what have you, and took up an empty seat. Much easier."

"I wanted to ask about that, actually," Noah said. He kept his question inside while they boarded, not eager to let his questions about the intricacies of fairy magic be overheard by the Bus Éireann driver.

Julien paused at the door to the bus and glanced over his shoulder at Lugh, who was standing back from the line. "You're not coming?"

"I do not ride the bus," Lugh answered simply, and he tilted his chin to urge Julien on his way.

The four of them took their seats near the back, Noah allowing Julien the window seat so that he could better talk to Ciaran—whether the fairy seemed interested or not.

"The invisibility," Noah went on. "It's inherent, isn't it? You have to make an effort to be seen."

"I don't know that I'd call it effort."

"But still—it's the nature of what you are."

Ciaran sighed and leaned his elbow on the armrest to peer over at the witch. "The Féth Fíada," he said. "It's a blessing. The mist that keeps us hidden from human sight. I allowed Trent to see me, so he sees me. Your hunter friend is a special case, of course. Perhaps only half-special now," he added, and Julien snorted at the jab while pretending not to listen.

"Did you do something to me? I could see you right away."

A teasing smile curled the fairy's lips. "Aye, but you're not exactly human, are you, lad?" Ciaran tapped his index finger on his own neck just behind his ear, and Noah instinctively reached up to touch the wine-colored stain.

He sat back in his seat as the bus started to move, and as they pulled away from the village, Noah paused and leaned over Julien's lap to get his face closer to the window. Just outside, speeding along beside the bus as it picked up momentum on the narrow road, he spotted a dappled grey horse and its burly rider. Noah took a glance around the worn, creaky bus, shifted in his lumpy seat, and sighed with longing. Why didn't he have a magic horse? Being on a fairy adventure should have some benefits, shouldn't it? The thumping of hooves, the wind in your face, a strong, living animal putting its trust in you—as sore as his ass had been after the ride from Vancouver to Ireland, he would still prefer it to sitting on a bus with a sticky-looking toddler peering over the seat ahead of him.

Julien looked down at Noah and followed his gaze to the fairy outside. Lugh looked calm and confident on horseback, slightly lifted from his saddle and leaned over the Enbarr's neck with a stoic stare. An involuntary frown twisted Julien's lips at Noah's sigh. He remembered the flustered look on the witch's face when Lugh had come to fetch them, the pink in his cheeks when the fairy had lifted him effortlessly and kept him secure in his arms. If Noah had a type, and Julien was it, then so was Lugh—and Julien wasn't quite so arrogant as to think he was in the same league.

He slipped a hand over to Noah's and gave him a soft squeeze as he interlaced their fingers. He tried to remind himself that Noah had chosen him. He wouldn't ruin it by being jealous. The witch settled back in his seat and laid his head on Julien's shoulder, his thumb brushing the hunter's knuckles, and Julien allowed himself a soft smile.

They moved from a bus to a train in Drogheda, which was only slightly more comfortable, and when they arrived in Belfast, Noah helped himself to Trent's laptop in a small coffee shop. While they waited, Ciaran helped himself to three slices of marble cake and a frozen coffee so heaped with whipped cream and chocolate sauce that Trent thought he might get diabetes just from looking at it.

"He says he can meet us here," Noah spoke up after exchanging a few messages on the laptop. "And he'll take trade, which is handy. He was very cooperative after I told him I had a small supply of mushrooms straight from Tír na nÓg."

"Just tell everyone where you've been, then," Ciaran scoffed. "Ní scéal rúin é nó rud ar bith," he added under his breath, glancing through the shop window at Lugh, who lingered near the door looking remarkably out of place.

"Oh, dún é. Mar má tá tú cúram," Noah snapped back. He froze, fingers poised over the keyboard, and then he covered his mouth with one hand as he looked up into Ciaran's startled face.

The fairy leaned both elbows on the table to peer across at the witch. "Just how much of me did you keep in there, lad?"

"I…some, I guess," Noah admitted. "What did I say?"

"You don't know?" Julien asked, his brow furrowing in concern. "That's a problem, right?"

Ciaran chuckled with a mouthful of cake. "You should be thankful. Not everyone's lucky enough to get me inside them."

Trent sighed beside him. "Really?" Ciaran shrugged.

Noah closed the laptop and pushed it back toward Trent to put away. "Let's just pretend that didn't happen. Cool? Cool."

"Noah," Julien cut in, "if there's some magic that's still connecting you—"

"I'm sure it's just...fragments," the witch assured him. "I don't feel any different." He smiled at Julien's skeptical frown. "I'm fine. Really. Let's just make this trade and head off for second fairyland, or wherever."

They waited, Trent relishing a cup of dark coffee without the sweetness of fairy food, and Noah stood when he spotted a figure approaching through the glass. He stood to meet him, and Julien followed immediately while Ciaran and Trent stayed at the table to guard the bags. Julien glanced at Lugh on their way by him, but the fairy only gave him the subtlest of acknowledging nods.

The man who arrived and greeted Noah with a smile was young, with messy brown curls pulled back into a short ponytail. Julien instantly spotted the dark reddish-purple stain at the right corner of his mouth, a thin pattern of splotches that extended the line of his smile. The stranger took Noah's hand and gave it a firm shake.

"Noah, eh? What about ye? Come a long way here, haven't you? Robert said from the far end of Canada."

"Feels like farther than that. You're Ethan?"

"Aye. I brought you a wee packet of goodies." He reached into the low-slung messenger bag at his hip and paused as he retrieved a zipped binder and a thick, leather-bound book, holding them slightly closer to himself and peering up at Julien. He seemed to have only just noticed the wary, eye-patched hunter. "Got a bodyguard, have you?" he asked.

"He's harmless," Noah said, earning himself a mildly offended frown. He nodded toward the binder. "What do you want for that?"

"Let's see these fairy mushrooms first, eh?"

Noah put a hand on Julien's arm to keep him still while he fished in their shared bag, and he offered the other witch one of the small, nondescript mushrooms, still faintly glowing blue even in the midday light. Ethan tucked his offerings under his arm and took the mushroom in both hands as though he thought it might shatter. He turned it in his palm, inspecting it with narrow eyes, and he even brought it to his nose to smell it.

"You said you got these in Tír na nÓg," he said. "I didn't think it was real. How'd you end up somewhere like that?"

"It's a long story involving smartasses and spells I shouldn't have been casting."

"You didn't just get stolen away and used for breeding, did you? I've heard they do that."

"What? No," Noah laughed. "I was just...helping someone. A friend. Kind of."

"Here's me wha? A friend? A fairy friend?"

"Is answering a hundred questions part of your price?" Julien cut in, and Ethan looked up at him with raised eyebrows.

"Just being friendly, me big lad. Not every day you hear about someone what's been down below." He returned his attention to Noah, gently worrying the mushroom in his hands. "So what are they like, then? The fairy folk?"

"Strange," Noah answered. "And...a little too bloody for my taste. I don't recommend getting involved with them." He turned when he noticed Trent and Ciaran approaching his side.

"Are you making a deal or a friend here, lad?" Ciaran asked. "We need to be off."

"Sorry. Just a minute." He turned back to Ethan, whose mouth had fallen open. Noah could see it in his face—he was taking in the pointed ears showing through Ciaran's messy hair, and slow realization pulled his lips into a smile.

"You're him, then!" he said, half laughing. "You're one of them!"

Ciaran didn't seem amused by being pointed out, and he kept his hands in the pockets of his jeans. He nodded his head toward the binder and book tucked under the witch's arm. "Is that for Noah?"

"Oh, aye." He held his mushroom carefully and finally offered the package to Noah. "Should be a fair collection of the basics—some herbs, incense, a few wee tokens." He hesitated and chewed his lip for a moment as he glanced between the witch and the fairy. "I'm glad to trade for an hour with your friend there," he said. He inched closer, reaching out a hand as though he meant to touch Ciaran and check if he was real. "There are so many things I could—"

"We don't have an hour," Trent interrupted, placing himself slightly in front of his lover. "And he doesn't have anything to do with you."

"My hero," Ciaran chuckled, and Trent snapped a glare back at him.

"Aye, wind yer neck in," Ethan answered, lifting his hands in surrender. "I don't mean any disrespect."

Noah moved forward to distance the two men from each other and pulled Julien closer to pick a few more mushrooms from his bag. He pushed them into Ethan's hands and leaned to catch his eye, breaking his curious staring at Ciaran. "This is enough, right? Look, thanks, but we really have to go."

"Sure," the other witch answered, pulling his gaze from Ciaran to offer Noah a smile. "We'll chat again when you finish your big adventure, eh?"

"Gladly." He offered Ethan his hand again, and when they parted, he caught the look of astonishment on the other witch's face as Lugh passed him. He suspected he would have a lot of messages waiting for him the next time he dared check Trent's laptop.

After another agonizing bus ride, they finally found themselves in a town called Coleraine, and from there, Lugh and Ciaran led them to a small village by the shore. They took the opportunity to gather supplies for the journey—Noah and Trent picked up bottles of water, granola bars, and some jerky and dried fruit, while Ciaran had apparently decided to live on nothing but a twelve pound bag of peach rings for the next nine days. Trent at least picked him out some breads and juice so that he wouldn't die of malnutrition halfway through the journey. Noah pretended not to notice the few chocolates that Julien slipped into the box he carried as the witch went in search of sleeping bags. They even found coats to fit them all, as Ciaran assured them that it was going to get cold.

Once they were as well-supplied as they could manage, the group walked the promenade by the water, father and son chatting in swift Gaelic that Noah couldn't make out, and then Lugh dropped down from the stone steps and onto the rocky shoreline.

"Are we going to swim?" Trent called out as Ciaran followed, the fairy splashing carelessly into a shallow tide pool.

"Don't be an ass," Ciaran scolded him. "Come along."

Julien went first, sparing a grateful glance at the empty street behind them, and he turned to offer Noah a hand down. The witch hopped from the steps, bracing himself with the hunter's hand as he landed. Trent brought up the rear, picking his way over the slick black stone toward the water. He would never ask for Ciaran's help anyway, but something still stung about seeing how gently Julien treated Noah.

Lugh stood just at the edge of the lapping waves, looking out over the empty, greenish blue sea, and his companions waited for a few beats of silence. When nothing happened, Julien leaned out to peer up at the fairy's stern face.

"Are fairy boats invisible, too?" he asked, and Lugh snorted in irritation but didn't answer. After a moment more, he glanced down at Julien with the faintest hint of amusement crinkling the corners of his eyes. The water beyond the rocks began to bubble, and with a roar of foam, a longboat burst forth from under the surface—first the bow, adorned with a bleached white ox skull, and then the massive hull covered in stitched, stretched animal skins. It was easily thirty feet long, with a towering mast and four rows of wooden benches separating the space inside. Thick, round beams separated the rear of the boat from the rest, lashed together to form a crude steering system, and a heavy anchor hung from loops of rope over one side.

Trent took a step back in shock as the wave washed toward them, and Ciaran had to put an arm out to keep him from tumbling to the rocks.

"Holy shit," Noah said, but he was laughing. "You have a magic boat?"

"Of course he has a magic boat," Julien muttered. "Why wouldn't he?"

"This is the Scuabtuinne," Lugh said. He waded into the shallow water and took hold of a rope at the bow of the ship to haul it closer to the rocks. "A gift from Manandán—the swiftest on the sea and unsinkable by man or beast. It can make the journey to Lochlann."

"You have a magic horse, a magic sword, a magic spear, a magic boat," Noah said, counting on his fingers. "How many enchanted artifacts do you own, exactly?"

"My share," Lugh answered simply.

"I assume one of you actually knows where this place is, right?" Trent asked. "We're not just sailing away and hoping we come across this mythical, possibly-abandoned country?"

Lugh glanced at his father, and Ciaran hesitated before answering.

"I know the way," he said. "Don't worry."

Trent wanted to ask him how, exactly, he knew the way to said mythical country full of brutal whatevers, but the fairy seemed somber, so he held his tongue.

They handed off the supplies to Lugh, who loaded them onto the ship, and then they waded out into the water after him, one by one accepting his help to climb aboard. Ciaran lifted himself up over the opposite side and set about pulling ropes and preparing the tall, dingy white sail. Lugh took his place beside his father without the need for words, and within minutes, the ship was skimming away from the shore, the rocky coastline disappearing behind them.

Trent settled himself on one of the boards that served as a seat near the center of the ship, attempting to keep his stomach steady as they lurched with every rolling wave. He should have remembered to buy Dramamine. Noah, on the other hand, seemed pleased as punch as he leaned far over the side, letting his fingertips brush the foaming surface and shutting his eyes in the wind. Julien looked ready to leap out and catch him at any moment, but he kept his place on the seat beside the witch and settled for watching him with a worried frown.

The air began to cool the further they went, but Ciaran didn't seem bothered. While Lugh tied off the ropes and secured the sails, Ciaran climbed up the dizzyingly-tall mast as easily as if it were a ladder. He stood in the narrow crow's nest and leaned against the railing, looking out over the endless ocean with a faint smile on his lips. Trent shielded his eyes with one hand to look up at him. The fairy seemed relaxed. It was a nice change from all the gloom and anxiety of the past few days—Trent just wished he didn't feel so sick to his stomach.

They'd been out for a couple of hours before Trent finally vomited. The swaying of the ship underneath him, the thick smell of salt water invading his nostrils, and the chill of the sea wind cutting down to his bones was too much to handle. He gripped the leather side of the boat and left a long trail of his breakfast in the water behind them, coughing and wiping at his mouth with the back of his hand. Ciaran dropped onto the seat beside him, startling him.

"Keeping well, a mhuirnín?" he asked as he laid a gentle hand on the other man's back.

"Peachy," Trent grunted, not daring to move from his place against the side of the boat.

"We've a long while to go yet, I fear. Perhaps you ought to lie down."

Trent wasn't eager to jostle his stomach with the movement, but, after pausing with his chin over the edge to settle himself, he took the fairy's advice and shifted onto his side on the long bench. Ciaran sat beside him and ran his fingers through his hair, and Trent tried to let his eyes close at the touch, but he could feel the stares of their companions and soon swatted away his lover's gentle hand.

"You can't be feeling too ill if you're still feisty," Ciaran chuckled. Trent spared the energy of turning his head to glare at him.

"The next time I throw up, I'm aiming for you."

"Yes, dear." Ciaran smiled and bent over him to touch a light kiss to his forehead, then busied himself with Lugh at the back of the boat.

Trent pressed his cheek against the wood and pretended that the sway of the ocean was comforting instead of sickening. They were going to be out here for nine days? He might throw himself overboard before they arrived.

He heard some shuffling behind him, and he tilted his head when he saw Noah's torn jeans pass in front of his face. The witch crouched down in front of him with a small smile.

"Here," he said. He held out a thin coin of what looked like ginger. "Hold this under your tongue. It'll help."

Trent eyed him skeptically, but when Noah nodded to urge him, Trent took the small disk and tucked it into his mouth. It didn't taste like ginger—it was almost like peppermint, somehow. As he slowly sat up, he expected his stomach to lurch again, but he felt fine. Noah smiled at the look of confusion on his face.

"Magic is good for more than causing trouble after all," he said as he rose. "Keep it under there for about half an hour, and you should be fine for a couple of days. Let me know when you start to feel sick again. I'll make you another one."

Trent sucked on the coin in his mouth as an excuse for not

answering, but before the witch could move away again, he muttered a reluctant "Thanks."

"Sure thing." Noah hesitated. "You guys…still wanting to try that binding spell? I noticed Ciaran is wearing his token again." When Trent only stared at him, he paused before giving a soft laugh. "Sorry. I just told you to leave a thing in your mouth. Anyway, as soon as Ciaran and Lugh stop arguing about who gets to steer, we can give it a try."

Trent nodded at him and looked out over the water, sucking on the maybe-not-actually-ginger the witch had given him. Nine days. In nine days, they would arrive in Lochlann, and Trent would—once again—be the most useless person in the group as they faced a people that made even Ciaran wary. Was it worth it to try and bind Ciaran's fate to his, not knowing what was waiting for them at the end of those nine days?

4

The night sky was beautiful this far away from the light pollution of civilization. Noah sat sideways on the seat near the tiller—the thick steering shaft attached to the ship's rudder. He supposed it must have been because of another remnant of Ciaran's memories that he knew what it was called. Ciaran had finally settled down and let Lugh steer after checking a dozen times that his son had the right bearings and wasn't going to stray from the course. Trent was lying on his bench, still recovering from his bout of seasickness.

Noah leaned against Julien's shoulder, arms wrapped around his knees, and tried to pick out constellations. They had left behind any sign of land and gone beyond the range of the sea birds. The sea was as smooth as glass, breaking only as the bow of their ship cut through the black water ahead of them. Noah thought he should have been worried about what was in store for them, and he was. He was worried about Airmed. But he also, just a little bit, wanted to stay out here forever.

He jumped as realization hit him, startling the man beside him, but he didn't see the confused frown on Julien's face because he was already bent halfway under the bench to check on the carefully tucked away box. A bright smile pulled his lips as he saw the dogs in their upright posture. A message must have been waiting for him.

Noah lifted the box into his lap and opened the lid, a laugh bubbling out of him as he spotted the folded paper inside. The handwriting on the page looked stiff, and a few dots of ink marked the paper near the edge, as though the boy had tapped his pen in thought for a while before forming his reply.

What was the first thing you ever gave me?

Noah smiled and crinkled the paper a little in his fingers. Good boy. Noah would have been supremely suspicious of a suddenly appearing magic fairy box, too. He bent down to take the pen he'd stolen from the hotel out of Julien's bag and twirled one finger in the air to urge the hunter to turn around, then spread the paper on the blond's broad back and managed to write his reply without piercing the paper.

A scolding, he wrote. *And then a hot bath. And then another scolding.*

Julien turned back to look at him when his duty as makeshift desk was over, and Noah beamed up at him.

"He actually answered me. I'm going to get to talk to him again, for real."

Julien nodded toward the note. "You told me you found him using magic in public," he said. "What was the second scolding for?"

"He tried to come onto me."

"He what?"

"I told him no, of course. Sabin was thirteen. He'd had...kind of a hard time before we met. So I guess he thought that was how I expected to be paid for my hospitality. But once he realized I wasn't interested, he stopped."

Julien frowned faintly as Noah folded the paper again. "Poor kid."

Noah shut the lid on his note and watched the dogs lie back down. "He'd probably hit you if he heard you pitying him," he chuckled, "but he hasn't had it easy. I'm glad he seems to at least be mostly safe where he is now."

Noah tried to count backwards to figure out what time it might be where Sabin was. Maybe he would be able to answer soon. He drummed his fingers on the top of the box, and a couple of minutes later, he heard a small click, and the dogs reared up again. Noah let out a small shout of excitement and hastily lifted the lid again, snatching the replaced sheet of paper. Two small bottles rolled to the back of the box, and Noah held them in his palm for inspection. One had a bit of white hair inside, and the other contained some thin curls of a brown substance he couldn't identify. He hummed to himself and looked back to the paper. The handwriting was more hurried this time, and Noah could picture Sabin's hand flying over the paper in his rush to get the words out.

Holy shit, this is real? I thought that Marla was stealing your letters when I stopped hearing back from you. I tried sneaking you notes from outside post boxes and I've started gathering materials for a transit spell. Where are you now? Are you still in fairy land? What was it like? What sort of magic did they do?

Also, thanks for the mushroom! Here is a bit of hair and antler shavings from a white stag we dealt with a while back. I've been holding onto it for you.

The box suddenly snapped shut on its own in Noah's lap, and he heard the soft telltale crack again. When he peeked under the lid, another small sheet of paper was inside that simply said *THIS IS SO AMAZING!* in scrawling handwriting.

Noah clutched the vials to his chest and read the first note over again. "A white stag," he repeated in a soft voice. "You've had some adventures of your own, haven't you?"

He moved to the floor of the boat rather than use Julien's back again, because this letter was going to be longer. He wrote in tiny letters and told Sabin everything that he was able to fit on the page— about the tall towers and sleek stone of Tír na nÓg, the beetle-drawn carriages and the endless darkness. He told him about Ciaran, and the spell that had connected them, but he left out the part about dying. He told him how Airmed had used singing and herbs to heal him, and how Julien had gone on a heroic quest and broken the spell. He turned a bit farther away from Julien and covered the paper with his arm like a student hiding his test from peering eyes as he wrote about how romantic Julien's confession had been, how the hunter had lost an eye to dangerous magic for his sake.

So, he added, *right now I'm actually on a boat heading toward a place called Lochlann to help settle my new fairy friend's blood debt. There's a sentence I never thought I'd write. But you've been doing exciting things! A white stag! I've always wanted to see one. Did you make a wish?*

He folded the paper again and shut it in the box, waiting anxiously for a response with his arms folded over the lid. He paused, then leaned back to look at Lugh, who stood at the tiller and watched the water ahead of them.

"I don't suppose," he began, smiling once he'd caught the man's attention, "that you have anything cool I could send to my friend? I didn't even think while I was dying to bring him a souvenir from Tír na nÓg. You know, a trinket, or something. Do you guys even have trinkets?"

Lugh considered for a moment, watching Noah's bright smile, and then he gave a soft grunt of agreement and jutted his chin toward his leather bag. "Check the leftmost pocket."

Noah gleefully jumped to his feet and climbed over the benches to reach the bag. The pocket held an assortment of various small tools, but at the very bottom, his fingertips touched a tiny metal object. He pulled it out and held it in his palm. The bright silver had been hammered into a coil with a curling spiral at each end, and minute lettering had been carved into one side—*Go n-éirí an bóthar leat.*

"What is it?" Noah asked as he stepped back over to his seat.

"There isn't any magic in it," Lugh said. "It's to be worn in the hair. Mine isn't long enough anymore."

"There are words here, too. What does it say?"

"May the road rise to meet you," the fairy answered. "It's simply for good luck."

"This is amazing," Noah said. "Thank you."

Lugh gave the smallest nod possible, clearly not overly interested in Noah's gratitude.

The witch tore a small sheet of paper from his hotel notepad and wrote on it, *May the road rise to meet you. A gift from Lugh Lámfada, who totally has his own Wikipedia page. I checked.*

He tucked the prize into the box and closed the lid again to wait. A few minutes passed before it clicked under his arms, and this note had a fun-sized Kit Kat sitting on top of it. Noah smiled as he took it and unfolded the carefully written letter.

So you finally bagged yourself a straight one, huh? You minx. Well I'm happy if you're happy, but you can tell Julien that if he steps like one toe out of line, I'll jinx his balls into his eye sockets.

I'm so jealous that he's there with you in Tír na nÓg and I'm stuck in a bunker. Did you get to touch any of the giant bugs? And what sorts of songs did the fairy girl use to heal people? That seems so useful. Is it something we can learn? I can't wait to get out of here. Even exciting things all seem to come with some sort of rule that makes them tedious. I had to sneak those white stag samples because Marla was flipping out thinking I was going to hurt it. I drew a little blood too, but it clotted on me before I could do anything with it. My friends got trapped in a cave a while back and we just spent a whole week in the middle of Nebraska fighting demon-possessed farmers.

The demon thing was pretty cool if I'm honest. I got to do a detection line up! Like the one you taught me. I managed to scrounge up something for every single region. I even pierced my tongue for it. My teammates looked like they were going to pass out. So that was a perk.

I miss you though. I'd rather be sitting in your apartment doing nothing but street tricks. Though going to fairy land would be cool too. Tell your friend I want to go some time. I guess that's what I had wished for when we caught that stag. Maybe it only granted half my wish since I stole samples from it. Please keep writing. This is the happiest I've been in years.

PS: Don't you dare give that candy to Julien! He doesn't get anything until I meet him in person.

PPS: I want so many of these fairy hair coils that I become an actual fairy! I'm going to live with this thing in my hair.

Noah laughed to himself, pressing his knuckles against his lips to stifle the little hiccup that threatened to escape. He turned the paper over to write his response, but he only got down four words before he had to stop and take a deep breath to collect himself.

I miss you, too.

The box gave another snap, and Noah lifted the lid to find a fresh Polaroid of the boy. The colors were still forming, so he shook it out of habit, and when it was finished, he laughed at the sight of his young friend with his tongue hanging out, showing off the new barbell in his tongue. Half of Sabin's head was shaved, the rest of his soft brown hair hanging down to his many-pierced ear, and he was holding up a lock of hair with Lugh's token fastened in it. Noah could see the smile in his blue eyes and felt his heart constrict. He'd had his septum pierced since the last time Noah saw him, and the two holes at the corners of his mouth seemed to have closed up. What little of the boy's room he could see in the background was a disaster, but that wasn't a surprise. Noah smiled and held the photo in one hand as he bent over the paper to reply. He answered all of Sabin's questions the best he knew how. He promised to try to learn some songs from Airmed the next time he saw her, told him how proud he was, and reminded the boy to rinse his mouth with salt water if he wanted to keep the tongue piercing. Noah chewed the ring in his own lip and hunkered down close to the paper to finish his note.

I'm going to see you again soon, one way or another.

P.S. Clean your room, you Garbador.

He slipped the paper back into the box and watched the silver dogs lie down again, then folded his arms on the bench and laid his forehead on them with a soft sigh.

"Es-tu correct, Noah?" Julien asked, leaning forward and resting a gentle hand in the witch's hair.

"I'm fine," he assured him as he raised his head again. "I just worry about him. He never talks as if he's made friends with any of the people he lives with. But he's a tough kid. And I know I'll see him again."

"This is him?" Julien nodded toward the photo still held tightly in Noah's hand, and the witch smiled and offered it to him. Julien inspected it for a moment, his lip twitching into a faint, skeptical frown. "He looks like a punk."

"He is a punk," Noah laughed. "But you like me, and he's my kind of punk. He's a good kid, really. He tries to hide it, but on the inside he's sweet, and very caring. I'm glad I can talk to him like this."

The box clicked beside him, and Noah found a much shorter note inside this time, tucked next to a squat glass jar.

I'll hold you to that promise. For now, hold onto this jar of spiders for me. I'm going to send you a cross in a few minutes. When you get it, take the cross out and dump all the spiders into the box.

I'll explain later.

Noah picked the jar out of the box and lifted it up to peer through the side. Sure enough, at least two dozen small spiders of various species crawled around inside, walking over each other and trying to scale the glass.

"Are those spiders?" Julien asked. "Why did he send you a jar of spiders?"

"I'm not sure," Noah admitted. "Maybe he's testing something?"

"Better question. Why did he have a jar of spiders?"

"It's not unheard of to use live insects and things, or webs, as spell components." Noah tilted his head at the jar. "But this does look like an unnecessary number of spiders."

"Your kid is weird."

"He's unique," Noah countered.

After a couple of minutes had passed, the box gave its small snapping noise, and Noah retrieved the palm-sized crucifix inside. He handed it off to Julien and dutifully emptied the jar of spiders into the box. He struggled to get them all out and the box shut without losing or crushing any of them, but when he closed the lid and saw the dogs resume their resting pose, he couldn't spot any unaccounted-for arachnids.

Just a minute or two later, Noah received another Polaroid, this one with the word "success" scrawled into the white space along the bottom. The picture showed what looked like a cafeteria, where a burly-looking black boy had clearly just tried to scramble his way across the room and tripped and toppled a chair in the attempt. A slender boy with flowing strawberry blond hair was standing nearby, but his amused surprise was the exact opposite reaction to that of the panicked teenager on the floor. Noah could see Sabin's identical box on the table and the black bodies of the spiders Noah had sent crawling across the tile, and suddenly the boy's innocent experiment made perfect sense.

"You little shit," Noah laughed to himself. When the box jostled again, he found a quick note with a photo of a terrarium full of spiders happily lounging in their underbrush.

I caught them all and put them back in their homes. Now I have a debriefing to go to. I'll write more soon.

Noah slipped Sabin one more note in return letting him know that he needed to sleep anyway. He promised to send something good from Lochlann, sent his love once more, and tucked the box away back into Julien's bag for safe keeping.

5

Noah kept an eye on Ciaran as the ship sailed on through the night, hoping for the right opportunity to test his new spell. The fairy had tried to urge Trent into his lap under the pretense of soothing his nauseated stomach, but the boy had shoved him away and snapped at him, so now the two sat at opposite ends of the long bench, both leaning against the sides of the boat and half glaring at each other. These were the two souls Noah was supposed to be binding together in eternal kinship and love. Great.

When Ciaran had made a significant dent in his giant bag of peach rings, Noah pushed away from the inviting warmth of Julien's body and stepped over some boxes of supplies so that he could plant himself between the two pouting men.

"So," he began brightly, "who wants to try some binding magic?"

Ciaran noticeably softened. "Is that still the plan, a mhuirnín?"

"We can always wait, if you guys would rather—"

"No," Trent interrupted. He was still frowning, but he didn't look so angry. "I'm still game if you are."

Noah smiled. "Excellent. Now if the two of you could maybe, you know, budge in a little bit here. Act like you like each other." He stood from the bench and pulled over a box of water bottles to sit on so that Trent and Ciaran could sit side by side on the bench. He ran his palms idly over his knees and looked up at the pair.

"This magic is...imprecise," he said. "Most magic is, to some extent, but it's a lot easier to deal with 'did the thing catch fire or not' than it is to say 'are these two souls properly aligned so that their destinies are permanently and irrevocably intertwined,' you get me?"

"What is it you're planning to do, exactly?" Trent asked. Noah could tell he was uncertain, and he didn't blame him. The kid hadn't had a great experience with magic so far, overall.

"It's more what you are going to do. I can facilitate, and I can channel the magic you need, but it's what's going on inside of you that matters."

"Don't," Trent snapped as soon as Ciaran opened his mouth, and the fairy let out a small laugh and bit his lip to keep in what was surely going to be a vulgar joke.

Noah sighed. He could be back in Vancouver guiding housewives into Virabhadrasana, he reminded himself. This was a challenge. Challenges were good, right?

"Let's start at the beginning," Noah tried again. "The idea is that every person—and every fairy, I'm hoping—has seven spots inside of them. Seven points running from the top of your head down. Each of these points of energy branches out into thousands and thousands of channels, and each of those branches out and branches out into the tiniest petals, until the whole body is full. It's this energy that makes up the soul. Now, what the two of you are aiming to do is to become like a ladder—two sides locked together at these points and supporting a single soul between you."

"That sounds like absolute bullshit," Trent scoffed.

"After what's happened to you over the last few weeks?" Noah snapped. He took a quick breath to soften his tone. "Look—if I could, I'd put you both in a circle and throw herbs at you until you were both immortal, okay? But that doesn't work. Do you want to be a vampire?"

Trent pressed his lips into a thin line and didn't answer.

"No, I didn't think you did. So shut up."

"You got scolded," Ciaran taunted, nudging Trent with his shoulder and getting a scowl in return.

"And you need to take this seriously," Noah went on, prodding the fairy in the knee with one finger. "All the magic in the world won't help you if you aren't sincere."

"Yes, boss."

"You can't fool me. I know you have a gooey center under all that sarcasm. Just let it show a little, will you?" He shifted on his box and straightened his back. "Now. For this to have any chance of working, you must approach each other with minds free of fear. Free of doubt. And free of lust. I know that last one may be the most difficult, given I've literally had Ciaran in my head and know what he's like. Not to mention your inability to keep your hands off of each other even when sharing a tiny hotel room with relative strangers."

All the color drained from Trent's face. "You heard?"

"Everyone heard," Julien noted from the back of the boat.

Trent turned to Ciaran in a fury, but no words quite made it out of his mouth. He just glared at him and huffed until he gave up, covering his face with his hands.

"Sexuality is a natural part of life," Noah assured him. Maybe he shouldn't have teased. "An important part," he added, but Trent kept his face covered and doubled over with his elbows on his knees. Noah couldn't help smiling. Trent was acerbic and cold and entirely too standoffish for Noah's taste, but knowing that his biting wit was a cover for being easily mortified made him understand a small part of what the fairy saw in him.

"Let's start over. We'll try simple," he said. Trent finally lowered his hands, and though he wouldn't meet Noah's eyes, the witch could see the flush in his cheeks. "We don't have to deal with that sort of thing right away. We begin at the entrance to the body and travel from there. That's the nostrils." He turned to look over his shoulder and held out a hand. "Julien, could you pass me the binder?"

Julien bent to take the zippered container from underneath his seat and tossed it lightly to Noah, who folded it open in his lap. Ethan had really delivered—the binder was full of neatly organized packets of herbs, incense, and various stones and chips of wood, all labeled and sorted by name. Everything he had asked for was inside. The other witch must have really wanted those fairy mushrooms.

Noah picked out the packets he needed and carefully lined them up in his lap, then he paused. He needed something safe to burn in.

After a bit of unsuccessful searching around, he finally convinced Lugh to loan him a silver cup from his pack. He touched the fairy's arm as he thanked him, not noticing Julien's frowning glance, and stepped back over to the bench where Trent and Ciaran waited.

He opened the first two herb packets and sprinkled the portions of rosemary and lemon rind into the borrowed cup.

"I don't suppose either of you are familiar with meditation in general?" he asked.

"I forgot to pack my lululemon," Ciaran quipped, and Trent sighed.

"Actually, you know, it used to be worth the price, but it's really gone downhill in quality over the last couple of years—and you totally don't actually care about yoga pants," Noah finished, tapping his lips with one finger as if to quiet himself. "Let's just get you relaxed first, okay?"

Trent wasn't sure how he was supposed to relax while on a fairy boat in the middle of the ocean, on the way to a place that was either abandoned or supremely dangerous and accompanied by two men who had tried to kill his lover a few days ago. Oh, and also said lover's war hero son. He was beginning to grow weary of spending all his time wondering what he'd gotten himself into. It couldn't hurt to at least try to follow the witch's lead. He had to believe that someday things would settle down, and it would just be him and Ciaran again, like the fairy had promised. He let out a soft sigh when Noah tilted his head at him in a silent question, and he nodded.

"You too," Noah said with a pointed glance at Ciaran. The fairy looked over at Trent and gave a small, private smile that wrinkled the corners of his eyes.

"Sure."

"Great. Okay. Now, close your eyes, and focus on your breathing."

Trent only hesitated for a moment before doing as he was told. He let his eyes slip shut and tried to relax his shoulders despite the rocking of the boat beneath him. The witch led them through slow, careful breaths, in through the nose and out through the mouth, counting each held breath and telling them when to release it.

"Notice the breath as it enters your nose," he said. "Feel it pass through, flowing down behind your throat. Down, and down, into your windpipe, filling your lungs. Feel the air expand your lungs with each breath. Now, as you exhale, feel the breath traveling up and out; feel it in your throat, your mouth, and across your lips. Each breath flowing in and out like a wave. Notice the pauses, the rests between those breaths. Let them settle in you and relax you, and then let them go, gently, taking your anxiety with them."

Trent would never admit it out loud, but the witch's voice was surprisingly soothing. He really did feel less tense when Noah told them they could open their eyes.

Noah lit a small fire in the palm of his hand, bathing the three of them in orange light that seemed brighter in the still night. The witch kept the flame small—just enough to light the contents of the cup when he closed his hand over the rim. As he moved his hand and scooted closer to the pair, pale smoke rose with his fingers and spiraled into the sky.

"Breathe deeply," he advised, holding the cup forward and guiding the smoke toward them.

Over what seemed like hours, Noah led the two of them through each imaginary point in their bodies—from the nostrils up over the top of the head and down into the chest, belly, and "root," which Trent suspected was a polite euphemism for the ass. With every step, Noah burned different herbs and touched their bodies with small shards of various stones. He spoke softly to them and focused their attention on the things that would connect them. Intellect, intuition, spirituality, trust, compassion, intimacy, and security. He encouraged them to think about themselves, and about each other, and about what they needed and what they could provide.

It all sounded like complete new age garbage to Trent, no matter how comforting Noah's voice was. He tried his best to focus, but when they finally finished, and Noah sat back on his box to look at them, Trent didn't feel different at all.

"Was that it?" Ciaran asked, voicing Trent's skepticism.

"You tell me," Noah answered. "You would know if it had worked."

Trent and Ciaran exchanged curious glances. The look on the fairy's face told Trent that he didn't feel any different, either.

"I guess not," Trent said.

"Well, I did say the magic is imprecise." Noah gave a soft sigh. "But everything I read last night indicated that this was a sound method. If it didn't work, then maybe there's something wrong…you know, on the inside. It's never going to happen if you aren't both fully committed."

Trent felt slightly sick to his stomach, but he didn't think it was the boat ride. Was it his own fear and uncertainty holding them back? He knew that he wanted to be with Ciaran—he loved Ciaran. Despite everything the fairy had put him through, Trent only wanted to stay beside him, to see those little lines form around his eyes when he smiled. He knew that. He was wary of the situation they were in and of what was waiting for them in this place called Lochlann, but that didn't have anything to do with how he felt about Ciaran.

He didn't want to look at the man beside him. Maybe it was Ciaran who wasn't feeling committed. The fairy had had so many lovers over the thousands of years he'd been alive—what could possibly make Trent the exception?

Noah seemed to sense the growing tension between them, because he noisily clanged the charred herb remnants over the side of the boat and cleared his throat as he turned back to them.

"Well," he said, "we can always try again. Maybe everyone just needs a good night's sleep. It is pretty late. Yeah," he agreed with himself, "we'll try again some other time. Let's just get a good night's sleep."

The witch busied himself with unpacking the rolled sleeping bags and distributing them, and Trent was happy to break away from Ciaran's side to help organize the sleeping arrangements on the narrow boat. When Noah stepped over the forwardmost bench on the pretense of handing Trent the last sleeping bag, he held onto it for a moment to catch the boy's attention.

"It really is okay," he said softly when Trent looked at him. "It would have been strange if you'd done it right the first time. Don't start doubting each other, okay?"

Trent hesitated with his hand on the sleeping bag, and he looked over Noah's shoulder at Ciaran, who had already picked a few more peach rings out of his massive bag and was casually chewing them as he leaned against the side of the boat.

"Yeah." Trent took the sleeping bag from Noah and rolled it out on the floor of the boat, but he couldn't look the witch in the eye. He took a place away from the others and kicked off his shoes before settling into his chosen sleeping bag. The bottom of the boat was hard through the thin cushioning, and the tar-covered wicker creaked under his cheek with every wave they bumped. He didn't want Noah's pity. He wasn't even sure he wanted his help.

Trent shut his eyes and pulled the sleeping bag tight around his chin, listening to the sloshing water as it broke against the bow. He had almost fallen asleep when he felt the quilt tugged away from him. Ciaran nudged his way inside the one-person sleeping bag and nestled himself against Trent, holding him close with one arm under the boy's head and the other wrapped around his waist.

"What are you doing?" Trent muttered even as he settled on the fairy's bicep. "It's too small."

"I spent too long away from you." Ciaran placed a soft kiss on Trent's hair. "Let me enjoy you now that I've returned. I love you, a mhuirnín."

Trent felt his cheeks flush even in the growing heat of the crowded sleeping bag. He murmured a muffled "I love you too" into the blanket, but he could feel the fairy smiling into his hair.

6

Julien shifted on the solid floor of the boat, trying to will himself to sleep a bit longer and delay the boredom of the day, but Noah's familiar laugh pulled him fully into consciousness.

"Easy, now," Lugh's rough voice said nearby, almost sounding at ease. Julien hadn't known him long—and would barely claim to know him now—but the fairy seemed anything but casual.

"Jesus," Noah laughed. "It's so thick. How do you get your hands around it?"

"Big hands," Lugh answered wryly. Julien tensed. He should get up. He should look. He was surely misunderstanding. But something kept him in place, listening.

"Doesn't it get in the way when you're on your horse? It seems like it would get beaten to death with all the galloping."

"Not if you tuck it close." Julien heard the soft shuffling of feet. "Here. Grip it firmly, like this."

Noah let out a faint satisfied sound, and he dropped his voice as though about to ask something he shouldn't. "Can I take it out?"

Julien sat up too quickly, fumbling as he tried to toss the half-zipped sleeping bag away from him, and he glared across at the pair on the bench nearby. Noah had the fairy's massive spear nestled in the crook of his elbow as he reached for the leather pouch concealing the bladed tip. He turned to Julien with a startled look on his face, but it quickly turned into a smile.

"You're up! Look at this thing. He says the blade catches fire on its own if it's not submerged in special water. Isn't that cool?"

Julien stood still for a moment, staring.

"Something frighten you, an duine?" Lugh asked.

"I'm fine," the hunter answered promptly. He kicked the sleeping bag away from his feet and bent to slip his boots back on. Noah was already bundled in his coat and sat cross-legged on the bench beside Lugh, looking up at him as if for permission to open the pouch.

"If you catch the sail on fire, it's going to take a lot longer to get there," Lugh warned, and Noah hesitated with the leather cord in his hand.

"Maybe...show me after we land," the witch said with a laugh.

Julien sighed and ran his fingers through his sleep-tangled hair. He was imagining things. Noah had slept soundly by his side all night, curled under his chin despite each of them being wrapped in their own sleeping bags. Noah loved him. He loved Noah. Just because Noah seemed to be the only person in the world not intimidated by Lugh aside from the fairy's own father—it didn't mean he was attracted to him. It didn't mean anything at all. Julien was being paranoid.

That's what he told himself, but seeing the easy way the witch chatted with and questioned the larger man still made his stomach feel uneasy. Had he always felt this possessive of Noah without realizing it?

Behind him, Ciaran had both hands on the beam controlling the rudder, keeping it steady with a firm grip as the sails pulled them farther and farther northward. Trent sat nearby, his back against the side of the boat and his elbows on his knees. He almost looked as if he was trying to avoid looking up at his lover.

"I want to know more about where we're going," Julien said, drawing the fairy's attention. "These Lochlannan—they're not human, obviously. Are they like you?"

"More true to say that *we* are like *them*," Ciaran answered. He glanced down at the hunter. "All you need to know is that if we do find anything still there, we aren't likely to get a warm reception. The

Lochlannan don't like visitors."

"But what are they? Spirits? Monsters? Why are you like them?"

"It's a long story, hunter."

"I want to hear it," Noah piped up. He returned Lugh's spear to him and moved to stand by Julien, stepping over the bench between them. "You can't just tell us that they're magical and secretive and whatever without sharing the goods. We ought to know what we're in for."

Ciaran looked about to argue, but then Trent spoke up from beside him.

"I want to know, too."

The fairy gave a sigh and let his shoulders droop. "All right," he said, and he paused to offer Trent a faint smile. "I don't want to be accused of keeping secrets."

"Just answer the question," Trent grumped, tugging his knees a little closer to his chest and staring pointedly out over the water.

"Long ago," Ciaran began, "long before my time or my father's father's time—so the story goes—my people were human. Our ancestors came from the East. They landed on the place they called Inisfail, the Island of Destiny. Ireland to you lot. They lived there for some time, but they were defeated by the Fomorians—a race of warlike giants that came from the sea itself. They kept my people as slaves for many years until we finally rose up against them. My understanding is that it didn't go well. Those who survived the rebellion and weren't recaptured as slaves fled the island. Some went to Britain and stayed there, and some went all the way to Greece. The people who would become my people sailed to the far North and found the island of Lochlann, with its four magnificent cities—Falias, Gorias, Murias, and Finias."

Noah climbed up onto the bench at the base of the steering shaft and stared up at the fairy like a child hearing a bedtime story. Julien found himself smiling. Noah never could resist learning about new magic.

"And the Lochlannan, they took you in?" the witch asked. "Well, your ancestors."

"Aye, so it's said. The others fleeing the Fomorians did simply that—they fled. My people 'met the Lochlannan with vengeance in their hearts,' as I was told. They liked that. There were very few of us, and we had suffered greatly to reach the northern isles. They agreed to help us become stronger in the best way they knew how. They taught us to use magic."

"But your people aren't just humans who can do magic," Julien said.

Ciaran chuckled. "The story's not over. My ancestors lived in Lochlann for centuries—studying magic, learning the Lochlannan's ways, and, of course, mixing with them in the most amorous fashion, until the men we were became something else entirely." Ciaran touched his own slightly elongated ear and tapped his lips as he smiled to indicate his sharp canines.

"We became more skilled in magic than men could ever be. Now, the story goes, the goddess Dana took notice of my people—of our will and our strength and our loyalty to our chosen island," he added in a stuffy voice that suggested he'd been told the dramatic story many times. "She blessed us and called us her children. The Tuatha Dé Danann. 'I shall make you a running river,' she told us, 'that you may wash over your foes and prosper in your rightful home.' She granted us eternal life and bore us safely back to Inisfail to claim our revenge."

"Have you actually seen her?" Noah asked, edging forward on his seat. "The goddess?"

"Not me, no." Ciaran shook his head. "It took some time after that for my people to prepare, and to actually leave Lochlann—a lifetime, probably, but time means much less once you've been given immortality. I was still a very young man when my people arrived in Ireland to take it back from the Fir Bolg—those were the descendants of the ones who had stayed behind."

Julien's brow furrowed slightly, and he could see in Trent and Noah's faces that he wasn't the only one having the thought. Trent was the one that voiced it.

"You weren't born in Ireland?"

"Well," Ciaran said with a scoffing chuckle, "how do you think I know how to reach the mystical Lochlann in the first place?" He turned his eyes on the boy at his side. "I was a child there."

"With these brutal and mysterious...proto-fairies?" Trent asked. He pushed to his feet and stared across at Ciaran with a frown.

"Please don't call them that once we arrive, if there's anyone to address at all."

"And hang on," Trent continued, his hands firmly gripping the edge of the boat. "Let me make sure I've got this all straight. Ethniu said she was one of those...the giants. The Fomorians? The people who kicked you out of Ireland to begin with?"

"Aye. They still gave us trouble when we got back, too. That's why it was decided that I should marry her. Our king had only daughters. I was the oldest son of one of our proudest nobles, and I'd done well in the battles against the Fir Bolg. Ethniu was the daughter of the Fomorian king. It was one last attempt at civility before the war. The Fomorians probably regretted it, all things considered," he chuckled.

"Why?" Noah spoke up.

"Because of me," Lugh answered in his father's place. Julien turned to look at him, and suddenly quite a few pieces fell into place. There was a very good reason why Lugh towered over his father and looked as though he could break him in half. He was literally half giant. The hunter paused, for a moment imagining the logistics of a man Ciaran's size with a giant woman, but he squeezed his one eye shut and shook his head to dispel the visual.

Noah spun on the bench, directing his curious stare at Lugh. "What did you do?"

The fairy hesitated as though he didn't really care to answer, but he seemed won over by the witch's eager smile. He spared a brief glance at Julien before he answered.

"When I returned from my fosterage under the care of Manandán, I took my place in King Nuada's court as Ollamh Érenn. It is a title equal only to the High King himself. When next we faced the Fomorians at Mag Tuired, I led the armies of the Tuath Dé and killed the Fomorian King myself."

Noah looked as though he might fall off his bench if he leaned forward any more. "But wait," he said, tilting his head, "wouldn't that be your grandfather? You killed your grandfather?"

"As prophecy said I would."

"Tell them how you did it," Ciaran pressed, his smile betraying a bit of his fatherly pride. "I only heard about it secondhand, of course, since I was dead—but it's an impressive story."

Lugh let out a faint, silent sigh, as though detailing his own heroic exploits was a chore. "Balor of the Evil Eye was called such because of his poisonous eye—it was said to always be covered by seven cloaks, and as each one was removed, plants would wither, trees would billow smoke, and the whole land would grow hot. When it was bare, the land itself would catch fire, and any man caught in its gaze would die instantly. Balor stood at the head of his army, prepared to lay waste to my people with this eye. So, before he could use it, I shot my sling-stone into it and drove it out the back of his head, so that his own army fell under his destructive eye."

Noah stared at him, teetering on the edge of his seat, mouth slightly open. Then he laughed. "That," he said, "is *awesome*. That's why they call you the Lonnbéimnech, isn't it? The fierce striker."

"Give me back the rest of my brain," Ciaran called, but for once, there wasn't much malice in his voice.

"That is why," Lugh agreed.

Julien glanced back at Ciaran to keep himself from acknowledging the admiring look on Noah's face. "So the Lochlannan, they're fairies, like you?"

"Not quite like me," Ciaran answered. "Lochlannan is only our name for them, anyway. They call themselves the Alfar. Either way, you'll see them for yourself or you won't have to worry about it, will you?"

"I don't see the point in being purposely evasive when you're leading us to people who very well might try to kill us."

"Hunter, if the Lochlannan want you dead, that's how you'll be, and there won't be a damned thing you can do about it. Seventh Son or not, you're just a man."

"Let's not get too optimistic about the trip, here," Noah muttered. He turned around on his bench again to face Ciaran. "If everybody thinks this place is abandoned, why do those other dick fairies think that the item they want will still be there?"

"It's likely not," he admitted. "I suppose I'll have to see what's left and try to bring them something they'll accept. They're mostly hoping I'll die along the way, I suspect," he added with a dry chuckle.

"But the Lochlannan can be killed," Julien pressed.

"Of course," Ciaran answered. "Anything can be killed. It's not dying in the process that's the tricky bit."

The hunter gave a quiet grunt and sat down beside Noah. That was something, at least. If a thing could be killed, than Julien could kill it—especially if Noah's safety was at stake.

The day passed slowly. Julien wished he had at least thought to bring a pack of cards. He'd already smoked three cigarettes, and there was only so much staring out at the ocean he could do before the rocking of the boat threatened to put him to sleep again. Ciaran seemed satisfied to hum a tune while he steered the ship, and Trent sat beside him in the small alcove behind the steering shafts, silent but looking deep in thought.

Noah sat cross-legged on the floor of the boat with the book Ethan had given him open in his lap. He traced the words on the pages with his fingertips, brow furrowed and lips moving in quiet whispers. Occasionally he paused to dig through the binder of supplies beside him, which usually ended in him putting his hands on his knees with his elbows jutting out and staring down at his book in consternation.

"Are you having trouble?" Julien asked. He leaned over the witch's shoulder and paused at the sight of the open book. It was in Sanskrit. "Having trouble...reading that at all?"

"Some of it's more archaic than I'm used to," Noah admitted, as though there was some shame to be had in only reading *most* Sanskrit. "This book is supposed to help me with Trent and Ciaran's problem, but I don't know how accurate it is. And a lot of this isn't exactly stuff I can readily test. It's stuff like success in gambling, guards against various diseases, blessings for different situations, that sort of thing. Or it's to fix a broken bone or to ward off arrows, which isn't super helpful right now, either. And if these spells don't work, I'd like to know that before I actually stand in front of someone aiming a bow at me and call their bluff, you know?"

"Is there anything I can do to help?"

"Well," the witch said with a sly smile, "there's a spell for a love charm in here, but I don't think it'll have much of an effect, do you?"

Julien's heart skipped, and he cleared his throat to try to hide it. "I...no. Probably not."

Noah chuckled at him and tugged the hunter down by his shirt to place a light kiss on his mouth. "Especially since I already used it," he whispered against the other man's lips.

"That was clever of you."

"Right? You never even knew."

Julien smiled, and despite the heat in his cheeks from the knowledge that they weren't alone, he pressed another soft kiss to Noah's lips. He wanted to do much more—he'd thought of very little else with the witch curled up against him the night before—but he wasn't flagrant enough to initiate anything with three other men aboard. It was going to be a long nine days.

"You two are quite cozy, hm?" Ciaran taunted from behind them.

Noah's fingers lingered in the fabric of Julien's shirt as the hunter pulled away, and he turned to narrow his eyes at Ciaran. "Maybe I should test this spell for 'consigning an enemy to the serpents?' That sounds fun, right?"

"Are you threatening me with magic, lad?"

"Actually, you might be able to help," Noah went on, all teasing forgotten as he flipped to a page toward the back of his book. "I totally forgot that there are other people here that can do magic. Do you think you could try to put some sort of curse on me?"

Julien leaned to catch Noah's eye, his eyebrows knit into a frown of disbelief. "Franchement? You want him to put a curse on you."

Noah shrugged. "Just a little one. He can undo it after. I just want to see how effective these spells are."

"Absolutely not," Julien objected instantly. "Why would you take that risk?"

Ciaran chuckled. "Better listen to your lover, lad. I'm far too busy to worry about him coming after me again if something happens to you."

Noah gave a heavy sigh. "There has to be something I can—" He stopped. He turned away from both of them and began to flip through the collection of herbs in his binder again. Julien watched him curiously as he plucked out a single packet, tipping a bell-shaped pink flower into his palm.

"What's that for?" Julien asked warily. The bright smile Noah flashed at him didn't comfort him.

"This is Digitalis purpurea. Witch's thimble."

"And what are you going to do with it?"

"Well, it's outrageously poisonous. So, I'm going to cast this spell that's supposed to render poisonous plants innocuous. Then I'm going to eat it."

Julien stared at him, waiting for the punchline, but the witch had already returned his attention to his book. "Noah, you can't be serious." The younger man didn't look up, so Julien bent closer. "Noah."

"It's not fatal," Noah assured him without turning from his chosen page. "Even if the spell doesn't work."

"Why do you have poison in the first place?"

"It's not *just* poison." Noah's fingers traced the lines of text as he spoke. "It can also be used as an antiarrhythmic agent. Some curses kill by cardiac arrest, and the Digitalis is a natural treatment for atrial fibrillation. It's a helpful thing to have in any witch's kit."

Julien paused. He found himself smiling, and without thinking, he reached out to put a gentle hand in Noah's dark hair. "Is there anything you don't know, mon râleur?"

Noah looked up then, and Julien was surprised to see a flush of embarrassment on the witch's face. "I just...plants are important," he grumbled as he focused on his book again. He didn't try to pull away from Julien's touch.

"There must still be a better way to test this book," Julien insisted. He couldn't quite bring himself to say it out loud, but the thought of Noah being in danger again so soon after Julien had gotten him back twisted the hunter's stomach.

"Well, let me know if you think of one in the time it takes me to work out this conjugation."

"Noah, please—"

"Julien," Noah spoke over the top of him, keeping his place on the page with one finger as he looked up at the other man. "I'll be fine. It's not a big deal."

Julien frowned as Noah leaned closer to his book, but he kept quiet. He watched his lover mouth the printed words a few times before sitting up and cupping the delicate flower in both hands. The words flowed from the witch's lips like a prayer, and a very faint light glowed between his fingers as he spoke.

When he finished, Noah lifted one hand and peered down at the flower, which didn't look different in the slightest to Julien. The hunter was teetering on the edge of the bench, prepared to act if the test went wrong—though what he could actually do about it, he hadn't the faintest idea. The Heimlich? Noah popped the delicate blossom into his mouth without hesitation. Julien watched him chew and swallow, and they both waited.

"Huh," the witch said after a minute or two had passed. "Neat." He looked down at his book and started flipping through the pages again, as though he hadn't just risked severe poisoning for the sake of curiosity.

Julien's shoulders slumped with relief. Noah was going to give him atrial fibrillation.

7

Ciaran drew great joy throughout the day from watching the hunter fret over his witch. He'd seen enough jealousy in his time to know exactly what was happening. Lugh was stoic, strapping, and mysterious in all the ways Julien could only dream of, and Noah seemed to have taken a liking to him. Whether it was curiosity or actual attraction didn't matter—it was fun either way to see the hunter's fists tighten every time Lugh gave the witch even a scrap of his attention.

When Ciaran caught Noah peering up at the tall crow's nest, he called to him, urging him to try making the climb. The boy seemed skeptical.

"Oh, go on," Ciaran said. "Lugh, give him a boost, will you?"

Lugh didn't argue. As soon as Noah stood to move toward the mast, Lugh lifted him easily by the waist, letting him steady himself on the fairy's broad shoulders as he reached for the lowest notch in the wood. Ciaran could practically hear Julien's teeth grinding. This would be a good way to pass the time.

In the evening, he traded steering duties with Lugh and helped himself to some candy and bottled water while Noah prepared the ingredients for their next attempt at his spell. He sat beside Trent, who had his hands pressed to the bench and his shoulders hunched as he stared at the bottom of the boat. He hadn't eaten anything all day. He'd just sat beside Ciaran and listened to him humming, either watching the distant waves or his own feet.

"All right, a mhuirnín?" he asked softly, nudging the boy with his shoulder. "You don't seem enthusiastic."

Trent kept his eyes on the floor. "Do you really think this spell has a chance of working? This whole…binding our souls together thing? It sounds like bullshit, right?"

Ciaran chuckled. "Aye, it does. But I've seen all manner of magic in my time, and plenty of it I wouldn't have believed before I saw it." He leaned forward to try and catch the boy's eye. "Do you not want to try?"

Trent's lips pulled into a thin frown, and he didn't answer right away. Ciaran waited with a slightly sick feeling in his belly. "I just…don't know."

Ciaran reached out to run a hand through Trent's hair, gently urging his lover to look him in the face. "Are you doubting the spell, a mhuirnín, or are you doubting us?"

"No," Trent answered a little too quickly.

"It's all right if you're uncertain, Trent," the fairy assured him, the lie tasting bitter on his tongue. "A lot has happened, and after all, it hasn't really been that long—"

Trent reached up to squeeze Ciaran's wrist, keeping his lover's hand at the back of his neck. It was a silent plea to stop talking. To not voice the truth they both knew—that they had met less than a month ago. That it was insane to talk about being bound together forever after such a short time.

"All right," Ciaran said. He tried not to let Trent hear the resignation in his voice. He'd suspected—should have known—that it was too much too fast. That Trent was still so young, and that everything Ciaran was would be overwhelming to him. It was what he'd feared would happen from the start. What always happened. Maybe someday soon, Trent would ask him for a wish after all, and they would part with only bittersweet memories left between them. He let his hand drop and stood to step over the bench away from him, giving a quick whistle to catch Noah's attention.

"I'm not feeling well," he said when the witch looked up. "We'll give it a miss tonight, hm?"

Noah paused with his hands full of herbs. "Oh. Sure, sure. No point in wasting it if you're not focused. We can try again when you're ready."

Ciaran nodded his thanks and moved to the bow of the ship, placing a soft hand on Trent's shoulder as he passed him. He settled himself in his own sleeping bag and stretched out with his hands under his head, watching the stars. He turned away when he saw Trent step closer to him, not wanting to make the boy feel bad by staring at him. But he soon heard the shifting of blanket behind him, and his shoulders finally relaxed as he felt Trent's fingers curl into the fabric of his shirt, his forehead pressed to the soft space between Ciaran's shoulderblades.

He allowed himself a faint smile as Trent shifted closer to him in the darkness. He reached back to draw the boy's arm around him, pressing a soft kiss to his knuckles and holding his hand close against his chest. "Good night, a mhuirnín," he whispered.

When he took over steering in the morning, he had to force Trent to eat a granola bar. He tried showing him how to steer the boat, letting him turn the tiller and feel the shift of the ship beneath him, but that almost made him vomit up his granola again. He settled against the back of the ship with another slip of Noah's ginger under his tongue and seemed liable to fall asleep again. Ciaran would try harder to cheer him up once he wasn't on the verge on being sick.

In the meantime, he leaned on the tiller and watched as Lugh tugged a heavy net from a crate at the side of the ship, drawing the attention of the curious witch once more.

"Is that a magic net?" Noah asked from his seat beside Julien.

Lugh didn't look up. "Yes," he answered dryly. "Its power is to catch fish."

"Did you just make a joke? Have you been out in the sun too long?"

Lugh spread the net over his knees, running his fingers over the knots to check for holes. When he didn't answer, Noah put a hand on Julien's knee to push himself up and climbed over the benches separating him from Lugh.

"Here." Noah picked up one corner of the net as he sat down

beside the fairy without hesitation. "It'll take you all day to untangle it. Let me." Lugh's brow creased in mild irritation, but he let the witch pluck the thick thread from his lap.

"It isn't a two-person job," he objected.

Noah tutted at him and gave his cheek a quick pat. "Just take help when it's offered."

Ciaran's eyes were on Julien as Noah murmured a soft spell to himself, pulling the net over his hand and smoothing it as he went. The poor hunter looked positively sick. Noah and Lugh spread the net between them and handily repaired the few loose knots in the thread, and every time their hands happened to touch, Julien would make a point of looking out at the water instead of at the pair of them. If he hadn't been an insufferable bastard for every moment they'd known each other, Ciaran might have felt a little sorry for him.

The fairy tilted his head, watching Noah grip the side of the boat while Lugh flung the wide net out over the water. The witch leaned over the edge to watch it disappear beneath the surface. A slow smile touched Ciaran's lips, and he cupped one hand to the side of his mouth and kept his eyes locked on Noah as he whispered, "Mí-ádh."

After barely a moment, Noah's hand slipped on the wet edge of the boat, and he tumbled head first into the sea, almost immediately left behind by the fast-moving ship. Julien was on his feet in an instant at the boy's startled shout. He whipped off his jacket and made for the side, already calling out for Noah, but before he could jump, a quiet splash sounded from the front of the ship. Lugh was already in the water. Julien looked as though he wanted to jump anyway, but he stayed put when Noah's head reappeared behind them.

Ciaran hopped over the tiller and snatched hold of the ropes securing the sails, drawing the canvas up with a practiced hand to slow the boat. Lugh appeared at the edge a few moments later with Noah's arms clinging tight to the larger man's shoulders. Julien bent to take the witch's hands and help him, but Lugh easily hefted the both of them up and over the edge. He placed Noah on the closest bench and patted his back to help him cough out some water, and the witch looked up at him with such gratitude that Julien seemed like he might lose what composure he had left. When Noah put a hand on Lugh's arm and earnestly thanked him, the fairy bent to look him in the face and pushed an almost caressing hand over Noah's wet hair to smooth it from his face.

"All right, mo óclach?"

"Yeah," Noah laughed. "I'm fine."

Julien moved between them, practically snatching Noah's hands away from Lugh on the pretense of checking them for chill.

"What the hell happened?" he demanded, a little too harshly. "You can't be careless like that!"

Noah seemed taken aback. "It was just an accident, Julien. I'm okay."

"You'll catch cold in those wet clothes," Lugh interrupted. He gestured at Noah's shirt and turned to pull his cloak from his satchel. Noah pulled his hands free of Julien's grip to strip off his shirt, and Lugh draped the heavy wool over the witch's shoulders. Julien fought to rein in his scowl, but even at a distance, Ciaran could see Julien's eye narrow with laser focus as he caught Lugh's gaze lingering on the witch's bare torso.

"Just stay away from the side," Julien insisted, tucking the cloak tighter around his lover to hide his skin.

Ciaran tapped Lugh's arm with the back of his hand, and together they lowered the sail again. As he stepped over the bench back toward the tiller, Ciaran gave Noah a brief pat on the head.

"Tá tú sábháilte, lad," he chuckled, undoing the simple jinx. He smiled broadly as he took over steering from Trent, who was glad to give up the responsibility.

Trent stayed near him with a frown on his face. "Why did you do that?" he asked in a low voice. "You made him fall, didn't you?"

"It's a long trip, a mhuirnín. I have to have some sort of entertainment." He nodded toward Julien and Noah. "See what just a little bit of jealousy can do?"

The hunter fussed over the younger man, speaking to him in a hushed voice and touching his hair. Finally, Noah snapped, "Julien, I'm fine," and he stood to separate himself from his lover, wringing his soaked shirt out over the side of the boat.

"You're an asshole," Trent muttered.

Ciaran smiled at him. "You knew that when you said you loved me." He paused, half expecting Trent to argue or to pull away from him—after their conversation the night before, perhaps it wasn't wise to joke about whether or not the boy loved him. But Trent actually smiled. Just a little.

"That's why I said it."

Ciaran's heart gave a heavy thud in his chest, and he released his hold on the tiller to tug Trent closer to him and press a heated kiss to his lover's lips. He let his forehead rest against Trent's, feeling the flustered heat in the boy's cheeks. "Mo ghrá thú, a mhuirnín," he murmured softly. "I love you."

Trent put his hands on Ciaran's chest to push him away, but they lingered, fingertips digging into the fabric of the fairy's shirt. He jumped at the sudden wet thump of Lugh's full net being dragged aboard and quickly distanced himself as though caught doing something he shouldn't.

"Just steer the boat," Trent said. His face was still slightly red.

Ciaran did as he was told. All wasn't lost for them. Not yet.

8

The next three days passed even more slowly than the first. They had underestimated how much water they would need, and the remaining bottles had to be carefully divided among the remaining days. They lived on granola, jerky, dried fruit, and packets of nuts, which none of them were satisfied with. The fish helped to break up the monotony of their diet, but only just. Ciaran's candy supplies had begun to run low despite the fact that no one else was eating them—with the exception of Lugh, who Trent had spotted sneaking some occasionally. Noah had even given in and eaten some of Lugh's freshly-caught fish, but he had regretted it when his stomach protested the meat and he spent the night curled up in his sleeping bag with his head in Julien's lap.

Now, on day seven of their seemingly endless voyage, Julien sat on the center bench while Noah practiced idle magic beside him—sparking tiny lights in his hands and changing the color of the buttons on Julien's coat. He had been exchanging longer letters with his young friend over the last few days. The boy had even sent him a couple of apples when he'd complained about how sick the fish had made him, which Noah had considered a blessing. Now he was waiting for a response, so he passed the time as best he could. He took one of the cigarettes the hunter offered him and laid across the length of the bench to breathe the smoke into the air.

Trent had another piece of ginger under his tongue, and he sat near the front of the ship with Ciaran, who was leaning over the edge to trail his hand in the water. They were all bored to tears, but none of them were willing to expend extra energy and risk reducing their already dwindling supplies.

The sky darkened in the afternoon, and as the wind picked up, Lugh gave a sharp whistle, and Ciaran turned to face him.

"Soon be on us," he called, tilting his chin forward to indicate the increasingly bleak sky ahead.

"Aye," Ciaran answered. He gave a resigned sigh through his nose. "You'll want to strap in, a mhuirnín," he said.

"Strap in? To what?"

"To the ship. We can't have you going overboard. That storm isn't natural."

Noah sat up on the bench with his cigarette in his fingers. "How do you know?"

Ciaran chuckled. "Because it's been there since I left. It's a barrier. I did tell you the Lochlannan don't like visitors."

"It's a magic storm?" Noah stood and brushed by Ciaran to lean on the bow of the ship, looking out toward the dark clouds. "But how is it maintained? The amount of energy that must be involved in creating something like that at all, and keeping it going, let alone for thousands of years—"

"I prefer not to think too in-depth about what the Lochlannan are capable of, lad."

"Incredible," Noah breathed. "How far does it go? How many square miles, I mean?"

"Concern yourself more with getting through it alive," Ciaran said. He put a hand on Trent's shoulder to guide him toward the back of the ship. "You just stay down, a mhuirnín. Here." He sat Trent down on the rear bench and gathered up a spare length of rope. He tugged on it to test the strength of the knot securing it to the ship, and then he looped the other end around Trent's waist, tying it deftly into a tight knot. He glanced over his shoulder at Julien and Noah. "You two ought to do the same."

"What about you?" Trent asked, hoping the question was too soft for the others to hear.

"Ach," Ciaran scoffed, a sly smile on his lips as he bent down with his hands on his knees to look Trent in the face. "Lugh will need my help to sail through the thing. Don't worry—a bit of wind and rain won't be enough to stop us. It is a magic boat, after all."

"Then why are you worried?"

"Because you can still fall off of a magic boat."

"Sure," Trent agreed. Ciaran's smile softened at his obvious uncertainty, and he placed a warm hand on Trent's cheek, just for a moment.

"It'll be all right, love." The fairy turned to gesture impatiently at Julien and Noah, urging them to tie themselves off as advised, and he positioned himself near the rigging with his eyes on the clouds ahead of them.

It was agonizing to wait, knowing that the storm was looming ever closer. Trent expected it to happen gradually—some rain, and then maybe some more rain, and the wind growing stronger and harder. But the sea was as calm as it had been so far. Until it wasn't. The storm hit them like a wall, pouring rain down on them and tossing the ship sideways on a sudden wave. Trent clung to the side of the ship to keep himself steady, suddenly grateful for the rope around his middle—although as soon as the thought occurred to him, he imagined himself thrown overboard and tangled in it like bait for a shark. Ciaran and Lugh shouted Gaelic at each other over the sound of the rushing wind, and Trent watched as Ciaran darted back and forth tying off canvas, hauling rope, and snapping at Julien whenever he tried to help. The rain pelted the fairy relentlessly, plastering his hair to his face and his shirt to his skin, but he barely seemed to notice. He only stopped to glance ahead of them, scanning the rolling sea— though what he hoped to see through the sheets of rain, Trent couldn't guess.

The ship lurched over a wave that was taller than the mast, and Trent lost his grip on the side as salt water rushed over the wicker rail, his glasses knocked from his face as he skidded across the bench toward the opposite edge. Before he reached the end of his lifeline, Ciaran appeared from nowhere to take a firm hold of his arm. Trent jerked to a stop in the center of the ship, and even in the chaos of the storm, the fairy paused to bend down and touch his lover's soaked hair, looking into his face as though checking him for injury. When he was satisfied, he straightened and pointed toward the floor, silently commanding Trent underneath the bench. Trent did as he was told, though he felt like a child for hiding away while Ciaran was so obviously in control.

He heard Noah shouting through the rain, and Ciaran turned to focus on the sound. The witch was pointing ahead of them toward a massive wave, easily twice the size of the ship and already cresting foamy white. Ciaran rushed toward Lugh, who heaved on the tiller to straighten their course, but they were too far turned to face the wave head on. Ciaran called for the others to brace themselves, but instead of obeying, Noah climbed up onto one of the benches and faced the wave with outstretched hands. Trent couldn't hear the words he shouted into the rain, but with a hard gesture as though he hoped to break the wave apart with his bare hands, the water in front of them burst into a shower of salt water, leaving the way clear for the ship to pass. Smaller waves drifted away from them on either side, rocking them gently in the heavy rain, but they stayed upright.

Julien moved to catch Noah as his legs crumpled beneath him. He held the witch in both arms and lowered him slowly to the floor of the ship, turning to look over his shoulder at Ciaran and Lugh. Ciaran offered him an approving nod on his way back to tending the sails, and even Lugh showed a touch of relief on his face.

Trent stayed in his place tucked between the benches and the floor, his hands turning raw from gripping the rope in an attempt to keep from hitting one side of the ship and then the other with every crashing wave. After what felt like hours, the sea began to calm, and the rain softened to a drizzle as the clouds grew pale above them. Trent was hesitant to look out from his cramped space, but he relaxed slightly when Ciaran dropped down on the bench beside him with a heavy sigh.

"All right down there, a mhuirnín?" he said, his voice rough from shouting.

"Yeah. I'm fine." Trent slowly crawled out of his hole, hiding the reddened palms of his hands from the fairy as he sat beside him. The last thing Ciaran needed was another reason to fuss over him. "Is it…over?"

"Aye," Ciaran answered, though he sounded weary. "For now."

"For now? What does that mean?"

"There's one more test between us and the isle of Lochlann. But never you mind just yet. We've time to rest." He noticed Trent shivering in his damp clothes and covered him with the driest of the sleeping bags, but once he was bundled, Ciaran tilted his head at him. "You've lost something."

Trent reached up to touch his face, feeling the empty space where his glasses should have been. He peered under the bench as Ciaran untied the knot around his waist, and once he was free, he crouched down near the floor and stretched to the far corner of the darkness. His fingertips touched cool metal, but when he retrieved the glasses and took his seat beside Ciaran again, he found that the frames had been crushed, one arm snapped loose and the other bent at the joint.

"Great," he sighed. "You think they have optometrists where we're going?"

Ciaran smiled at him and took the broken glasses from his hands. He set the pieces on the bench between them and held one hand over them. "Dheisiú," he said softly, and before Trent's eyes, the parts shifted on the wood, clicking quietly as they reconnected with each other. When the frames were whole again, Ciaran picked them up and offered them to Trent with an easy smile.

"Fairy bullshit's good for something on occasion," he chuckled, and Trent lowered his eyes to hide his smile as he took his glasses back and slid them onto his face.

"Thanks."

Ciaran reached out for Trent's hands, turning them palm up for inspection. "You've hurt yourself," he said in a gentle voice. He held on when Trent tried to pull away. "Let me see. You don't want it getting infected." He scooted closer to the younger man and urged him toward the edge of the boat, where he pulled his hands forward and dunked them into the passing water.

Trent hissed as the stinging salt water touched his open scrapes, and Ciaran tutted softly at him, holding his lover's hands in his lap while he reached into their dripping duffel bag. The shirt he retrieved was damp but mostly clean, so he tore it without hesitation and wrapped it carefully around Trent's abused palms.

"Now don't bang them about," Ciaran commanded. "Maybe the herbologist over there can give you something better when he wakes."

"What, no fairy bullshit for this?"

Ciaran frowned insincerely at him and put a brief hand on the other man's knee before standing again. He stepped over the next bench to call to Julien. "Oi, hunter. How's our witch?"

Noah lifted one arm and gave a half-hearted thumbs up, his head in his lover's lap and his other hand dangling from the seat to brush the floor of the ship.

"He's all right," Julien answered. "Just exhausted."

"As well he should be," Ciaran snorted. "That was impressive magic. He may well have saved our hides. Perhaps it was worthwhile to bring him along after all."

"Glad you approve," Julien muttered, his gaze on Noah's sleeping face as he brushed the hair from his lover's eyes. He shifted the witch on his lap so that he could face Ciaran better. "You said there's another test. What is it?"

"A monster," the fairy answered simply.

Trent leaned forward in his seat to stare at the back of Ciaran's head. "It's a monster, and you just told me not to worry about it?"

Ciaran offered him an apologetic smile. "There isn't any point to worrying. It's not the sort of monster you can really do anything about."

"There's always something to be done about monsters," Julien cut in, his lips pulled into a thin frown.

"Don't get riled up, hunter. When we get there, you're more than welcome to take your chances. In the meantime, let's rest up, hm? We've a ways to go, yet."

Trent wanted to ask more questions, but he had to admit that he was exhausted, too. He didn't feel he had any right to be, since he hadn't been the one raising sails, steering, or casting ridiculous Moses-level magic—but he realized that his shoulders hadn't relaxed since they'd first seen the brewing storm clouds. He'd been a little afraid, though he'd never say it out loud, but Ciaran had been watching him the whole time. Making sure he was safe. He hesitated as Ciaran took a place beside him, but after a moment, he leaned his head on the fairy's shoulder and let himself rest. He didn't even mind the light touch of the other man's lips against the top of his head. Not right now.

9

It was almost dawn of the next day before Noah stirred again. The afternoon sun had mostly dried the bottom of the boat, so his sleeping bag only felt a little damp. Julien still laid beside him, one hand fixed around Noah's fingers as he slept. The witch smiled down at his hunter's face, still stern and frowning even in sleep.

Noah scooted slightly closer to him and nuzzled the growing blond scruff on Julien's chin. The larger man gave a soft grunt at the movement and opened his one good eye to peer down at him.

"Morning," Noah whispered, the faint light of the coming dawn making him feel like he ought to keep his voice low.

"Good morning." Julien reached up to touch the witch's cheek. His brow was furrowed in concern despite Noah's sleepy smile. "Are you feeling all right?"

"Still a little tired. But I'm fine."

"You scared me to death," the hunter said in a hushed voice. "When you just collapsed, I thought—"

Noah exhaled an embarrassed laugh through his nose. "I might have overdone it a little. But I'm all right. It just...took a lot out of me."

"You can't take risks like that," Julien insisted. "We don't know what side effects you might still be having from the spell, and if you overexert yourself—"

"You would prefer we all got knocked into the ocean and died? Come on, Julien."

"Just be more careful."

Noah leaned back from Julien with a disgruntled frown twisting his lips and one distancing hand on the hunter's chest. "I'm not a child, Julien. What is your deal? When I fell overboard the other day, you acted like I'd thrown myself into a volcano. And now I use my magic to keep us all from drowning and you're telling me not to take risks? The risk would have been doing nothing and letting that wave hit us. It's not your place to tell me what to do."

Julien opened his mouth, ready to snap back, but then he shut it. He pressed his lips together to keep his words from escaping and took a quick breath, then he nodded. "You're right. Désolé."

"Don't just apologize when you clearly don't agree with me. I'm a grown man. I'm going to do what I think is right. I know that you worry for me, and that's great, I love that you worry—you just need to worry...a little less. Okay?"

Julien put a hand on the side of Noah's neck, gently pulling him close again so that their noses touched. "I'm sorry, Noah. I'll try."

Noah felt a slight flush in his cheeks, and he couldn't stop the smile that pulled his lips. How was he supposed to stay angry at that? Julien wasn't exactly forthcoming about his previous relationships, but Noah could guess that they were few and far between. He tried to remember that Julien was just a little gruff, and that to say he wasn't good at using his words was an understatement. Noah could be patient with that—but it started a bubbling of nauseous nostalgia in his stomach to think that the hunter might start to think he could control him. He'd had enough experience with men who tried and who weren't afraid to use force.

He let out a soft sigh and pressed a kiss to Julien's lips. Julien was just worrying. Noah had been attracted to his stoic, hardworking nature. It would be unreasonable to pretend he didn't know that personality would come with a certain level of seriousness. He couldn't blame Julien for his past self's bad judgment. Julien wasn't Travis.

"It's fine," he said softly. "Thank you for worrying about me." He let Julien draw him close with an arm around his waist and settled his head under the hunter's chin. This was the warmth he'd wanted. This was the gentleness and the devotion he'd known was hiding in Julien all along. He could forgive him being a little overprotective.

Noah's hand flattened against the other man's chest, feeling the heat of the firm muscle there. This was just what he'd imagined all along, too. The stubbled jaw, the scarred skin, the rough hands, battle-worn and calloused, that touched him so timidly when they were alone. The witch shifted slightly as he felt a stirring in his belly, hoping to distance himself from the other man before he made it awkward for both of them, but as soon as he moved, Julien snatched him tightly against him in one sudden movement. Noah sucked in a silent gasp as he felt the hunter's erection pressed firmly into his hip, and his grip tightened in Julien's shirt.

"I hate this fucking boat," Julien muttered against Noah's ear, the husky promise in the deep voice sending a longing shudder through the witch.

"I do too," he sighed. He let one hand snake between them and smiled at the start the hunter gave as Noah cupped him. The stifled, guttural sound caught in Julien's throat was torturous, but Noah simply leaned up to touch a teasing kiss to the outside edge of his lover's lips. "But when I get you alone, I'm going to have a lot of lost time to make up for."

Julien gripped the witch by the hip, and it took all Noah had not to grind against him. They'd only had one night together—one short, perfect night—and this forced communal living made it impossible to continue their relationship the way Noah wanted. He hoped that whatever was waiting for them on this lost island, they would at least be able to finally get some privacy. He wasn't going to be able to take much more teasing.

"We'd better stop before we do something embarrassing," Noah said with a smile, and he reluctantly pulled away from his lover and sat up with his sleeping bag pulled modestly over his lap. Julien gave a soft grunt of irritation as he pushed himself up to sitting, but then he froze, and Noah followed his gaze toward the back of the ship, where Ciaran stood casually leaning his elbows on the tiller and staring down at them with an easy smile.

"Don't stop on my account," he said, and Julien scowled up at him with red staining his cheeks.

Noah put a hand on Julien's shoulder to push himself to his feet and tilted his head at Ciaran. "Well I wouldn't want you getting envious—or have you forgotten that, having had you in my brain, I know exactly how you two measure up? Or rather, don't?"

Ciaran paused, a momentary look of offended disbelief on his face, but then he brushed it off with a laugh. "You're full of shit," he said, but he didn't seem entirely convinced. He frowned and cleared his throat as he returned his full attention to steering the ship.

Noah smiled and bent down to touch a light kiss to Julien's lips, the hunter staring up at him with a mixture of embarrassment and admiration. "Don't mind him," he whispered against the hunter's cheek, and he set about rummaging in their bags in search of what remaining food they had.

The day passed lazily, and everyone on board was glad for the rest after the excitement of the storm. Noah poured some oils over the scrapes in Trent's hands to seal them, but the group didn't exactly have any pressing business aboard the boat. Trent worked up the nerve to climb to the top of the crow's nest with Ciaran's assistance; Julien helped Lugh haul in the afternoon's net full of fish; Noah studied his book for the tenth time and did what stretches he could manage balanced on the long seats. The conversation on the ship had almost completely died—after seven days together, none of them had very much left to say to the others, and it had grown too cold for any of them to be too energetic. Noah was a little grateful for the peace, if he was honest. Even with Julien, talking had become a lesson in patience. He loved the hunter's company, but it wasn't his conversation that he wanted. The only person he still wanted to chat with was Lugh, and the fairy was less than eager to talk about his adventures. Still, Noah was certain he'd seen a faint smile on the other man's face once or twice while they were talking. He considered each one an accomplishment.

He slept uncomfortably that night. It was nice to lie next to Julien, to feel his warmth nearby and listen to his breathing, but it was also awful. Noah ended up scooting away from him and stuffing his hands between his own knees to keep them from wandering. Tomorrow would be day eight of their supposed nine-day journey. He could wait a little more.

The next afternoon, just when Noah was considering curling up under a bench for a nap to take his mind off of his hunger, Ciaran suddenly shouted at Lugh from the rear of the ship. Lugh raised the sails to slow their progress, and Ciaran left the tiller in Trent's uncertain hands as he darted up the mast to the crow's nest. Noah scanned the horizon in an attempt to find what the fairy was looking for, and his heart leapt at the sight of distant rocks jutting out of the sea in front of them.

"Is that land?" he asked, climbing up onto one of the benches and balancing himself on Lugh's shoulder as they both looked out over the water. "Oh, thank god," he breathed, the words coming out as puffs of steam in the frigid air.

"We need to get through that passage," Ciaran answered from above them. He pointed toward the fjord ahead of them, the water between the tall stone cliffs at least a mile wide. "Lochlann is beyond."

"So, let's go," Julien spoke up. "It's not like we won't fit."

"No." Ciaran dropped down from the high perch and moved to the front of the ship. "This is trouble."

Noah turned to him with a curious frown. "What, the rocks?"

"Those aren't rocks. That is the Hafgufa."

"The what?" Julien asked, but Noah already had an excited grip on the fairy's sleeve.

"Are you serious? It's real?"

"Look there," Ciaran said. He leaned close to Noah to direct his sight, pointing out one of the massive stones near the base of the cliffs. "See the way the water moves, washing steadily, not like the splashing at the cliffside. That's breathing."

Julien took a step forward to look. "Breathing?" he echoed. "That rock is breathing?" He stared at Ciaran with an accusing frown. "That is the monster we have to fight?"

"I did say you might not want to fight it, hunter. The Hafgufa is the mother of all sea monsters. Literally." Ciaran turned to face his companions, his hands weary on his hips as he took a short breath. "Those two rocks are its open mouth, waiting for the sea to fill with fish for it to eat. So we have two options. If we wait for it to close its mouth, we're likely to get sucked into the whirlpool as it sinks. Or we risk just sailing through and hope it doesn't close with us in it."

"These aren't exactly great options," Noah said.

Trent stepped away from the tiller since the ship wasn't moving, and he frowned at Ciaran. "Why not just move far away and wait for it to close? One of you must have packed a set of binoculars, right? Then we can wait for it to come back up, and we'll know it won't close again for a while."

"Because we don't know when it closed last," the fairy answered. "It could be days. And we're running out of supplies."

The group stood in silence for a few long moments, until Lugh finally folded his arms and gave a shrug.

"So we sail through now." The others turned to look at him. "It is the only option. We take the risk."

Julien nodded, though his jaw seemed tight. "He's right. We have to chance it."

"Well," Noah said, "at least we have a super-fast magic boat, right? Let's go for it."

Ciaran glanced up at his son. "You take the rudder. I'll direct you from above."

The two men took their places, Lugh at the helm and Ciaran dropping the sails, and soon the ship was moving forward again, toward the mile-wide maw of the monster. Trent stayed near the mast, his eyes warily on Ciaran in the crow's nest above him, and Julien kept a watchful eye on the water as the ship rocked gently on the low waves. Noah immediately moved to kneel on one of the benches, leaning out as far over the edge as he dared and peering down toward the murky depths. He knew the water was too dark to see very far, but he imagined that he could see the creature's massive teeth deep down below.

The ship's exhausted crew stayed dead silent as they went. The air was tense, and none of them seemed willing to risk making a sound and rousing the beast underneath them. Ciaran guided Lugh forward with gestures and exchanged glances, and Lugh turned the ship with a gentle hand at his father's commands, keeping them heading through the passage as directly as possible. The cliffs blocked them in on either side, and monster or not, Noah was relieved to see something other than flat ocean for the first time in a week.

They slipped forward as quickly as the wind would take them, and they passed right between the two matching rocks, all of them letting out a tentative sigh of relief as the open jaws began to drift behind them. Noah paused, listening, as something began to pulse underneath the water. It began as a churning, low and distant, but then it grew louder, and Noah reached out to put a warning hand on Julien's arm.

"It's moving," he whispered.

Ciaran seemed to have already noticed. He dropped from the crow's nest, sliding down a dangling rope to speed his trip, and shouted at Lugh, "Ní mór dúinn a bhogadh níos tapúla!"

Noah frowned at the words, the gist of their meaning clear in his head. They needed to go faster.

"I can't control the wind!" Lugh snapped back.

The water around them began to swirl, the rocks shifting and groaning as they edged closer. It was like watching it happen in slow motion, but they were definitely moving. The mouth was closing. Noah could already feel the ship lurching to the side with the downward current. They weren't going to make it. He jumped when he felt Ciaran's firm hand on his shoulder.

"Can you?"

Noah didn't hesitate. "Hold onto something." He rushed to the rear of the ship, bounding over the rows of benches, and he stood beside Lugh and lifted his hands.

Julien swayed on his feet as the witch began his incantation, producing a swift gust of air from behind them that filled the sails and pushed them forward. The ship's bow lifted out of the water from the force of the wind, and Ciaran took hold of a rope securing the sails when it started to slip. Julien rushed to help him, though his footing was unsure. The ship leaned so far to the side, pushed by the wind and pulled by the whirling water, that he almost slipped on the wicker floor as he grabbed for the rope.

"I have it," Ciaran assured him, but the metal fastening holding the rope snapped free as he tied it off, and the fairy had to snatch it from the air. He twisted it around his arm and held onto it with both hands, leaning the full weight of his body against the pull of the straining sail. "Mind Trent!" he shouted over the wind when Julien tried to help.

"But I can—"

"Julien!" the fairy snapped, distracting himself long enough to look the hunter in the eye. "Take care of him. *Please.*"

Julien's eye widened for a moment, but then he set his jaw and moved toward the mast, where Trent clung tightly to the wood in an attempt to brace himself against the lean of the ship. He held the boy tightly around the shoulders, urging him to hunker down near the floor away from the worst of the wind.

The roar of the water around them was deafening, the whirlpool opening to the depths of the ocean as the rocks of the creature's jaws finally began to slip beneath the surface. Lugh had drawn Noah close to him, letting the witch lean back against him for support as he struggled to maintain the spell pushing them forward. He held Noah's slender body easily with one arm and kept the tiller stable with the other, guiding them steadily away from the swirling epicenter threatening to suck them to the bottom.

Something struck the hull of the ship and slammed them sideways toward the deepening maw, and Trent was knocked out of Julien's grip and sent tumbling toward the edge. Julien snatched him by the arm as their last half-empty case of bottled water fell over the side in his place. He kept one hand on the rigging to secure himself, and with a quick heave, he pulled the boy back against his chest and held him around the waist. Trent felt small and trembling in his grip, young and unsuited to ocean voyages, sea monsters, and magic quests.

"We'll make it," he said close to Trent's ear, and the boy nodded against him with a tight hold on his coat.

Distantly, he heard Noah cry out in exhausted determination, and the boat shifted underneath them again. The ship rushed forward over a looming wave, and with a final push, the bow of the ship crashed back to the water, free of the whirling current. Noah didn't let up until the sea boomed shut behind them and the waves grew still, and then he finally stopped his constant murmuring and collapsed over Lugh's waiting arm. The ocean seemed eerily silent in the wake of the maelstrom, only the lingering echoes of the heavy waves sounding off of the stony cliffs. Julien passed Trent off to Ciaran, who held him tightly and touched his hair, and he rushed to the back of the boat to tend to Noah.

Lugh settled the witch in the nook behind the helm, snatching up his cloak from nearby and folding it into a pillow under Noah's head. He crouched beside him and pushed damp hair away from his sweat-soaked forehead. He looked up as Julien appeared at his side, but he put out a hand to keep the hunter from touching Noah.

"Leave him be," the fairy said in a low voice. "He'll come around soon."

Julien bristled at being blocked, and when Lugh rose to his feet again, Julien glared at him, drawing as close to the other man's face as the difference in their height would allow.

"You and I need to talk," he said through gritted teeth. Lugh tilted his head just slightly but didn't respond. "You think I don't see what you're doing? Noah has nothing to do with you. He's my responsibility. I will protect him, and you will keep your hands off of him."

Lugh lifted his eyebrows in mild surprise. "I'm only helping a comrade."

"I'm not blind," Julien snapped. "Anyone can see that you're interested in him—and not as a comrade," he added with a sneer. "You need to forget about him."

"You're walking a fine line, an duine, threatening me."

"You don't frighten me. Just keep your distance."

Julien turned away without waiting for Lugh's answer, and he took his place beside Noah, one gentle hand on his chest to check the steadiness of his breathing. For all his talk, Julien didn't seem to be doing a very good job keeping Noah out of trouble.

10

Trent stayed by Ciaran's side when he took over steering after sunset. He didn't mind staying up; he doubted he would have been able to sleep after the day they'd had in any case. He still had too much adrenaline pumping through him. Ciaran had fussed over him and asked him repeatedly if he was all right, but all Trent had been able to think about was how close he'd come to tumbling into the water and how he'd clung like a frightened child to the chest of a man who had very recently been trying to kill Ciaran. He felt like an idiot. Ciaran at least seemed to understand that he wasn't in the mood to talk, and they passed the night quietly. Trent leaned against the fairy's legs and watched the ribbons of green light that passed overhead in the winter sky.

Just as the sun was rising and Trent was beginning to drift off to sleep, he heard Ciaran softly call his name, the fairy's fingertips brushing his hair to rouse him.

"We're here."

Trent lifted his head and stretched upwards to peer over the tiller at the approaching land in the distance. The cliffs hid the horizon, a mass of cold, grey stone closing them in on both sides. Ahead of them, the cliffs dropped off into a low natural harbor leading to rugged hills covered with dying grass. The land beyond seemed empty and deserted.

"That's it?" Trent asked. "It…doesn't look very magical."

"Well I did tell you there might not be anyone here, didn't I? If we're lucky, Lochlann is abandoned."

Trent pulled himself to his feet with Ciaran's offered hand and leaned on his shoulder to look out over the water.

"Hold the tiller, will you?" Ciaran left Trent in charge of the helm and clambered up the mast, his movement stirring their sleeping companions. The fairy stared ahead, watching for any signs of life, but the foggy hills were barren even of trees. He could see some crumbling ruins in the distance, fallen ages past, stone pillars worn smooth by wind and the passage of time. Ciaran leaned against the crow's nest railing and took a deep breath of the saltwater air. He'd hoped the island would be empty, hadn't he? There wouldn't be anyone there to potentially kill them. They could go ashore, say they'd had a look around, and go back to Tír na nÓg empty-handed and apologetic. That was the sensible thing to hope for. So why did he still feel a little disappointed?

"Oi, mo mhac," he called down. "Tabhair dúinn i."

Lugh ran a hand through his hair to smooth the tousle of sleep as he pulled to his feet, and he relieved Trent from steering duty with a brief, sleepy pat to the boy's head. At his father's guidance, he eased the ship toward the island, and he dropped the anchor as soon as the bow touched the curving sandbar.

Ciaran dropped from the crow's nest and stood on one of the long benches to take one final look at the desolate island. He glanced back at Trent, who approached him with a cautious frown.

"You lot ought to stay here," the fairy said. "I'll have a look around first."

"The hell you will," Trent answered immediately. "You're not just going by yourself."

"I am putting my feet on solid ground in about ten seconds," Noah added, already scooping up his binder full of herbs and tokens. "It's been nine days, and I am getting off this boat, scary ancient magic people or no scary ancient magic people."

Ciaran sighed. "All right," he said with reluctance in his voice. His expression softened slightly as he looked at Trent. "But keep your eyes open. This place may not be as empty as it looks."

Trent nodded, and he even took the fairy's hand when he offered it, following him over the side of the ship with the others following close behind. They waded through the gentle surf and headed up the slope to the grassy hill, Ciaran taking the lead as they approached the toppled stones. They all watched, waiting for something to happen, but the island was silent except for the cold wind rushing through the fjord. There weren't even any birds or animals darting away from them as they passed—just dying grass and salt-scented mist.

Ciaran walked between the rows of worn pillars with a knot in his stomach. It should be empty. No one had heard from the Lochlannan in thousands of years. Something must have happened to them. Ruins were all he could have reasonably expected to find. It was better this way. They could make camp, find some fresh water and gather some food, and head back the way they came without incident. He would have another journey back to figure out what he was going to tell Gaibhne. He couldn't very well be expected to retrieve something from a people who were no longer here.

Behind them, a tiny pebble ticked its way down a pile of fallen pillars, and Ciaran stopped, putting out a hand to halt the others behind him. His eyes narrowed, and he tilted his ear toward the piled stones.

"Taispeáin díbh féin," he called.

A few beats of silence passed. The mist stirred ahead of them, and a dozen dark figures appeared through the fog, seeming to climb from the stones themselves. They crept over the rocks like spiders, slow and purposeful, with longbows drawn and arrow tips trained on the group of strangers. Every one was clad from head to toe in shades of dreary grey, hoods drawn low over their eyes and long braids of black hair trailing down over their shoulders. One of them shouted what sounded like an angry question, but Ciaran couldn't understand the words.

Ciaran put a wary hand on Trent's arm to guide the boy behind him, and Julien and Noah instinctively drew closer together. Lugh had a tight grip on the shaft of his spear, but he didn't make a move to free it from its cover. Not yet.

"Tá mé Cian mac Cainte na Tuatha Dé Danann," Ciaran said,

eyeing the hidden faces surrounding him.

After a moment, one of the men touched the arm of the shadow beside him, urging him to lower his bow, and he took a step toward them as he pulled back his heavy hood. The face underneath was harsh and narrow, with slate grey skin and empty, pitch black eyes without a sign of surrounding white. His ears were long, with a more exaggerated point than Ciaran or Lugh's, and Trent caught a glimpse of sharp canines as the man spoke, his voice low and rumbling like grinding stones.

"Hvað leiddi þig?"

Ciaran frowned. He placed himself purposefully between the staring stranger and Trent, but he didn't understand the other man's words enough to answer. The leader of the party narrowed his eyes as he studied the travel-weary group, and Ciaran felt a faint pulse in the air before the man spoke again, this time in clear, slightly accented English.

"You have no business here, Nemedian."

"We come seeking the aid of the Alfar," Ciaran answered. "I am sent by the Trí Dé Dána."

The man's lip curled in a faint sneer at the title, but his black, sharklike eyes focused on Ciaran's face. He studied them all in turn, inspecting their faces with skepticism written on his frowning lips. "High King Huldrekall will decide," he said after a long pause, and the scouts around him straightened as they lowered their bows. He tilted his head toward them. "Your weapons."

A pair of men approached from either side, and Lugh and Julien warily handed over the weapons they carried. Neither of them looked very pleased about the idea, but Ciaran nodded quiet encouragement at them, and they complied. One of the scouts even took Noah's binder, tucking it into his satchel and giving the witch a suspicious look. The leader gestured to them to follow, and the group moved forward over the low hill, encircled by dark, silent figures.

Trent leaned around Ciaran to try to get a look ahead of them through the cloaked shoulders of their guards, but they didn't seem to actually be walking toward anything. The mist grew thicker as they walked, but there was no sign of civilization that Trent could see.

The scout closest to him edged nearer with each step, and Trent moved away as he noticed, glancing up at the black eyes studying him.

"Nemedian," the man said, drawing Ciaran's attention. "If our King doesn't kill you, how much will you take for your pet? He's a pretty one." He reached out and brushed a thin knuckle down Trent's cheek to his chin, and Ciaran snapped out a hand to knock away the offending touch.

"Nach bhfuil sé ar díol," the fairy growled. He urged Trent closer to him with a light hand on his back, placing himself between his lover and the smirking stranger.

Trent frowned up at Ciaran, his voice low as they walked. "Pet?"

"Don't mind it, a mhuirnín."

"Is this because I'm Chinese again? Have none of you people ever seen someone not white? Or…grey, or whatever?"

"It's because you're human," the fairy answered softly. He kept a protective hand on the small of Trent's back, but he didn't look at him again.

Despite the mist around them becoming almost too thick to see through, the scouts walked forward with sure steps, until Trent was certain that they were leading them right off the side of a cliff. Then, just as he began to squint to try to see through the fog, he felt a wash of cool air flow over him as though passing through a curtain, and the mist was gone. In front of them, an entire city came into view—rows of low, thatched roofs in a semicircle surrounding a wide moat and a tall two-level rampart lined with heavy, rough-cut tree trunks.

"Falias," Ciaran said softly, but Trent wasn't sure if he was explaining or admiring.

A broad path led through the center of the pattern of houses and over the moat, and as they traveled through the village, Ciaran took note of the eyes on them from all sides. Lochlannan stopped in their tracks to stare at them, pausing with their baskets or satchels and watching the strangers through their cold, black eyes. They whispered amongst themselves in hushed voices. How many centuries had it been since outsiders walked this path?

Ciaran kept Trent close to him as they approached the broad rampart walls, but there didn't seem to be an entrance at the end of the bridge. Their guard led them forward without care. At the last moment, a heavy grinding sound startled Trent, and the stones forming the wall shifted and turned until an arch large enough for them to pass through opened up in the heavy wall. Only the pull of Ciaran's gentle hand kept Trent moving forward under the rampart gate and the watchful gaze of the guards standing along the wooden fence. There was no getting out of this now. There would be no turning back if they changed their minds. When they entered the compound, the houses became sturdier and more ornate, with curling eaves carved with notched geometric patterns. The scout leading them turned a corner, and the longhouse clearly belonging to the King came into view. It was twice the size of the homes around it, and coarse carvings of animals lined the walls of the longhouse. Two wooden wolves taller than Trent guarded the door.

The leader of their group snapped out a quick word to his followers and positioned them near the door. He gestured to Ciaran with a wary eye on the others, and all five of them filed into the longhouse behind their guide. In the entry room, thick tapestries covered the wooden walls, and a variety of furs were stacked on the low bench on the far side of the room. Ciaran glanced back at his companions and held out a hand to keep them from following him.

"Wait here. Please," he added with a soft look in Trent's direction. "I'll talk to them."

Trent nodded, but he seemed reluctant to obey. He watched Ciaran step through the doorway and immediately moved up behind him to peer around the corner. He didn't even mind Noah leaning against his shoulder to get a better look. Their guard touched Ciaran's shoulder to stop him just inside the room.

"The King is in audience," he said under his breath, so they waited. The hall was large but simpler than Trent would have imagined a King's longhouse to be. The room was lit with candles placed in worn metal chandeliers that hung in the air near the ceiling without the support of chains, and hammered sconces lined the walls and gave off a low orange light as they gently bobbed in place. Low tables stretched the length of the room on either side with a massive fire burning in a pit between them, on which some kind of half-butchered animal was skewered on a spit. People eating and drinking filled the benches on both sides of the room, but no one spoke. All eyes were on the far end of the room, where Trent spotted a raised wooden platform and a high-backed seat illuminated by flanking braziers.

Sitting in the sturdy, knot-carved chair sat a man with the same smooth, ash-colored skin as the others, his pitch black eyes focused sharply on a cloaked figure in front of him. Trent assumed the waiting man would be the same as the others, but he did a double-take as he realized that the figure had thick horns growing from his head, curving close to his skull and twisting upward in a grand arc at the back of his head. The dark horns were adorned with thin gold bands at intervals along the ridged surface, and heavier rings at the lowest base of the curve bore the weight of an inky veil that flowed from his horns down his back, covering his bone-straight black hair and ending just above his floor-length cloak.

The King of the Lochlannan was broad-shouldered, with dark kohl marking his eyes and long, black braids framing his stern face. A heavy silver crown rested on his head, a simple ring of metal covered in swirling carvings and adorned with a red oval stone. The King's long ears were decorated with silver clips and thin chains looping from a number of piercings, and his thick fur cloak was fastened with carved silver brooches. He sat tall on his throne, fingers slightly curled on the arms of his seat, watching the man before him with his faintly scarred mouth set into a firm line. He seemed to be considering something, and the entire hall waited in tense silence for his answer.

"Very well," he said at last, his voice low and steady. He offered a single nod. "The Alfar are pleased to accept your proposal, Lord Ashmodai."

The figure in the dark cloak gave a deep bow with one long-fingered hand to his chest, and he took a respectful step backward before turning toward the door. He took long strides down the hall, passing the men watching him from the tables without a glance. He wasn't one of them. As he approached the doorway, their guide urged them to make way for him, so Trent and Noah stepped backward to let him pass. When he drew near, Trent noted his long, sharp features, his straight nose and narrow chin, and the distant, superior look on his face. He kept his eyes ahead as though their presence wasn't the slightest concern to him.

The man breezed by them and out of the hall in silence. Trent noticed Noah staring after him with a curious frown on his face, but when he heard Ciaran announced in the next room, both of them crowded up to the doorway again. Ciaran stopped a polite distance from the platform where the King sat and gave a low bow. His presence drew almost the same surprised quiet as the horned man before him had. Trent reminded himself not to hold his breath.

"Beannú mé tú i síocháin, mo Thiarna," Ciaran said, and the King's empty eyes narrowed faintly.

"You have no business here, Nemedian. Your people left our shores long ago."

"I am Cian mac Cainte, Lord. I have come to settle a blood debt, and I require aid to—"

"You think you are owed favors." King Huldrekall leaned forward in his seat, ever so slightly. "Do not mistake a distant past for current kinship. You come unbidden to our island, bringing strangers to us, and you think you deserve to stand before me and make demands?" His gaze snapped to the doorway at the end of the hall, and Trent felt a chill run down his spine as the man's eyes landed on him.

"I ought to have you and your companions put in gibbets for the crows," The King said with a tight jaw.

"My Lord," a new voice spoke up from the low table to the King's right, drawing the attention of both Ciaran and the King himself. A man stood and took a small step forward, greying hair spilling over his shoulders as he bowed. He looked thin, with wrinkles at the edges of his eyes, but his gaze was still sharp. "I recognize this boy. His father was a strong man, a good physician, and a personal friend to me. The laws of hospitality demand that I at least offer his son my welcome."

The King's mouth twisted into a grimace, but he sighed, his eyes studying Ciaran as he pondered. "They would be your responsibility, Gunvard," he said after a long pause.

"I would expect no less, Lord."

King Huldrekall leaned an elbow on the arm of his throne and tapped his scarred lip with one finger before answering. "Very well." He sat up straight and focused on Ciaran again. "Three days. You may rest and resupply, and then you may leave whole with my blessing. But that is the only grace you shall receive from me. And if you or your companions cause any trouble—especially your Seventh Son—

both you and Gunvard will pay for it. Do I make myself clear, Nemedian?"

"My Lord is generous, and I am grateful," Ciaran answered with another bow.

"May I escort them, my Lord?" the man called Gunvard asked, and the King waved them away with an impatient gesture. Gunvard approached Ciaran and placed an open hand on his back to guide him away from the throne and back to the others.

11

A simple nod was all it took for their scout guard to bow and excuse himself. Their weapons were returned to them, and then the five of them stood in the entry hall under the scrutinizing eye of a man who claimed to have known Ciaran's father.

"You did bring quite an entourage," Gunvard said, scanning each of them in turn before returning his attention to Ciaran. "You don't remember me, do you?"

Ciaran shook his head with an apologetic frown. "I'm sorry."

"No matter. It was some time ago, wasn't it?" He gestured toward the door. "If you please. I'm sure it was no easy task to get here. You must be tired."

The alfar led them from the great hall and down a wide stone path, into the rows of smaller homes nearer the ramparts. All around them, people passed with suspicious eyes as they hurried on their way, some lifting their chins or pulling long skirts aside as though to avoid touching the same ground as the intruders. Others only scowled at them as they led wagons piled high with grain or fabrics, the wooden wheels seeming to turn on their own to move the carts down the path.

Trent and the others trailed behind Ciaran as he walked beside Gunvard. His head was held high, but Trent was certain he could see a faint trembling in the fairy's clenched fists.

"Is your father still living, Cian?" Gunvard asked as they walked, carrying his hands loosely clasped behind his back.

"Yes, he is."

"And did you grow up like him, I wonder?"

Ciaran scoffed and instantly tried to stifle it. "I tried not to," he answered in what he clearly hoped was a sober tone, and Gunvard gave a soft chuckle.

"When I knew Dian Cecht, he was a more than capable healer, but he was also jealous, untrusting, and quick to anger. I'm glad to hear that you haven't followed in his footsteps." He glanced over his shoulder at the motley crew of followers behind them. "But you're still a troublemaker, I see. Gotten yourself a blood debt, hm? And a son as well."

"Yes." Ciaran turned his head to look at Lugh. "This is—"

"I know who he is. We do still hear such stories here, you know." Gunvard stopped outside one of the longhouses and stepped inside ahead of them.

The inside of the house was spacious and luxuriously furnished, with woven tapestries on the walls, thick furs on the floor, and an open fire pit at one side of the main room. A figure in a shabby blue tunic and pants was crouched by the fire, tending it with a metal rod to stoke the flames, and Trent froze as he noticed the young man's face. He wasn't the same pale grey as the others. He was dirty, but his lightly tanned, rosy cheeks, closely shorn brown hair, and perfectly normal ears gave him away in an instant. He was human. He kept his eyes on the floor as the group passed him, and Gunvard didn't even spare him a glance. It was like he didn't exist.

"We will have fine accommodations for you and your son, of course," Gunvard assured Ciaran as he reached a fur-lined chair and took a seat. "You are welcome in my home. Your humans will be escorted to the slave quarters, but you may call for them at any time."

Trent took a half-step back on instinct, but Ciaran instantly placed himself in front of the boy. "He is not a slave," he said, reaching back to take Trent's hand in his. Trent could feel the cold sweat in the fairy's palm, but his voice was steady. "He must stay with me."

Gunvard's placid expression faltered. "You've taken it for a lover?"

"He's not an 'it,' either," Ciaran countered.

Gunvard seemed to consider for a moment. "Well. It is uncouth. But if it's your preference to keep the boy with you, then it isn't my place to forbid it. I will allow him to stay in the house. As for the others—the witch, for example…"

Lugh put a hand on Noah's back and pulled him toward him, causing the smaller man to jump. "This one is mine," he said easily, and he leaned down close to the witch's cheek with his hand on Noah's waist. "I won't be apart from him."

Julien moved forward with his mouth already open to protest, but Lugh took hold of his shoulder and squeezed it so hard that the man flinched. "This one too. I need both of them quite close, do you understand?" He turned his pale eyes on Julien at the indignant scowl on the hunter's face, but instead of scolding him, he let the faintest of smiles touch his lips and reached up to ruffle Julien's hair. "Now now, pet," he said in a voice softer than Trent ever expected to hear from him, "don't get feisty until we're alone."

Trent could see Noah biting his bottom lip so hard it must have been close to bleeding, his shoulders trembling with barely restrained laughter.

"You really don't want to separate them," Ciaran added, completely deadpan. "The muscly one doesn't look it, but if you try to put him off too long, he'll show up panting for it." If Ciaran noticed the hole Julien was trying to burn into his head with his one good eye, he didn't pay it any mind.

Gunvard lifted a hand to quiet them, his brows furrowed in distaste. "I do not need to be convinced of your…preferences. There are two guest rooms. You may arrange yourselves as you please."

"Thank you, Gunvard," Ciaran said. "Sincerely. You may have saved our lives."

"Doubtless. But save your thanks. I am only doing what is right. Get some rest, and in the morning, we can discuss what brought you back here."

"We will. I'm in your debt," he added as Gunvard gestured for the boy in the blue tunic.

"Also doubtless," the alfar said with a small smile.

The whole group gave a small start as the door to the longhouse burst open, and six pairs of eyes turned to the figure in the doorway. Another alfar stood with one hand on the heavy wooden door he'd just shoved, panting for breath. He was half doubled over, his free hand on his hip and his long black hair tumbling over his shoulder. It was tied back from his face on the left side by rows of small braids that led into a messy knot, but soft bangs brushed his face on the other side, and the length of it fell in thick locks down to his back. When he spoke, he sounded winded and paused between words to breathe.

"Faðir," he gasped, "Heyrðiru? Það eru—"

He finally looked up, and his black eyes widened at the sight of the crowd in the room. He looked young—though Trent supposed that didn't necessarily mean anything to these people. He was still probably older than Trent could really wrap his brain around.

"Af Æsir," the stranger breathed as he slowly straightened. Gunvard raised a hand, and as their host moved toward the door, Trent felt the same faint pulse in the air as he had on the shore.

"Rathgeirr, these are our guests," Gunvard said, the faint lift of his eyebrows suggesting that he expected the younger man to behave himself. "Cian mac Cainte and Lugh mac Cein of the Tuatha Dé Danann," he went on, gesturing to them both in turn. The humans in the party apparently didn't merit an introduction. Gunvard touched the other alfar on the shoulder. "This is my youngest son, Rathgeirr. Please excuse his...exuberance."

"Tuatha Dé Danann," Rathgeirr repeated. "Really?" He stepped out from under his father's hand and approached the group with a broad smile on his face. It was strange to see such a friendly expression after the sea of staring black eyes and blank grey faces that had greeted them thus far—and the sharp canines in Rathgeirr's smile didn't help lessen the dichotomy.

"Really," Ciaran chuckled.

"How have you come here? Why did you come? Did you see the Hafgufa? What was it like? How do you know my father? How long will you stay?" Questions poured out of him like water, but Gunvard stopped him with a pointed clearing of his throat.

"Our guests are tired," the older man said with a scolding tone, and Rathgeirr seemed to shrink slightly under the admonishment.

"My apologies," he said. His disappointment was written on his face.

"We will have time for conversation in the morning, I'm sure. Please, make yourselves at home." At his nod, the boy in the dirty blue tunic approached to lead them to their rooms.

"Thank you, Gunvard," Ciaran said again, though Trent saw him offer the younger alfar a small smile as he turned. They followed the human through a short hallway and to a pair of doors.

Trent couldn't take his eyes off of him—he must have been a slave. He showed them into their room, bowed, and took his leave, all without raising his eyes from the floor. Ciaran released his lover's hand only once the bedroom door was closed, and he dropped down onto the fur-lined bed with an unsteady sigh.

"Are you okay?" Trent asked softly, though he couldn't quite bring himself to move from the door. He didn't feel at home here.

"I was so afraid," the fairy answered with an empty laugh. He leaned his elbows on his knees and hid his face in his hands for a moment before looking back up at the younger man.

"I didn't know you could be afraid."

"Not for me, a mhuirnín." Ciaran's brow knit together, and he held his hands out for Trent. When the boy approached, Ciaran put his arms around his lover's waist and laid his forehead against his stomach. "If I couldn't convince them...if Gunvard hadn't—" He shook his head, hiding his face in Trent's shirt. "They'd have killed you," he whispered. "Or worse."

Trent's chest tightened at the way Ciaran's fingers twisted in the fabric at his back. He put his arms around the fairy's head and doubled over, smelling the traces of seawater in the other man's hair as he kissed it. "I'm fine. I'm here," he assured him, and he felt the fairy's shoulders relax, just slightly. He pulled away when Ciaran's grip on him loosened and sat down beside him instead.

"Anyway," Ciaran said, his cheerfulness only sounding mostly forced, "this is much better than Lugh's boat, hm?"

Trent nodded, but he kept glancing at the door. "Ciaran," he said after a pause. "There are humans here."

Ciaran pressed his hands into the mattress, his shoulders hunching as he leaned on them. "Aye, there are. They've kept humans for centuries. For manual labor, mostly. In my time, they used to go on raids to the mainland and bring people back. I suppose these are their descendants."

Trent watched the floor. They'd come here to keep Ciaran's sister from being killed. They'd been through a storm, escaped a sea monster, and had their lives threatened more than once by angry dark elves. Even the kind older one who had taken them in had wanted to put Trent in the slave quarters. He knew that Ciaran must be a hundred times more stressed than he was—but Ciaran was also a hundred times more equipped to deal with all of this than he was.

"This place is awful," he said, and Ciaran put a gentle arm around him and leaned in close to kiss his temple.

"You're safe here with me, a mhuirnín. You're always safe with me. No matter what else comes, I will keep you safe if it takes everything I have. I didn't mean to make you feel otherwise."

"I'm fine," Trent murmured, but he wasn't sure Ciaran was convinced.

"Let's just get some sleep, hm? Everything will seem better after a good night's sleep."

"Yeah. Sleep sounds…pretty good." He let Ciaran kiss his cheek, and together they undressed and settled in the surprisingly comfortable bed of down and furs. Trent hid his face in the crook of the fairy's neck and shut his eyes, hoping that the bubbling dread in his gut would be gone by morning.

12

In the room next door, Julien, Noah, and Lugh stood in a similarly-styled bedroom—a woven rug on the floor, a small fire pit in one corner to warm the room, and in the other corner, a large bed covered in fur blankets. One large bed. The three of them stood silently uncertain for a moment, but then Lugh brushed by them and dropped his satchel and his heavy spear beside the bed, rattling the floorboards.

"Don't get any ideas," he said dryly. "You two are supposed to be servants, remember?" He settled on the bed, cradling his head with one arm behind him, and he glanced over at them. "Noah's small enough, though; he can share with me if he wants."

Julien's hackles went up immediately, his hands tightening into fists at his side, but Lugh only stared at him with slightly raised eyebrows and an indifferent expression. The hunter would have snapped at him again if he hadn't noticed Noah standing near the wall with his eyes on the floor and a frown on his lips. The witch was rubbing the back of his neck, clearly deep in thought. Julien softened immediately and took a step closer to catch the other man's attention.

"Something wrong?"

Noah reached out and put a hand on Julien's arm, looking up at him with a furrowed brow. "That person that was leaving as we arrived. I can't stop thinking about it."

"I'm not sure I'd call something with horns a 'person,' Noah," Julien answered, but the witch waved away his sarcasm.

"When he passed...I thought I could smell demon."

Julien tilted his head with a frown. "Demon? How do you 'smell' demon? How would you even know what a demon smells like at all?"

Noah released Julien's sleeve to rub at his own arm, shrugging one shoulder and breaking the hunter's gaze. "A few years ago, I helped out a friend of a friend. His niece was possessed, and he asked me if I could do anything. So Sabin and I...fixed it."

Julien stared at him. "You performed an exorcism? An actual exorcism."

"I lived a very full life before you came to Vancouver, Monsieur Fournier," Noah shot back, but he had a faint smile on his lips. "Anyway, once you've smelled demon, you never forget it. It's...rotten. Sick. What would a demon be doing here? I'm getting all mixed up with all these different mythologies all...intermingling."

"Mythologies?"

"Well, these Alfar, they're...pretty Norse looking, aren't they? Did you see the embroidery of Árvakr and Alsviðr on that tapestry in the High King's hall?"

Julien didn't want to admit that he had no idea what Noah was talking about—but he had no idea what Noah was talking about. "Did I...?"

Noah sighed. "How can you know so much about how to kill things and not know anything about actual myths?"

"Because mythology never tries to kill me. Monsters try to kill me. I hunt monsters, not gods."

"I'm not sure the two don't overlap more than you'd think," Noah mused. "Árvakr and Alsviðr are the horses who pull the sun across the sky in a chariot. It's fairly common for ancient myths to have a solar deity that drives the sun in a vehicle of some kind—Surya, Apollo, Ra, Mithras. It's a reasonable explanation for people who haven't figured out that the Earth goes around the sun and not vice versa, but I wonder if any of them are based in truth? Do you think there are actual dogs, or horses, or whatever, that have the right kind of powers that ancient people might have believed them to be personifications of the sun itself?"

Julien found himself smiling as the witch rambled. "I think we're getting off topic," he said gently, and Noah blinked up at him for a moment before looking down at the floor with a slight flush of embarrassment in his cheeks. He began to pace the length of the room as he started again.

"Sorry. Anyway—we always knew to assume that every kind of mythology got at least some things right, right? You've been hunting long enough to learn that. Remember the gumiho we found in Shaughnessy? And that owl-woman back in Vancouver was obviously some kind of Inuit spirit. Ciaran—and our current roommate—are literal Tuatha Dé Danann. I *know* demons are real. And they're never good news. If one of them is here—first of all, how? That didn't look like a possession to me. Not with the...you know." He gestured around his head to indicate the demon's curling horns.

"It's here on its own, then?"

"That's even worse. That means it's someone important. I mean, he looked important, right? Why is it here? And why is it meeting with ancient secluded Norse things? Ugh," he groaned, lightly slapping his thighs in irritation. "Ashmodai, Ashmodai...I know the name, but I can't—ugh. Do you think there's Wi-Fi down here?"

"Probably not," Julien chuckled. "You mean there's some information not in that brain of yours?"

"Hey, there are literally hundreds of demons that we know the names of, and hundreds of thousands more that we don't. Give me a break."

The hunter raised his hands in surrender.

"This is the worst. We need to stop hanging around in secret magic places that don't have Internet." He glanced toward Julien's bag on the floor. "Sabin said he'd seen some demons recently. He must have some books he could check for me. I'll have to write him and ask."

"Do you think the demon is still here? I've never hunted a demon before, but I'd be willing to give it a try."

Lugh sat up on the bed, drawing their attention. "I would advise remaining focused on the task at hand. We have a goal in mind being here, and it isn't to hunt creatures that have nothing to do with us. Remember that we are guests here, and misbehavior will reflect dangerously poorly on our host."

Noah's shoulders slumped, and he let out a sigh. "You're right. It's been a long day." He moved to the empty corner of the room and stripped off his shirt without hesitation, then unfastened the button on his jeans. Julien's eye snapped to Lugh as the witch slid his jeans down his hips, and he bristled to see the fairy watching Noah out of the corner of his eye.

"What are you doing?" Julien asked, edging forward and hoping he could position himself to break Lugh's line of sight without giving himself away.

"Oh!" Noah seemed to realize he wasn't alone, but he still kicked off his jeans anyway and stood in his slightly worn grey boxer briefs. "I'm just going to get a practice in. Jeans get in the way. I'm so stiff after being on that boat for all that time. And, you know, being dead. Plus I'm finally warm enough to get some feeling back in my fingers and toes. Don't mind me. I'll be quiet; you guys can get some sleep."

Noah dropped into an easy stretch, not bothered in the slightest that he was being watched. Julien attempted to place himself between Noah and Lugh, but the fairy wasn't even being subtle about staring. He sat half-reclined on the bed and watched with mild amusement as Noah flattened himself on the floor, legs stretched wide and forehead pressed to the wood in the space between them. Julien was going to need his own distraction.

He busied himself by going through his bag, which looked more and more like it was being slowly beaten to death, and he sorted his guns and cleaned them each in turn. The saltwater hadn't been kind to them. He did his best to focus on his task, but his eye kept drifting back to Noah. The witch was taking slow, steady breaths, his eyes gently closed as his body bent into positions that made Julien hurt just to look at them. He watched the lean muscles shift the tattoos on his lover's skin and admired the way his back arched, the solid tension in his shoulders as he lifted and inverted his body weight with practiced ease.

Julien stared pointedly down at the weapon in his hands and pressed his lips into a tight line as he pieced it back together. This wasn't the time for thoughts about all the ways Noah's very naked body was capable of twisting. They were in a strange and dangerous place and apparently sharing a room with Lugh—who was still looking, Julien noted with a scowl. It had been torture to lie next to Noah on the boat for nine days, but at least that hadn't involved an abundance of bare skin. He hadn't been able to touch the witch since their first night together—not really. And Julien was having difficulty ignoring the gnawing ache in his belly as Noah arched into a bridge, his flat stomach stretched tight and tantalizingly close. He very much wanted to touch him now.

When Noah was finished, he pulled to his feet and gave one final roll of his shoulders, then let out a satisfied breath.

"You're quite flexible, aren't you?" Lugh spoke up from the bed, and Noah smiled at him.

"It's no big deal. Anyone can do this if they practice. It just takes time and dedication. I could teach you some stretches if you wanted. It's really good for relieving stress."

"I do have a lot of stress that needs working out," the fairy answered. Julien didn't like the low rumble in his voice.

The hunter practically threw his guns back into his bag and set about building a makeshift bed out of spare blankets and furs. "We really ought to get some sleep," he said a little too loudly. He piled the furs together and folded up his coat for Noah to use as a pillow. The witch yawned his agreement and crawled into the mess of a bed, and Julien followed him. He only pulled off his shirt, not willing to get too undressed with Lugh in the room.

The fairy didn't share his modesty. Apparently the Tuatha Dé Danann didn't believe in underwear. Julien only caught a glimpse of bare ass before Lugh settled himself in the bed, but it was enough to make him scowl and turn his back on the other man.

He tried to sleep. He felt time ticking slowly by in the quiet room, the firelight flickering on the dark wood surrounding them, but he couldn't relax. Regardless of how Lugh had brushed aside Julien's concern, the fairy clearly had an interest in Noah. And Noah was so friendly with him. Julien tried to tell himself that Noah was friendly with most people—but this was different. It felt different. Now Noah was curled up beside him, his head tucked neatly under the blond's chin as though it was made to be there, soft breaths puffing against Julien's neck and bare skin warm and soft under his hand. Noah was next to Julien, but was he dreaming of Lugh?

He shouldn't have agreed to come. He shouldn't have let Noah come. He'd just gotten him back, and he'd been through falling overboard, a storm, a sea monster—and now they were in this place where the only other humans were slaves, and the fairy leading them seemed to think they were on the verge of getting killed any minute.

Julien squeezed Noah tightly against him. What would he do if something happened to Noah now? He'd failed him before. He'd forced him to cast that spell in the first place, and he'd failed to bring back Manandán's apple in time to save him. The thing still sat in his bag, a reminder of his uselessness. He couldn't let Noah down again.

Noah squirmed subtly against him at the pressure of his embrace, and he tilted his head up just enough to press a warm kiss to the hunter's scratchy-haired jaw.

"You're still awake?" he whispered. "Everything okay?"

Julien had to ask. He had to talk to him about Lugh—ask him what was going on, ask him to reassure him and tell him that he was just imagining things. But he couldn't do it here. He leaned down to touch his cheek to Noah's and whisper in his ear.

"Can we go outside? I need to talk to you. Alone."

"Of course."

The pair of them sat up and quietly dressed well enough to step outside. Julien put his coat around Noah's shoulders and took the witch by the hand to lead him from the room, both of them creeping silently through the common room and out the front door. The air outside was cold, and Noah stuck to Julien's side as they moved to the back of the longhouse. Hopefully there wouldn't be anyone passing by out there. The grass was sparse, and the wind from the sea cut right to Julien's bones, but the stars above them were bright and clear, sharing the night sky with the shining full moon. If Julien had had time to think of anything other than the worry in his gut, he might have thought it was beautiful.

"Are we hunting for demons after all?" Noah asked, his voice hushed in the darkness.

Julien stopped at the back wall of the longhouse, knowing his grip on Noah's hand was a little too tight. "No," he answered. "I need to talk to you. There are things I need to say."

Noah looked up at him, his brow knit softly in concern, and he reached up to take Julien's face in both hands. His thumbs stroked the bristle of beard on the hunter's jaw. "You can tell me anything. I'm listening."

Julien's resolve was weakened by the gentle caress. His eye drifted to the tiny shadows on Noah's collarbone, his slightly parted lips, his dark eyes swallowing the moonlight. He was looking up at Julien with such love on his face that he could barely remember what he'd brought him out here to ask. Instead of speaking, he slid an arm around Noah's waist and kissed him. The witch melted instantly into the kiss, and Julien found himself pushing him back against the wall— eager, hungry, and desperate for the taste of Noah's lips. Noah clung to him, just as needy, Julien's coat slipping off his shoulders as he wrapped his arms around the hunter's neck.

Julien lifted Noah up with his hands under the smaller man's thighs. He pressed him to the wood of the house, unable to stop himself from rolling his hips against his lover's once he felt the witch's growing erection and heard the quiet whine from his throat. He knew, somewhere in the back of his mind, that he ought to stop. That they were outdoors and unwelcome. But Noah's fingers tangled in his hair, tugging him deeper into the kiss, made a stronger argument than logic.

He shifted the witch's weight in his arms, and Noah leaned his shoulders against the wall to hold himself up with his legs around Julien's waist. Julien's hands worked quickly on Noah's jeans. He didn't feel timid about touching him now. He pulled away the denim and the soft cotton of his underwear and let his fingers slip around the base of Noah's already straining cock. Every movement of his hand made the younger man jump and gasp, and he gripped Julien's shoulder to keep himself steady while the hunter stroked him. His breath came in eager pants that dissolved into whimpers when Julien gave him a pointed squeeze, and he watched his lover's hand on him through lowered lashes.

Noah's shirt rode up as he lifted his hips into the touch, exposing a line of soft skin above his hips. Julien pushed the fabric farther up to show more of the boy's smooth stomach, his palm flattening on the lean, twitching muscles. The night made Noah look paler than he was, the wash of moonlight illuminating the soft dips his hipbones made with each tightening breath. Noah was beautiful.

Without hesitation, Julien tugged his lover's jeans down his thighs and supported him with one arm underneath him, the other reluctantly relinquishing its hold on the heated skin of his dick. He slid his hand between them and pressed a finger to Noah's entrance, a growl of satisfaction forming in his chest at the gentle cry the younger man gave. Noah immediately bucked against him, whimpering and wanton, and he supported himself on Julien's shoulder while he reached to cover the hunter's hand with his own. With a quick, breathy incantation, cool liquid flowed from Noah's fingers, coating Julien with slippery fluid that allowed him to push two fingers easily inside the other man.

Noah arched his back against the touch with a shaky cry slipping from his open mouth. He whined and ground his hips in time with Julien's movements, gasping as the hunter brushed the bundle of nerves inside him.

"There," he moaned. He twisted to meet Julien's touch and guided his hand deeper, urging him to press his thumb against the sensitive spot just above the slowly stretching ring of muscle. As the hunter slid a third finger inside, the witch's clenching heat almost making him dizzy, Noah cried out and clutched at his lover's neck, lifting himself away from the wall to let his full weight push down against Julien's fingers.

A soft swear fell from the witch's lips. "Please," he whispered, taking biting kisses from Julien's mouth and letting his tongue wet the hunter's top lip. "Please, Julien." His voice was weak and breathless against his lover's lips. "I've been wanting you to fuck me for so long."

What little restraint Julien had left flew out of him as soon as Noah's words reached his ears. He pulled his fingers free and crushed his lover against the back wall again, holding him up with one arm only long enough to unfasten his own pants and shove them out of the way. The witch whimpered with need and tightened his grip as Julien pushed into him in one quick motion. Julien buried his face in Noah's neck, leaving hot kisses and tasting the hint of salt on the other man's skin. He was helpless against the younger man's begging voice—Noah's clinging hands urged him faster and harder, until

Julien was sure he was going to hurt him, but the younger man only panted for more.

Neither of them cared that they were out in the open and exposed. Every breath Julien took was overpowering with Noah's scent, and the heat and the pressure of the witch's body around him made him ache with need. He held Noah firmly by the waist and began to stroke him again with his still slick hand, adjusting his hips until he touched the spot inside that made the other man hiss and moan and jerk against him. Noah scrambled to keep from falling, clutching Julien's shoulder with one hand and the wall behind him with the other as he fumbled in search of stability.

"I've got you," Julien promised in a husky whisper against Noah's cheek, and the witch relaxed, trusting in the larger man to support him. He did his best to grind back against Julien's forceful thrusts, but the hunter kept him steady, setting a pace guided by his lover's gasping demands. Noah began to shake in his grip and whispered a warning that went unheeded as Julien gripped him tighter.

He watched the hot droplets stain Noah's stomach as he stroked him to completion, the pulsing of the muscle around him almost too much to take. He kept up his rhythm until he could barely stand it, but it was Noah's soft whisper of "Come in me, Julien, please," that finally tipped him over the edge. He clutched the witch tightly to him as the rush of orgasm washed over him, drawing a groan from him that was muffled by Noah's shoulder.

They stayed still for a few long moments, neither of them having the strength to move. Finally, Julien slipped free of the other man and eased him back to the ground, unclamping his stiff hands from his lover's hips. Noah leaned against his chest to catch his breath and placed one more kiss to Julien's collarbone.

"What was it you wanted to talk about?"

A low chuckle rumbled through Julien's chest. "I've forgotten."

13

Ciaran left Trent sleeping in the morning, curled up under the heavy furs and breathing softly through parted lips. He ran a loving hand through the boy's hair, kissed the top of his head, and moved to the fire to pick at the breakfast Gunvard's servant must have left for them while they slept. He hoped that the alfar would be able to point him in the right direction with regard to settling his debt, but he recognized that the chances were slim. He didn't know what he'd do if Gunvard didn't have any leads.

He'd eaten every bit of fruit on the tray by the time Trent woke up with a slow stretch.

"Good morning, a mhuirnín. Look—it's not even gruel. Well, it's not only gruel. They've also brought fish and bread."

Trent pulled himself out of bed and squinted down at the tray on the table for a moment before he remembered to take up his glasses and slip them on. "Thanks for leaving me the stuff you didn't want. How much honey and fruit was here before you got to it?"

"You don't like sweets anyway."

"It's your fault if I get scurvy."

"But we aren't on the boat anymore. Scurvy is something sailors get."

Trent narrowed his eyes at him. "Are you actually an idiot?"

"Time will tell," Ciaran chuckled. He gave the boy's temple a peck and smiled as he was shoved away in irritation. When Trent had eaten his fill of breakfast, he moved to the basin on the dresser to wash himself. This much, at least, he'd gotten used to in Tír na nÓg. He looked for a pitcher to fill the bowl with, but as he stepped close, water swirled up from the bottom of the basin in a soft splash. Steam poured from the water, and the liquid was hot when Trent dipped his fingers into it. He guessed this was the kind of thing he should expect from the people who taught the fairies to do magic. Tír na nÓg seemed almost mundane compared to this place. Trent scrubbed at his hands and face, and no matter how much sea salt and dust he cleaned away, the water stayed clear and hot. When both he and Ciaran had washed themselves, Trent peeked over his shoulder as he dressed and found the bowl clean and empty again, as though there had never been water in it at all.

The pair left their room and found their host sitting at his own table, his tray in the process of being cleared away by the human slave. Rathgeirr sat at the far end of the table with a half-eaten bowl of murky gruel in front of him. He perked up instantly at the sound of Ciaran and Trent entering the room.

"Cian," Gunvard said. He gestured to the seat across from him. "I trust you slept well."

"I did. Thank you." Ciaran took the offered place, but Trent hung back with a frown on his face. He didn't think the alfar would appreciate sharing a table with him. Ciaran glanced at him but didn't comment.

Within moments, the others appeared. Lugh sat down beside his father without hesitation, and Noah and Julien took seats farther down the table. Gunvard eyed them, but then cleared his throat and said nothing.

"Well," he said. "Why don't we start with why you came here, Cian? Your debt."

Ciaran gave a short sigh, and he told the whole story from top to bottom—his attempted murder, leaving Tír na nÓg to live freely on his own, Lugh's vengeance, and the death of the men who had tried to kill Ciaran in the first place. Rathgeirr had been edging closer down the long bench throughout the story, and now he sat so close to his father that the older man had started to frown down at him. By the time Ciaran got to his return with Trent and being taken captive by Gaibhne and his brothers, his voice was slightly rough with exhaustion.

"So now, they have my sister, and if I don't bring them what they want to pay the debt, they're going to kill her."

"And what is it they've asked you to bring them?" Gunvard asked.

"Something called the Gambanteinn. It's apparently a rod that purifies any metal."

The alfar's eyebrows lifted in surprise. "That is absolutely not what the Gambanteinn does. That staff has been hidden away for centuries, and for good reason. It can enslave a man's mind and force him to do the wielder's bidding. What would they want with that, after all this time?"

Ciaran paused, letting the information sink in as a scowl formed on his lips. "They lied. They sent me out here on a quest likely to kill me, and they didn't even tell me the truth about why? I don't trust Gaibhne with a weapon like that, either—not as far as I can throw him." He leaned his elbows on the table and slid his fingers through his hair. "What do I do? If I go back empty-handed, they'll kill Airmed."

The alfar stroked his bottom lip with his knuckle. "I wonder how they even came to know about it. These men, these brothers—you said they're artisans?"

"They make the Tuath Dé's weapons," Ciaran answered, finally looking up from the table. "And gold and silver jewelry prized by the nobles in Tír na nÓg."

"Perhaps they were merely misinformed."

"I don't think anyone at this table is that naive, Gunvard."

"Then what could their purpose be? If they only wanted you to die on the journey, there are deadly creatures they could have sent you after. They sent you here for a specific item, and they hid its true nature from you, besides." He frowned, his black eyes scanning Ciaran's face, and then he nodded as though he'd made a decision. "We should consult the seeress."

"A seeress?" Ciaran asked.

The alfar nodded. "She will be able to provide an answer. But these things are best performed at night. I will speak to the seeress and arrange for her to prepare the ritual. We will see what she can divine about the men who sent you here."

Ciaran reached out for the other man's hand, clasping it earnestly in both of his own. "Thank you. I'll repay your kindness, I swear."

"Oh, I'll keep you in mind," the older man answered with a wry smile. "I will come to fetch you at sunset. In the meantime, keep out of trouble. Stay to my grounds, and don't make a fuss. Absolutely no venturing to the other cities—the guards will cut you down as sure as look at you. You may ask Blíður for anything that you require," he added, gesturing toward the slave standing in the corner, who gave a deep bow at the mention of his name. "And keep your humans in line, Cian. We don't need them getting into places they shouldn't. None of you have any business outside of the borders of Falias."

"We won't give you any trouble, Gunvard," Ciaran said, choosing not to address whether or not his companions were "his" humans. "Thank you again." He stood from the table and glanced at the others, urging them to follow him with a slight tilt of his head, but turned at the sound of Rathgeirr's end of the bench scraping suddenly across the stone floor.

"Ah," he started, holding out a hand toward Ciaran's back. "If I may—"

The fairy paused to look at him.

"Rathgeirr," Gunvard sighed, "please do not bother my guests."

"I only have a little time before I have to report back to the outpost," the younger man countered as he edged around the table to approach the group. He took a moment to study each of their faces, but he settled on Ciaran, obviously judging him to be the leader. "Please—I have questions."

"About what?"

"About...about everything," the alfar admitted. "About where you came from, about the world outside—"

"There is nothing beyond our shores that is worthy of the Alfar's attention," Gunvard cut in. "And nothing that needs concern a boy like you, regardless."

"A boy like—" Rathgeirr stopped himself before he said something he would regret, but Trent could see the alfar's hands clenching tightly at his sides. "They're only questions, father. Even a boy like me might be curious."

Gunvard gave a soft sigh and looked up to Ciaran as though he needed to apologize for his son's behavior. "Do not let him concern you needlessly, Cian; he is too inquisitive for his own good."

"I don't mind," Ciaran insisted. "I'm happy to share what I can."

Rathgeirr's face brightened. "Thank you," he said earnestly. He glanced over his shoulder at his father, but Ciaran noted his reluctance to speak, so he gestured for the alfar to follow the group into their provided room.

He really did seem to have questions about everything—but because of it, he also didn't quite know what to ask. He frequently paused mid-sentence and drifted onto another subject before he even got the first answer. He wanted to know all there was to know about the world beyond his island, but even if Ciaran had known everything about everything, there was no way to condense the information into something palatable. The fairy tried to be patient with him, but he had too much on his mind to have much patience left. He was grateful when a distant bell sounded from outside, and Rathgeirr leapt to his feet in a panic.

"Oh, I'll be late. Thank you," he said again, already heading for the door. "I'll come back when my shift is done."

"Take notes for next time," Ciaran advised, and the alfar gave a slightly sheepish grin on his way out of the room. Once the five of them were in the room, Ciaran gave a soft sigh.

"Oh, I had questions for him, too," Noah lamented in a soft voice.

"What now?" Julien asked. The question had clearly been on the tip of his tongue ever since their conversation with Gunvard. He folded his arms as he glanced between Ciaran and Lugh. "We came here for a purpose. We're supposed to just wait?"

"At least until tonight," Ciaran answered. "I don't know that we've much of a choice. The seeress may be able to help. We were given three days here, so we may as well use them. Gaibhne knows it takes nine days to sail here and who knows how long to get back. They won't assume I've died—not yet. We have a little time."

"In that case," Noah spoke up, "how serious is he about that whole 'keep to the grounds' thing? Because I'm sure there's all kinds of new magic here, and I'd really, really like to do some investigating. Do they have a library?"

Ciaran frowned at him. "The library is in Falias, yes. But you need to keep your head down here. All of you. Some of them may know me, but Lugh is a stranger, and you lot doubly so. I don't have any sway here, and distasteful or not, humans are not citizens in Lochlann. If you get into trouble, they'll take it upon themselves to punish you, and you don't want a slave's punishment, believe me. So try to behave, lad."

"I can behave at the library," Noah objected, but Ciaran shook his head at him, and the witch snorted out an indignant sigh. "Well what are we supposed to do all day? Just stare at the wall?" He paused, tilting his head and glancing at Trent, who hadn't said a word since they returned to the room. "We could try the spell again. It might go better now that we're not on a boat and Trent's not on the verge of puking."

Trent tried to hide his slight flinch. They had attempted the spell three times on the trip, and each time, they had failed. Noah had tried talking them through it over and over again—he wanted them to open up, to think about themselves and their love for each other and everything they had been through together. He had helped them meditate and breathe, and he had even tried to give Trent a head massage to relax him, which had only made things worse. Trent still felt anxious.

He couldn't let go of his worries, no matter how much Ciaran assured him of his feelings. Aside from still feeling a gnawing shame in his gut every time someone found out about the nature of their relationship, he still worried that Ciaran was too old for him in every way. That he would only ever see Trent as a boring human— something that he apparently had grown up thinking of as a slave. Ciaran was literally magical. He was immortal, and handsome, and clever, and perfect. Trent didn't know anything about magic or how to sail a boat. He wasn't strong, or brave, or athletic, or even especially smart. He was afraid that they would never be on equal footing. He was afraid of what would happen to him if Ciaran ever came to his senses.

He was afraid, above all, that someday Ciaran would see him the way Trent saw himself.

Ciaran was watching him, waiting for his answer. Trent didn't want to disappoint him. He didn't want to tell him that he didn't see much chance of the spell working while his head was full of thoughts like this. So he nodded.

"Let's try," he said.

Noah kicked Julien and Lugh out of the room, and he settled cross-legged on the floor with Trent and Ciaran in front of him. They went through the motions that were frustratingly familiar to Trent by now—the witch lighting incense, burning herbs, touching the line of points down their heads and torsos. Trent truly did his best to clear his mind as Noah asked. He tried to focus on Ciaran's gentle breathing beside him and to imagine they were back at his apartment, sitting on the couch together, comfortable and content. But Trent hadn't known then the full extent of what he was getting into.

The attempt ended the same as all the others—only this time, Noah seemed more frustrated than before as Ciaran and Trent stared at him in unchanged silence. He did a decent job of hiding it behind an encouraging smile, but Trent could see the crease in his brow.

"You can't rush these things," Noah said, not for the first time. "I'm sure it's partly my fault. I've never done this before either, so that's probably it. And maybe I'm reading it wrong, or maybe the spell doesn't work at all. I'll keep looking, okay? Maybe I missed something." He gathered up the ashes of his used herbs, frowning down at the floor as he scraped them into his palm. "I said I'd help," he added in a softer voice. "So I'll figure something out. I'll find an answer for you. I promise."

"Thanks for trying, lad," Ciaran said. He could see the tight-lipped sadness in his lover's face. Trent wasn't going to speak up with the other man in the room. Ciaran glanced sidelong at Noah, hoping he would get the hint, and the witch stood and edged toward the door.

"I'll just...do some more reading. Keep positive, okay?" Noah slipped through the door, leaving them alone in the bedroom.

Ciaran waited. He hoped that Trent would speak first, but the boy kept his eyes on the rug underneath him.

"We don't have to keep trying," the fairy said after a pause. His voice was quieter than he'd meant it to be. "I know that I tried to make this decision for you by giving you my pendant in the first place. If you don't feel up to it…I'd rather not push."

"I'm fine," Trent promised, each time less convincing than the last. But Ciaran didn't want to argue.

"All right," he said. "I'm going to see if I can help Gunvard prepare for this ritual. Will you be fine on your own for a bit?"

"I'll stay here and be quiet like a good human," Trent snapped before he could stop himself. Ciaran opened his mouth to reply and then thought better of it. He stood and put one hand on the door.

"I'll be back later then," he said, forcing calmness into his tone, and then he opened the door and shut it behind him, leaving Trent alone on the floor.

14

Ciaran stayed away from the room for most of the day, following Gunvard through the low, sprawling city. They talked about the past and about Ciaran's life outside of Tír na nÓg. Ciaran told him about his siblings, about his wife, and about how he'd fallen in with his current companions. He didn't have any memories of Gunvard that weren't heavily fogged by time, but the older man listened so patiently and spoke so kindly that Ciaran didn't hesitate to tell him his story. It was nice to speak to someone who understood the passage of time the same way he did, who could discuss events from a thousand years ago without a disbelieving stare.

When it was time for them to visit the seeress, Noah practically begged to go, but Gunvard insisted that humans were absolutely not allowed—even ones that could do magic. So Ciaran went with him alone.

"This woman is what we call a *spákona*," Gunvard explained while they walked toward the squat temple near the back of the enclosed town where the nobility lived. "She is one who sees. If anyone can tell us about the men who sent you, she can."

He opened the heavy wooden door to the temple and stepped inside ahead of Ciaran. The room was small and stuffy with smoke that poured from a carved basin in the center of the floor. Beyond it, an Alfar woman sat in a high-backed chair, the kohl around her eyes smeared messily over her cheeks and her black hair knotted at the back of her head and spilling matted braids over her shoulders. She wore a simple wrapped skirt, but she was bare-chested, her breasts only partially hidden by necklaces of silver and glass beads. Her black gaze was distant and cold as she regarded them in silence.

Gunvard urged Ciaran to the floor opposite the basin curling pale smoke up to the roof, and he spoke to the woman in the language of the Alfar, which Ciaran remembered only as if in a dream—it felt familiar, but he could barely make out a few words.

Apparently satisfied with his request, the seeress slipped from her seat to kneel on the floor. She leaned forward, breathing in the smoke and letting it out in a low chant. Her back snapped into a deep arch, first forward, then back, and her limbs fell limp at her sides as she stretched toward the floor. The voice that came out of her was ragged and distant, and Ciaran found that he could understand the words she spoke.

"Three brothers," she began, her rough breath seeming to echo in the small room, "the last living of nine. A family destroyed by deception and intrigue, once respected, now forgotten in times of stagnant peace. Bitterness seeps, lost glory beckons. Greed, and bloodlust, and ambition. These roil the kingdom, and many would see their will done. Three kings sit where three would stand. And one long dead will bring them victory."

Ciaran's brow knit in confusion. He leaned back with a start as the woman's head jerked suddenly, her pitch-colored eyes looking emptily through him.

"Three paths lay before you," she hissed, fingertips twitching against the floor. "Return that which the brothers seek, and blood shall run through the halls of your fathers, spilling out into the world of men. Flee, and an innocent will die in suffering. You will be hunted to the ends of the earth by those eager for vengeance. Fight, and peace will reign in your ancestral home, but you will lose something dear to your soul."

"Dear to me?" Ciaran asked despite Gunvard's warning hand on his arm. "What something dear to me?"

"That which binds you to this world—forever severed."

"What the hell does that mean?"

Gunvard shushed him, gripping his elbow firmly, so Ciaran shut his mouth.

"The fate of the people of Dana hangs in the balance." Her body twisted, the movement more languid than sudden now. "The fate you choose for yourself, you also choose for your kind. Choose wisely, Scal Balb."

Before Ciaran could question her again, she collapsed, slumping over onto the floor in a deep sleep. He almost reached out for her, but Gunvard pulled him to his feet with an encouraging hand.

"Our audience is complete," he muttered near Ciaran's ear. He walked him to the door and let the fairy out ahead of him, then shut the door quietly once they were back on the path outside.

Ciaran paced a small circle in the worn road, running his hand over his face as he let out a frustrated grunt. "What the hell am I supposed to do with those three shitty options? What do they even mean?"

"That's for you to decide," Gunvard answered in a significantly calmer voice than his younger companion. "I can tell you that actually obtaining the Gambanteinn from King Huldrekall, if you're considering it, is going to be a nearly impossible feat."

"To hell with that," Ciaran snapped immediately. "I'm not likely to bring Gaibhne something that's going to make 'blood run through the halls of my fathers.' Ugh," he groaned, slowing to a stop and letting his hands fall to his sides. "I need...I need time to think about this. Thank you. For your help."

Gunvard put a heavy hand on the fairy's shoulder. "You still have two days. Use them carefully, child."

Back in the guest room he shared with Trent, Ciaran fell face first onto the bed and fisted his hands in his hair. He felt Trent sit down beside him, and he told him, half muffled by the fur blankets, what the seeress had said. At least, he told him what she said about the brothers apparently trying to stage a coup. He left out the part about the promised consequences of his choices.

His options were to help Gaibhne and his brothers overthrow the High Kings and start a war with the world above, to let Airmed die and have his enemies chase him and Trent to the ends of the earth, or he could do something to put a stop to all of it—and lose that which bound him to this world. Something dear to him—that meant something would happen to Trent, didn't it? The number of people Ciaran cared about wasn't exactly vast. If it came to that, choosing between saving Trent's life or Airmed's...how could he make that choice?

Even if he chose to fight, what could he actually do? Fight? Fight what? The seeress made it seem like Gaibhne had allies in this plot. If Ciaran wanted to fight them all, he couldn't hope to do it alone—and as far as the rest of his people were concerned, Cian mac Cainte was long since dead. He would have to reveal himself.

The fairy let out a long groan into the blanket, but he softened slightly when he felt Trent's hand on his shoulder.

"Why don't you tell the King?" Trent asked. "I mean, your King. Not this creepy one. If you tell him something's happening, they'll do something about it themselves, won't they? And they'll forgive all this blood debt stuff if you're literally warning them about a hostile takeover attempt, right?"

"Maybe," Ciaran answered as he sat up to face the boy. "But I can't be sure. And even if I did tell them, I don't have any proof. Why should the High Kings believe a damned thing I say? I don't imagine they'd take 'a Lochlannan seeress told me so' as solid evidence."

Trent frowned, but he didn't have an answer. "We'll need to tell the others. Maybe Lugh will know what to do—he's been around them a lot more than you have, right?"

"I'm not sure that's true. But I'm tired now," the fairy sighed. "And I need some quiet to think. Let's have a bath."

Trent paused, glancing around the room as though expecting to find a bathtub he hadn't noticed until now, but Ciaran was already on his feet. He stuck his head out the door and called to Blíður, the blue-clad slave, and the young man appeared promptly at the doorway as though brought into existence by Ciaran's voice.

"Where is there a bath?" Ciaran asked, but the boy only slightly lifted his head, daring to raise his eyes to Ciaran's face to express his confusion. "Oh," Ciaran added, letting out a brief laugh. "I assumed you would—hm. Oh, what's the word?"

The slave waited patiently while Ciaran tapped his forehead with his balled fist, hoping to dislodge the long-buried vocabulary. "Hei...heitr?" Ciaran looked back at Blíður with hope on his face only to be met with an apologetic frown. "No? You know, where is the...laug—lauga! Yes! Ek lysta lauga. Yes?"

"Ah!" Blíður's lips curled into a smile that quickly died as he seemed to remember himself and dropped his gaze to the floor again. "Já, herra minn. Þessa leið."

Ciaran held a hand out for Trent's to guide him from the room, but as soon as Blíður noticed the boy following, he stopped and turned to Ciaran again, already in a deep bow.

"Herra minn, ég bið náðugur fyrirgefa," the slave said quickly. He seemed to notice that Ciaran didn't understand, so he risked gesturing toward Trent. "Nei," he said. "Nei lauga. Mann-ligr."

Ciaran stopped walking, but he didn't let go of Trent's hand. "Nei?"

"What's he saying?" Trent asked in a slightly subdued voice.

"I think he just doesn't understand," the fairy said. He didn't want to tell Trent that he was fairly certain the slave was trying to tell him that humans weren't allowed in the baths. He reached out to lift the boy's dirty chin, forcing him to lock eyes with him. "Ek lysta lauga," he said again, his tone lower and quieter. "Hjá minn leannán—friðill," he corrected himself. He kept slipping into Gaelic. Too many languages he'd stopped using years ago. "Understand?"

The slave's face turned suddenly red from his hairline to his neck, and his eyes darted downward to Ciaran's hand lightly touching his chin. He didn't dare pull away, but a stream of words began to flow out of him, quicker than Ciaran could hope to catch. He was clearly apologizing, and the fairy saw the flinching anticipation in the boy's face, so he removed his hand to let him drop his gaze again.

"It's all right," he said. "Just show us the way. Gjörðu svo vel."

Blíður lowered his head in a deeper bow and hastily slipped away, leading them down a curving path toward the stone ring in the ground that marked the hot spring. Worn steps led down into the water and formed seats around the edge of the spring, allowing the use of the naturally heated water as a bath. Ciaran thanked the boy as he bowed and darted off again, but he returned before either Trent or Ciaran could blink. He left them each a change of clothes on the edge of the stone, then gave one final bow and disappeared around the turn in the path.

"This is the bath?" Trent asked, leaning over to peer into the water. It was opaque in the darkness of the night, but he could see steam rising from it into the chilled air. "Just...out here, outside?"

"There's no one here but you and I at this hour, a mhuirnín." Ciaran tugged his tunic up over his head without hesitation and slipped his fingers through the lacing holding up his trousers. A faint smile touched his lips as he noticed Trent turning away from the sight. As much as Ciaran wished the boy was more comfortable in his own skin, it was still cute to see him so shy.

The fairy stepped into the water and settled himself on the ridge of stone below the surface, and he looked up to find a determined frown on Trent's face. The younger man wouldn't meet Ciaran's eyes, but he pulled off his shirt and pants and hurried into the water to sit beside him.

"Good job," Ciaran chuckled, and Trent snorted at him.

"What did you say to him, anyway? The...kid."

Ciaran scooted closer to Trent and put an arm around the boy's narrow shoulders. He leaned in to touch a kiss just below his ear and whispered, "I told him I wanted to take a bath with my lover." He smiled at the heat that bloomed in the younger man's skin.

"Ugh," Trent scoffed, turning his head to hide the embarrassed frown on his face. "Can we not use that word? It sounds gross."

Ciaran laughed. "What are you, then, if you're not my lover?"

"I don't know, your...boyfriend, I guess?"

"That isn't a mite juvenile?"

"You're the one applying labels at all," Trent grumped. He seemed to hesitate, so Ciaran held off teasing him until the boy looked up at him through the swirling steam. "Was it strange for you?" he asked after a heavy pause. "To go out into the world, to leave Tír na nÓg and live with humans...when the only humans you'd ever known were slaves?"

Ciaran was startled into silence long enough for Trent's expression to fall.

"Here, and your people too," Trent went on, "they kidnap people, don't they? That's something that fairies do, isn't it?"

"Not *my* people," Ciaran clarified. He gave a soft sigh and let his thumb brush the damp skin of Trent's arm. He wished the boy would relax against him, and that they could have a comfortable bath together and look at the stars. But he supposed they both had too much on their minds.

"There are many kinds of things that live in Tír na nÓg, Trent. Some of them are like my people—we think of ourselves as too important to meddle in human affairs anymore, and instead spend our time bickering amongst ourselves. But some of the others...some of them take human lovers whether they want to go or not. Some of them have strange rules about fighting their own kind, and the solution is to take a human champion to fight in their name. Sometimes the humans get to go home. Sometimes they don't."

"But these people are slaves, Ciaran. Generations and generations of slaves."

"The Lochlannan...they were a menace in their day. Did I tell you what the word 'Lochlannan' means? It means 'raider.' It isn't a word you'll hear them use. We called them that because their ships would appear at the shore in a mist, their warriors would pour out over the countryside, and they would take whatever they wanted. Animals, weapons, food—even men and women. To be taken by the Lochlannan was a fate worse than death. That's what I heard, anyway. By my time, my people had already been on this island for hundreds of years." A faint crease formed in his brow as he tilted his head back to look up at the green ribbon of light trailing across the black sky. "I remember when I was a child, sometimes there would be new people. I knew that the men of the island went away and came back with them, but I didn't think anything of it. It was just the way things were. I never thought to question it. Humans weren't us."

"That's fucking awful, you know that," Trent snapped, and the fairy frowned at him.

"Of course I know it. I said I was a child. If nothing else, humans were the ones who forced my people underground. Any one of us who still thinks of them as less than we are is an idiot. The Tuath Dé should recognize an equal in battle even if they don't have the morals to see the evil in slavery." Ciaran stopped at the silent sadness written on Trent's face. He touched the boy's dark hair and ran his thumb over his cheek to urge him to look up. "You don't think I think of you that way?"

Trent took a moment to swallow down the lump in his throat before answering. "We're just...very different," he said. He sounded so sullen that Ciaran's chest ached.

Ciaran could barely make his voice work. "Too different?"

"I don't know."

Ciaran's stomach twisted painfully as he removed his hand from the other man. He put a little distance between them and sat silently beside him, neither of them able to bear looking at the other. He wanted to tell Trent no. That he didn't accept that they were too different. That he loved him, and that he would do anything to see the smile Trent only showed to him. He wanted to tell him that he had never felt this way about anyone before—man, woman, fairy, human—and that the thought of losing Trent was making him consider allowing a full-blown war break out between his people and the world above.

But he didn't want to scare him. He couldn't pressure him anymore; Trent had to make his own choice. But Ciaran didn't have words to express how afraid he was that, after all the fairy had put him through, Trent wouldn't choose him.

15

Noah paced the length of the guest room for the fifth or sixth time. He had been pausing at the door with every lap to press his ear to the wood and listen, and this time he stopped completely.

"I think they're finally leaving," he murmured. He had waited patiently for hours for Ciaran and Gunvard to leave to see the seeress—it would be his opportunity to sneak out. He darted back to Julien's bag and crouched to retrieve his quickly-filling notebook. He had exchanged a few letters with Sabin while he waited and written down every seemingly-pertinent detail from the boy's recent demon encounter.

Julien watched him from near the fire. "Can I say again that I think this is a bad idea?"

"I need to know what a demon was doing here. I'll just have a look around. Anything I find might be helpful—any traces there might still be. If he stayed somewhere, maybe he left something behind. And, you know, if I happen to find the library while I'm on my way, maybe I'll check it out. It'll be fine."

"I'm going with you, at least."

"I can't stop you," Noah answered without looking up from the bag, "but it'll be much sneakier if I'm alone. Just saying." He let out a small victorious sound as he located his book, and he stood to move toward the bedroom door. He listened a moment longer and eased the door open, but as soon as he did, he was face to face with Lugh's broad chest.

The fairy looked down at him, one eyebrow lifted in mild curiosity. "Where are you going, exactly?"

Noah's shoulders slumped in frustration. "I just want to do some looking around, okay? We aren't going to be here very long and I don't expect to ever get back to Mysterious Viking Elf Island. So can you move?"

"Did you forget that you're of the slave class here? And that you are supposed to be my servant?"

"No, but—"

"Enough," Lugh cut him off. Noah looked about to argue again, but then the fairy gave a short sigh through his nose. "I will go with you. At least if they catch us, you'll be with me, and not just a runaway servant."

Noah brightened instantly. He looked back at Julien, but the hunter didn't share his enthusiasm. He would definitely have to go now. He didn't like the idea of Lugh and Noah getting any time whatsoever alone in the dark together. But he couldn't say that.

"Why don't I just go?" Julien suggested. "You can stay here and avoid the risk altogether, and I'll tell you what I find."

"Oh," Noah laughed, "because you know so much about seeking spells and demons that it'll be totally useful for you to go by yourself."

Julien sighed. "Fine," he agreed at last. "But I'm still coming with you."

Lugh led the way from the longhouse with Julien's accusing eye on his back the entire way. They walked slowly, allowing Noah to softly murmur his spell as they went. There were still some people milling about even after sunset—some human slaves in dark blue tunics following their straight-backed nobles, some less-proud-looking Alfar heading to and fro on whatever business Alfar might have. Most concerning were the hooded men who were armed with heavy steel swords at their hips and longbows on their backs. They watched the humans carefully as they passed, and Julien could feel their mistrust. These were the ones who would cause trouble if any strangers stepped out of line.

"Why can't we just go where we want to go?" Julien muttered as he and Noah walked behind Lugh. "These humans might be slaves, but we aren't."

"But we're human just the same," Noah answered easily, pausing his incantation to look up at the hunter. "It isn't right, but we're in a strange place. If we make a ruckus, we'll just get Ciaran and Gunvard in trouble. And who knows what they'd do to us?"

Julien sighed. "Isn't that a good indication that we shouldn't be doing this at all?"

"Don't act like you don't care that a demon was here, Mr. Hunter." He leaned in closer to him and dropped his voice. "Besides, it's exciting to sneak, right?"

Julien couldn't keep the small smile from his lips. "You used to be such a good boy."

"When was that? It's your fault anyway for taking me on an adventure."

Lugh glanced over his shoulder and narrowed his eyes at them, staring them into silence, so they just walked the paths between the longhouses while Noah whispered his seeking spell. When they passed a small guest house, Noah felt the tingle of magic and caught the sickly scent he knew too well. He put a hand on Lugh's back to stop him, and the three of them approached the house. They waited for a break in pedestrians before Noah touched the door and slid open the lock, allowing them to duck inside without being seen.

Noah held out a hand as he moved through the rooms, taking slow steps and pausing every so often to smell the air. Julien helped as he could by checking the physical things in the room—a small cabinet by the bed and a shelf above the cold fire pit. Lugh lingered near the door, apparently not very interested in demon mysteries.

After a thorough search of the house, Noah stood in the center of the room and let his hands slap against his thighs in irritation.

"Fuck," he said. "It's totally empty. It's hard to tell since there's so much magic all over the place here, but there's just enough...I know it was here. At least for a while, the demon was definitely here. But there's nothing left now. Even the bed is clean. If it was even used at all." He groaned and crossed his arms and frowned at the floor. "What sort of agreement could it make with the Alfar? What could they have that it wants?" He perked up and put a hand on Lugh's arm. "Gunvard was at the meeting with the king; maybe you could ask him what happened?"

"But I don't care what happened," the fairy answered. Noah pursed his lips at him.

"You're no help." He sighed. "It's driving me nuts that I can't remember anything about that name—Ashmodai," he said again, as though repeating it would help him remember. "But it's a name I recognize at all, which means it's an important demon. And Sabin said he'd heard the name recently, too. That isn't good, right? The same demon popping up in two places, starting trouble? Maybe," he added with a sidelong smirk in Lugh's direction, "if we could check the library, we'd be able to find something…?"

Lugh watched him in silence for a moment. "Fine," he agreed. "If it pleases you." The fairy's tone was a little too soft—it made the hairs on the back of Julien's neck stand up to hear him speaking so gently to Noah. He kept his mouth shut. He didn't want to start an argument in the middle of a stealth mission.

They walked the paths again, avoiding the glaring patrolmen as well as they could, until they spotted the sprawling building marked with words that Julien couldn't read, but Noah apparently recognized. The witch was practically trembling with glee beside him as they drew near it. The roads were mostly empty now, though, and the building was dark inside. It was definitely time for strangers and humans to be indoors. Julien looked down at Noah with a wary frown, but the witch stared at him with such excited hope that he couldn't bear to suggest they go back now.

Lugh opened the door and ushered them both inside ahead of him. The long room was cold and dark, but even with only the faint light of the moon outside, Julien could make out the rows upon rows of leather-bound books and scrolls that reached all the way to the rear wall of the building. Noah rushed ahead, snatching up one of the magic lanterns floating near the wall and lighting the wick with a quiet spell.

"Keep that low," Julien warned as he glanced over his shoulder at one of the narrow windows. "Someone outside might see."

"Got it," the witch whispered back, but Julien got the distinct impression that he wasn't listening. Noah ran loving fingers over the shelves of books, some of which had suspiciously non-cowhide leather covers, and he pulled one down whenever it caught his fancy. The books that were too high for him to reach pulled themselves from the shelf of their own accord, but Julien couldn't tell if it was Noah's magic or their own that moved them. Noah passed the lantern off to Julien when his arms started to fill, and eventually he had a pile surrounding him as he sat on the floor at the back of the library and thumbed through the pages.

"Of course, they're in runes," he lamented. He bent close to the book in his lap to peer at it. "I'm such shit at reading runes. I didn't have any warning that we'd be coming somewhere Norse-ish. God, I wish I had Internet access." He sighed and pushed the book aside in favor of the next in the stack. "This is Old Irish," he murmured. Julien wasn't sure if he should answer or if the witch was just talking to himself. "This I can actually read. Thanks, Ciaran's brain. Oh—but this is a history. It's not a spellbook. Fuck." He moved to toss it aside, but then paused as something caught his eye. "Huh. But did you know they're supposed to be from Scythia? Someone named Nemed is, I mean. He must be some sort of patriarch figure. Hence Nemedians. I wouldn't have guessed a Kazakh background for the fairies. Although it would have been so long ago it would be so different...huh," he said again, as though his curiosity had been sated, and then he snapped the book shut and set it back on the pile.

Julien watched, adjusting the light as Noah directed him, and he waited while Noah scratched scraps of information into his little lined notebook. He felt the passage of time and grew slightly anxious, so when Noah began to draw close to the bottom of his stack, he finally spoke up.

"It's getting late, Noah. They'll notice that we're missing."

"Just one more minute," the witch answered without looking up. "I think I've found something that might help Trent and Ciaran. I need to take some notes."

Julien glanced toward the door, where Lugh waited with his arms folded. He was getting impatient, too. He turned back when he heard Noah rolling up his scroll and stopped him before he could reach for the next.

TO KEEP YOU NEAR

"We really need to go."

"I know, I know. Sorry."

Julien helped him to his feet and carried a share of the books. He wasn't sure in the slightest that they were going back in the right places, but at least they wouldn't be found strewn all over the floor in the morning.

"Quietly," Lugh urged them as he opened the door and stepped outside.

They slipped away from the building and made their way back toward Gunvard's house. They went far enough that Julien thought they would actually make it back without incident, but as they crept around a corner, he heard a harsh voice calling out from behind them. The footsteps following them came up fast, and before Julien even had time to consider his options, he felt a powerful arm around his waist. He caught a brief glimpse of Noah, pressed tightly against Lugh's chest with the fairy's fingers tangled in his hair, and then suddenly Julien had another man's lips on his.

The hunter couldn't help the startled sound of panic that escaped him. His hands instantly shoved against the assaulting fairy's chest, but it was like trying to move stone. He was locked in Lugh's grip as the larger man kept his mouth firmly against Julien's.

The guard's voice started rough and then faltered as he rounded the corner. "You shouldn't be out here," he snapped, the command sounding a little like a question in his confusion.

Lugh finally broke the kiss, but he kept close to Julien while he stared across at the guard. "Can't a man get some privacy?" he murmured. Julien was uncomfortably aware of the growling voice rumbling in the chest under his palms.

Noah's eyes lit up with understanding, and he kept an arm freely slung around Lugh's neck as he leaned close to Julien. He took the hunter by the collar, turning a lidded gaze toward the guard as he licked a slow, purposeful line across Julien's upper lip. Julien felt frozen in place—torn between the shiver Noah's tongue shot through him and the unwelcome hardness of Lugh's arm around him. He knew his face would be red, and he was glad for the darkness hiding it.

The guard seemed to hesitate uncertainly, glancing between the three men with growing discomfort. "Just...get back to where you belong," he said finally, and Lugh gave a sigh of annoyance.

The fairy slid an arm around Noah's shoulders, keeping the witch pressed against his side as they began to walk, but he guided Julien forward with a casual hand on his ass and hissed into the hunter's ear when he balked.

"Just walk," he whispered, so Julien shut his mouth. He kept quiet until they got back to Gunvard's longhouse, but as soon as they were inside, he pushed Lugh's hand away from him with a scornful snort.

"What the hell did you think you were doing?" he growled.

"Keeping you out of a cell," the fairy answered languidly. "You're welcome."

The flush on Julien's face only made him angrier. "But you didn't have to—why would you—and get your hands off of Noah already!"

Noah laughed as Lugh removed his arm from the smaller man's shoulders. "Julien, it's fine. We didn't get in trouble, right?"

Julien knew he shouldn't say what was really on his mind. He knew that he shouldn't tell Noah not to let other men look at him, let alone touch him. He shouldn't tell him to stay away from Lugh in every circumstance.

"This isn't what we came here for, Noah!" he said instead, knowing his tone was too harsh. "We've risked our lives for Ciaran and Trent's sake, and we're only making it worse by sneaking around where we shouldn't! For what? For your curiosity about what you claim must have been a demon? Maudit, Noah, you can't fuck around like this!"

"What I *claim*—" Noah stopped himself and took a step toward Julien with a scowl on his face. "If you recall, I didn't want you to come with me in the first place."

"I was supposed to let you out alone?" Julien bent close to him, hearing his voice grow too loud as though he was outside his body looking in. He saw the slight flinch in Noah's face but couldn't stop the anger rushing out of him. "After everything that's happened? I'm supposed to trust you on your own in this place?"

"Everything's fine, isn't it?" Noah snapped back. Julien could tell he was doing his best not to waver. "So why are you losing your shit now? Because of Lugh? It was just a kiss, Julien! It didn't mean anything!"

Julien opened his mouth to reply and finally hesitated at the touch of fear in Noah's eyes. The last time Julien had shouted at him like this, Noah had trembled and agreed to cast that deadly spell for the hunter's sake. Julien had sworn that he wouldn't ever make Noah feel that way again. But he said kisses didn't mean anything. If kisses didn't mean anything, then what did? How much would Noah let Lugh get away with if it was just harmless flirting? How close would he let the fairy come before it meant something? And what happened when it did mean something?

The hunter pressed his lips together to keep his frustration inside. "You're right," he said, forcing his voice to sound softer. "I'm sorry. I'm just tired," he added to cut off Noah's reply. "I'm going to get some sleep." He moved away from Noah and kept his back to him while he undressed and got into the makeshift bed on the floor.

Noah would think he was pouting, and Julien knew it, but he couldn't talk about it anymore. He could hear the witch taking a place beside the fire and the quiet turn of the pages in his notebook as he looked through them. A jolt hit his spine at the sound of Lugh's soft voice, too quiet for Julien to make out. He knew, rationally, that Noah was probably just asking the fairy about the spells he'd found, but he still couldn't sleep. He could only picture the two of them sitting close together near the warm, flickering firelight, shoulders touching, sharing magical secrets that Julien could never be a part of.

He knew better than this. He'd never expected himself to be such a jealous person. But he couldn't stop the worry in his gut. They couldn't have been through all this just to have Noah leave him because they couldn't understand each other. Julien shut his eye, hid his face in the fur blanket, and tried to pretend he couldn't hear the quiet conversation going on behind him.

16

Trent sat up in bed the next morning and rubbed his hands over his face. He had sat beside Ciaran in the open bath for what felt like an eternity, trying to find his voice and failing. He couldn't even imagine the weight that was on the fairy's shoulders right now, and Trent was only adding to his problems with his own insecurities. Trent wanted to help him somehow, but he was only human—in the most literal, practical sense. Ciaran was too distant from him, too magical, and too comfortable with all of the insanity they'd been through over the last few weeks. How was Trent supposed to keep up? Everything had been so busy and so dramatic that Trent had almost forgotten how good it felt to just sit on the couch with Ciaran and watch trashy television.

The boy from the night before gave a very soft knock before pushing open the bedroom door and poking his head inside. He balanced a tray of food in one hand as he shut the door behind him, and he didn't raise his eyes to Trent until he'd placed the breakfast on the small table near the fire. Even then he only briefly glanced up without meeting Trent's eyes.

Trent was uncomfortably aware that he was a half-naked human in bed with an also half-naked fairy. He felt like he should say something, but what was he supposed to say? Just so you know, I'm not his slave? I'm not fucking him for better treatment? Trent's stomach twisted with an emotion he couldn't quite name. Since when did he care what other people thought of him, anyway? Maybe he felt guilty because Gunvard hadn't seemed to approve of his relationship with Ciaran—or maybe it was the fact that he was one of only three humans on the island who weren't slaves and whose families hadn't been slaves for generations.

"Thank you," he said, because he couldn't say nothing to someone who had just brought him breakfast.

The boy paused near the door, looking up at Trent's face as though he was surprised he'd been addressed at all. Trent caught the quick glance the slave gave to Ciaran's bare torso and tried not to grimace.

"Fyrirgef mik, herra," the boy said in a gentle voice. "Ek skil eigi."

The only part of that Trent caught was 'herra,' and only that because he'd heard it used to address Ciaran before. He guessed it was some sort of honorable title, and the thought made him a little sick. He let out a soft sigh.

"Never mind," he said. The boy didn't leave. Trent tried again. "I don't...I'm not asking you for—"

Ciaran stirred beside him, lazily waving a dismissive hand in the slave's direction. "Þǫkk, Blíður," he said without opening his eyes. "Sagði Þǫkk."

The boy gave a deep bow and scurried out of the room, the heavy rattle of the metal in the door the only sound of his leaving.

Ciaran pushed himself up and leaned his weight behind him on the balls of his hands. "Þǫkk," he said again, "is thank you."

A small frown twisted Trent's lips. "Did you have to...send him away like that?"

"Like what?" Trent gestured in an impersonation of Ciaran's dismissal, and the fairy chuckled softly. "I was just translating. He would have stood there all day if he'd thought you wanted something."

"I feel sorry for him."

"I'd be shocked if you didn't." Ciaran hesitated when Trent only shook his head in disgust, but then he stood and fetched the tray of food, placing it on the bed between them. "Let's not waste his efforts. He'll be disappointed if you don't eat."

Trent's nose wrinkled at the obvious cajoling. "I know what you're doing."

"I'll use whatever methods necessary to make sure you keep your strength up. Even playing on your guilt about innocent-looking slave boys."

Trent gave in. He only managed to steal a single berry before Ciaran claimed them all for himself, but the bread and salted fish were fresh and filling. As he ate, he tried to avoid the fairy's persistently peering gaze. Eventually, with a mouthful of bread, Trent sighed. "Why are you staring at me?"

"I've had a thought," Ciaran said, tapping his bottom lip with one thoughtful finger.

"It's about time."

"Shut up. I'm thinking that you've seen very little of what good there is in this world. Both at home with your father and with me, in Tír na nÓg and here. I needed to leave Tír na nÓg, but that doesn't mean that it doesn't have any good qualities. It's the same here. You think it's awful—and you're right, keeping slaves is awful—but there is beauty here. Everything that's happened to you since you joined up with me has been gloom and doom. Today let's do something else."

Trent couldn't help the skeptical frown on his lips. "Something else?"

"Yes. Finish up and get dressed." The fairy dusted his hands and pushed to his feet to fetch the stack of clothing that had been left for them.

Trent's personal clothes hadn't been washed since they left Vancouver, and every article he had now smelled like salt water and weeks of wear. He was reluctant to put on the clothes offered to him, but since the alternative was being naked in the cold cliffside air, he did it anyway. There weren't any mirrors in the bedroom, but Trent felt awkward enough without seeing himself. The wool pants, long tunic, and thick leather boots were rough against his skin, and they hung slightly long from his shoulders. He knew he looked ridiculous.

Ciaran, of course, Trent thought with a frown, looked perfectly dashing. The shades of black and grey suited him, the tunic split just enough at the neck to show his sharp collarbones, and the tall, dark boots were snug against his lean calves. The corners of his eyes crinkled in a smile as he offered Trent his hand.

"Come along then."

Trent let himself enjoy the warmth of the fairy's fingers in his as he was led from the longhouse. In the light of day, there were many more eyes on them, but when Trent stared at the ground in embarrassment, Ciaran reached over to lightly touch his chin and draw his gaze upward.

"You look them in the eyes, a mhuirnín. You've nothing to be ashamed of."

Trent frowned away the heat in his cheeks and squeezed Ciaran's hand. He managed to keep his chin high as they walked.

Ciaran turned a corner, and his pace quickened as they approached a long wooden building set apart from the others. The smell of animals hit Trent's nose when they got close. He leaned closer to Ciaran to see around the corner of the wide doorway and almost stopped walking as he caught sight of the endless row of stalls. It was a horse stable. Ciaran approached without hesitation, releasing Trent's hand to catch the attention of a young man brushing the coat of the horse closest to the entrance.

The boy gave a polite bow at the light touch to his shoulder. He was wearing the same faded blue tunic as Gunvard's servant, and he was just as dirty, but he seemed a little more composed. Trent wondered if that meant he'd been beaten more, or less. He had seen the healing bruises on Blíður's arms the night before—even Ciaran's hospitable friend wasn't above leaving marks on his slaves.

Ciaran opened his mouth to speak and then paused. The slave waited patiently with lowered eyes until the fairy started again. "Ek lysta...ugh," he sighed. "I didn't realize how much language I'd lost. Ek lysta...hoster? Histir?" When the slave dared a confused glance up at him, Ciaran reached out to pat the nose of the horse beside him, hoping the boy would understand.

"...Hestr?"

"Já!" Ciaran laughed. "So close. Hestr. Svá vel." He held up two fingers and chose to simply gesture to Trent and himself rather than try to remember more words. The young man hesitated as his eyes flicked reluctantly to Ciaran's obviously human companion, but the fairy tilted his head to keep the slave's attention on him. "Don't look at him," he said. "He's no concern of yours. We're guests of Gunvard.

Understand? Gunvard selga fínt."

The boy paused for only a moment more before offering another quick bow and rushing off down the corridor. Trent sighed and folded his arms as Ciaran turned back to face him.

"This is great and everything, but are you thinking for some reason that I know how to ride a horse?"

"Oh, it's easy," the fairy assured him. He stroked the soft nose of the horse in the stall beside him, rubbing his fingertips affectionately down the fat line of white on its face. "The horse does all the work, doesn't she? Don't you, a leanbh?" He smiled as he bent to touch a kiss to the animal's snout.

"I'm not sure that's true at all, actually."

"Don't worry, a mhuirnín; we're just going to have a bit of fun. Nobody's asking you to win a race." He pulled away from the horse to lift his eyebrows hopefully at the younger man. "Unless you'd like to race."

"I absolutely do not want to race."

"Suit yourself," he chuckled. He turned his head as the slave returned with reins in each hand, leading two saddled and bridled horses down the broad aisle. "Ah. Here we are." Ciaran thanked the boy as he took the reins from him, and he tilted his head to urge Trent to follow as he walked the horses from the stable.

Trent walked behind them, giving the animals a wide berth. He stared warily at them even after Ciaran stopped walking.

"Have you ever been on a horse before at all?" the fairy asked.

Trent flinched and took a half step back as the horse closest to him snorted and shook its head. "No," he said, as though the answer should have been obvious. "No, I have not." One more thing that was an easy part of Ciaran's world and that Trent knew nothing about.

"Just be confident," Ciaran advised. He looped one set of reins around a standing post and reached out a hand to draw Trent closer to the horse he still held. "And gentle. Do you need a lift getting on?"

Trent frowned. He liked to think he'd at least seen enough movies to know—theoretically—how to mount a horse. He took a step forward and put a hand on the saddle. Ciaran steadied the animal by the bridle while Trent put one foot in the stirrup, and after only a little bit of embarrassing struggle, Trent situated himself on the horse's back. Ciaran politely said nothing about the performance; he just handed Trent the reins.

The fairy mounted his horse with flawless grace. He sat tall in the saddle and held the reins with an easy grip, as comfortable as if he was on a plush sofa instead of an unfamiliar 800 pound animal. Ciaran clicked his tongue at the horse and eased it forward, but Trent's horse didn't move.

Ciaran looked over his shoulder at him with a smile. "Just lean forward. Give her a little squeeze with your legs."

Trent tried. The horse idled forward, and Trent kept one white-knuckled hand on the pommel to stop himself from slipping sideways. The horse at least seemed to know enough on its own to follow Ciaran's mount out of the compound, for which Trent was grateful.

The fields outside of the towering ramparts were covered in dull grass faded by the cold, misty air, and dark stone rocks lined the distant cliffs. Trent could hear the crash of ocean waves far below them as they drew nearer to the coast. Rows of wheat stretched far on either side of the path they rode, bent figures in muddy blue tunics tending to the growing stalks. None of them looked up as the horses passed. Trent risked shifting on his saddle to call to Ciaran ahead of him.

"What are we doing out here?"

"We're having fun, a mhuirnín," Ciaran answered with a soft laugh. "You do remember fun, don't you? I don't want to worry about tomorrow today. Today, I want to go for a ride."

Trent wasn't sure that this adventure was going to be any fun at all for him, but he could see the hopefulness in Ciaran's face, so he did his best to smile. The fairy was trying to cheer him up, and probably trying to get his own mind off of the decision he was being forced to make. Just for a little while. Maybe they both needed it.

Once they were outside of the farmlands surrounding the city, the fields opened up into sprawling, tree-spotted hills. In the far distance, Trent could see the faint outline of another massive city through the mist. Ciaran urged his horse a little faster with a gentle tut, calling back to Trent to encourage him to try out a trot. Trent held on tightly and tried to do as he was told, but every time the horse sped up, he panicked and clutched at the reins so tightly that it snorted to a halt again. After the fifth time Ciaran left him behind and had to circle back for him, Trent was just as annoyed as the animal underneath him.

"Why don't you just go?" he said. "I'll get the hang of it. You go run or whatever, and I'll catch up."

Ciaran stopped his horse a few feet from Trent's. "It's fine, a mhuirnín. We'll stay together."

"Ciaran," Trent sighed. "You clearly want to go. So just go. I'll catch up—I promise."

The fairy hesitated a moment longer, but then, with a grin on his lips, he turned his horse, leaned forward in the saddle, and gave a quick whistle that sent the animal bounding forward into an eager gallop. Trent's horse started slightly at the sudden movement, but he managed to settle it enough to avoid falling off. He walked the horse to the top of the next hill to look for Ciaran and could already barely see him.

Ciaran rode across the field at what Trent considered a terrifying pace. He was lifted a little in his saddle, balanced perfectly on the stirrups, the icy wind blowing his hair from his face as the horse galloped close to the cliff's edge. Even at this distance, Trent could tell the fairy had a smile on his face. He looked perfectly at home in his dark tunic and boots, running wild in the grassy countryside, guiding the animal beneath him like he'd been born doing it. This *was* where he was born. This was where he belonged.

Trent watched his lover until he was almost out of sight, the horse running full tilt as it circled a distant crop of trees along the cliff. He thought that the sight of Ciaran in his natural element—on horseback in some secret magical land full of totally-not-proto-fairies—should upset him. It should remind him of how different he was from the man he loved. Back at the apartment, when they'd first met, it had been easy to forget what he was, and being plunged head first into Ireland's magical underbelly had been like getting dunked in ice water. It was overwhelming trying to reconcile the two Ciarans he knew—the Ciaran who drank heavy cream and ate chocolate cake at Trent's kitchen island, and Cian mac Cainte, the fairy with more titles than Trent could hope to pronounce. Seeing how happy, how young, how wild Ciaran looked as the horse's hooves pounded the earth beneath him—it should scare him. But suddenly Trent didn't feel afraid at all.

He was only human. The man he loved was immortal. He was four thousand years old; he was stronger than a human could ever be; he could do magic; he came from a place underground where there were carriages drawn by beetles. They had come here together on a magic boat, through a storm and past a sea monster, on a mission to fetch a mind-controlling staff to settle a thousand-year-old blood debt.

Trent found himself laughing, and he lifted a hand to cover his mouth as his shoulders shook. How had he ever thought he'd be happy working at a bank?

He paused. He hadn't, he realized. He had never thought he'd be happy at all. Not until he met Ciaran.

With his jaw set tight with determination, Trent tried to urge his horse forward to meet the other man. He managed to guide the animal into a trot, but the quick step made him slip, and when he squeezed the horse with his legs to keep upright, it bolted. Trent's life flashed before his eyes as he scrambled to hold on, but before he could slam into a tree or run off the edge of the cliff, Ciaran was beside him, leaning from his own saddle to take hold of Trent's reins. He slowed both of them to a stop with a soft laugh.

"Easy, there," he murmured, but Trent wasn't sure whether he was talking to him or the horse.

Trent watched the man beside him, panting and sweaty and grinning, with sun-darkened freckles and hair wild in the wind. This man had convinced Trent of his own worth when everyone around him had scolded him and forced him into line. He'd offered Trent his freedom and held his hand while he took the first frightening steps away from the only life he'd ever known. Ciaran was sarcastic and affectionate and challenging and gentle, and he looked at his lover with a childlike smile crinkling the corners of his eyes.

Trent loved him. Without even fully understanding what that meant, he'd fallen in love with him, and no matter how many ridiculous things happened from here—how many beetle-carriage rides or sea monsters—he knew that Ciaran would be there to take his hand when he was afraid. Trent had been an outsider all his life—and he would always be an outsider in Ciaran's world.

But it didn't matter whether other people thought he belonged. He belonged wherever Ciaran was.

Ciaran tilted his head, lifting his eyebrows and nodding toward the smile Trent knew was on his face. "Something good happen while I was gone, a mhuirnín?"

Trent reached out for the other man, took him by the collar to tug him close, and kissed him. The fairy let out a little noise of surprise, but Trent felt his hand against his cheek, his thumb brushing the line of the boy's jaw.

"I love you," Trent whispered without pulling away. He felt Ciaran smile against his lips.

"I love you, too."

Trent's fingers curled into the fairy's tunic. "I've been...afraid," he said. "But I want you to know, I'm...I'm all in. For real. I don't ever want to leave you. Whatever that means. I'm going to be by your side."

Ciaran pressed another heated kiss to his lips. "That's exactly where I want you." He leaned back from the boy with a warm smile on his face. "Come. Let's rest a while."

Trent nodded, so Ciaran let his horse move forward, leading Trent's mount along behind him by the reins. They walked at an easy pace until they reached an outcropping of rocks jutting out over the churning ocean. Ciaran dismounted first, then held Trent's horse steady for him so that he could climb down. He let the horses wander, the pair of them idling over to a patch of slightly greener grass and bending their heads down to eat.

Ciaran held Trent's hand and sat beside him on the rocks, close enough to the edge that Trent could see the waves hitting the side of the cliff below them. He leaned his shoulder against Ciaran's, his arms around his bent knees, and watched the strips of sunlight glinting off of the water through the clouds.

"I guess it is pretty here," he admitted after a while. "You know, if you ignore the whole slavery thing."

Ciaran nudged his shoulder and gave him a sidelong smirk. "You know," he said, "I used to come out here a lot when I was young." He twisted just enough to point out a massive nearby tree with thick, sprawling roots. "When I was first learning to ride, the horse tripped over a root from that very tree, and I went face first into the rocks. Blood everywhere. The way I cried—" He laughed. "My father scolded me, of course. For crying, not for falling. But the next day I came right back out again, broken nose and all."

"That sounds like you."

Ciaran looked over at him and ran a hand through the boy's hair. His smile was as gentle as his touch, and Trent couldn't help returning it as he leaned into the fairy's caress.

"That's what I've been missing," Ciaran murmured. "Don't show that look to anyone else."

He moved closer and touched a kiss to Trent's faint smile, and the boy melted against him, hands moving up to wrap around the fairy's shoulders. He let his fingers slip through Ciaran's hair as the other man eased him back onto the smooth stone.

Ciaran slid a hand under Trent's heavy shirt, his fingers brushing the soft skin at his side, and he opened his mouth to the kiss to taste the younger man's tongue. Trent shuddered against him and tightened his grip in Ciaran's hair, the thought that they were out in the open far from his mind. This was what Trent wanted. None of the rest of it mattered—only being with Ciaran. Only feeling this warmth that Trent never thought he'd get to have.

Trent paused as Ciaran's kisses moved down his jaw to his neck. He didn't feel hesitant. He gasped softly as the pad of the fairy's thumb ran over his nipple, but he didn't feel embarrassed.

"Wait," he said, touching Ciaran's cheek to urge him away so that he could look him in the face. He knew that there was a faint smile on his lips, and he tried to resist the urge to bite it away. "Let's...save this."

Ciaran tilted his head in confusion.

"We should try the spell again," Trent explained. "I...have a good feeling about it this time."

A sly grin pulled the fairy's lips as he leaned closer, giving the corner of Trent's mouth a tiny lick. "You want to wait until I'm spiritually inside you before I get physically inside you?"

Trent let his head fall back against the stone as he rolled his eyes. He pushed Ciaran away by the shoulder. "And you've ruined it. Get off me."

Ciaran laughed and settled beside the boy again, and Trent didn't even mind the teasing look the fairy gave him as their fingers laced together between them.

17

Noah ran his fingers along his lines of notes countless times while he stretched on the bed, studying his findings and doing his best not to seem like he noticed Julien's pouting. He felt guilty, but he was determined not to be the one to apologize for their little spat. Even if Julien was worrying about him, he didn't have the right to control him. He certainly didn't have the right to shout at him. Still, the sight of the hunter across the room from him, clearly trying to keep out of his way, gnawed at his belly. Noah had never told him about Travis. It was unreasonable to expect Julien to understand how his heart began to pound at the first sign of anger. Noah didn't believe that Julien would ever lay a violent hand on him, but he couldn't help the way his skin trembled when the hunter raised his voice.

When Lugh left them to find something to eat, a few more minutes of silence passed before Julien finally approached the bed.

"Are you angry with me?" he asked.

Noah's gut twisted at the softness of the other man's voice. He sat up with his legs curled under him and pushed his notes aside. "I'm not angry with you," he answered honestly. "But I do wish you would trust me more. I got along just fine for a long time before I met you, you know? I'm not helpless."

"I know that."

"I want to be partners with you, Julien. It's been all drama and hero quests and passionate confessions…and that stuff is great, but when we wake up the next morning, I'm just going to be Noah, and you're just going to be Julien. If we want to make this work…you know, long term, then we need to be equals. And I want this to work long term."

Julien let out a soft sigh, and he dropped onto the bed a polite distance from the younger man. After a moment, he laughed softly and shook his head. "You're so much better at this than I am."

"It's not any different from dating a woman, you know. Any girl who was attracted to you wouldn't want to be treated like a delicate flower, either."

"You think I'm any better with women?"

"I mean, at least you have more practice, right?" Julien didn't answer. Noah's eyes narrowed as he spotted a telltale splash of pink on the other man's cheekbones, and he crawled forward on the bed to look him in the face. "You have practice, right?" he asked again.

"I have practice," the hunter grumped. "Just—" He sighed in resignation and looked into Noah's dark eyes. "Just not a lot of it. And never with anything like this. Not because you're a man. Because— before, it was always temporary. We both knew it was. I never…loved any of them, and they never loved me. There was never anyone that I actually…wanted to stay."

"It's fine if you're afraid, Julien. I am, too. But relationships are work, you know? I know you know how to work. So we'll both work hard, and we'll figure it out as we go, okay? We just have to trust each other."

Julien still seemed anxious, so Noah crept closer and took the hunter's face in his hands, lifting his gaze and leaning in to kiss him. The soft little growl in Julien's throat made Noah's heart skip. A few weeks ago, Noah had been lamenting his hopeless state and resigning himself to gazing at Julien from a distance forever, and now it was his touch—*his*—that was drawing that sweet sound from the larger man. For that, he could work through some anger issues.

A knock on the door startled their kiss apart, and Noah gave Julien's jaw one more light brush with his thumb before standing to answer it.

Ciaran stood in the open doorway with Trent's hand in his. "We'd like to try again," he said. "The spell."

"Oh. Oh, sure." Noah waved them inside and crouched to fetch his binder from Julien's bag. "How did it go with the seeress, by the way? Any answers?"

"Not very helpful ones," Ciaran answered. "But Gaibhne and his brothers are definitely planning something. I'm thinking on what to do."

Julien seemed less than satisfied with that answer, but Noah didn't push. If they were in the right mindset to attempt the joining spell, he didn't want to shake them out of it.

"Well keep us in the loop, right? You know," he went on immediately, "I've actually been doing some thinking about this soul joining. I think I found something in the—" He stopped himself from saying 'library' and glanced over his shoulder at Ciaran like a guilty child. He cleared his throat before continuing. "In, you know, my book. Something that might work too. But it seems…riskier. So before we go that far, there's one more thing I'd like to try." He stood and held the binder close to his chest as he faced them. "And since I only have enough supplies to try this particular spell once more, I really think we should."

Ciaran tilted his head skeptically. "And yet the look on your face tells me you think we won't agree."

"Well, it's…I don't suppose either of you have ever heard of Maithuna." Noah continued when he saw the blank looks on their faces. "It's sex. Well, it's more than sex. It's tantric. But I really think it would help you two come together. I mean—" He snorted out a laugh and held up a hand to excuse himself. "Not like that. It will help you to join properly. That sounds dirty too—sorry. You know what I mean. It'll help your minds meet the right way. There."

"I'm pretty sure we know how to have sex, lad."

"I told you it's not just sex. There are specific ways to do everything, and it's usually done with an experienced guide. So I'd have to…you know, guide you."

A slightly strangled sound came out of Trent before he spoke. "You want to help us have sex?"

"I want to help you perform a ritual," Noah corrected.

"Noah," Julien spoke up as he stood. "This is a bit—"

"It's their choice." Noah gave a small shrug. "I still can't guarantee it'll work. For all I know, this spell will never work. I'm still looking into other options. But if it's possible to complete the joining this way, Maithuna will better your chances of success. I know how to do it. If you're comfortable with it, I'll guide you."

Ciaran turned to look at Trent with his eyebrows raised in a question. Noah expected Trent to object immediately and vehemently, but he wanted to make the offer regardless. A few beats of silence passed, and Trent's mouth slowly formed into a tight frown.

"Let's try," he said.

"Are you sure, a mhuirnín?" The fairy's voice was soft, but Trent shook his head and let out a quick, determined breath.

"I want to try. If we can only do the spell one more time, we should do whatever we can to make it work, right?"

"All right then." Ciaran looked back at the witch and nodded. "Let's be guided, I suppose."

Noah smiled. "Great. I promise it won't be as awkward as you think. But—let's go into your room. Lugh won't want to come back and see this." He let Ciaran and Trent out ahead of him, but when he tried to follow, Julien took him gently by the arm.

"You're not going to—not really," he said in a hushed voice, his eye darting into the hall and back to Noah's face.

Noah chuckled. "It's a tantric ritual, Julien, not a three-way. I'm just showing them what to do. I'll still have my clothes on, even." He stood on tiptoe to press a light kiss to the blond's lips. "But it's cute that you're jealous."

"I am not—I just—"

Noah gave the hunter's chest a light pat with his free hand and headed out the door toward Ciaran's room. He shut the door behind him and laid out his supplies while Trent and Ciaran stood awkwardly nearby. The witch laughed softly as he noticed them.

"Relax," he said. "This is just like the meditation. You have to try to clear your mind." He sparked a small fire in his palm and lit the incense, shaking his hand to put out the flame as he turned to them. "You're also going to have to get naked."

Ciaran began pulling off his tunic without a care, but Trent hesitated, his fingers rolling the hem of his own shirt.

"Trent," Noah added, "I have helped fifty-somethings who don't think they need to wear underwear with their white yoga pants into downward dog. You don't have anything I haven't seen before. I promise."

The boy didn't crack a smile, but he did pull off his shirt and drop it with Ciaran's in one quick motion. Noah waited while Ciaran stripped naked and dropped onto the bed; Trent followed noticeably slower but managed to tug off his boots and pants. His skin was flushed from his cheeks down to his neck, and he didn't make eye contact with Noah, but he finally stood naked in the quiet bedroom. Ciaran had a lean frame with strong-looking shoulders and thighs, but Trent was bordering on what Noah might call "slight." Even if he hadn't known their preferences through cloudy borrowed memories, Noah could guess how they would prefer to arrange themselves for this exercise.

"First, breathing," Noah said in a low voice. He pulled the roughly-sewn curtains closed over the narrow windows, leaving only the fire in the corner to light the room. He put a hand up to guide Trent onto the bed without actually touching him. "Kneel facing each other," he advised. "Look your lover in the eyes. Softly, half-focused. Breathe deeply, like before—in through the nose, out through the mouth. Try to synchronize your breathing; feel the rhythm of them in front of you. And relax," he said again. He stood near the bed between the two of them, watching their chests slowly rise and fall.

Just when they were beginning to settle into a pattern, a heavy thump sounded outside the door followed by a whispered curse that sounded suspiciously French. Noah frowned over his shoulder, but the hallway went quiet, so he turned back to Trent and Ciaran and encouraged them to continue their breathing. He knew that Julien was outside, probably with his ear pressed to the door, but the hunter's suspicion couldn't distract him.

"When you're ready," the witch went on, "we can proceed to worship." He kept his voice soft when both pairs of eyes flicked over to him in silent confusion. "The tongue has many energy points, and the goal is to transfer and exchange that energy between you. Usually the woman is worshipped first, but that doesn't really apply, so you choose who begins."

Ciaran looked up at Noah, clearly trying to keep a straight face. "You mean a blowjob. You're sure this isn't just you wanting to watch?"

"It's not just a blowjob, you walnut. Focus." He gestured toward Trent, who seemed to be shrinking away from the very idea of blowjobs. "Worship him. Show him how much you love him and how beautiful he is. Tell him. Orgasm is not the goal—only ecstasy, mutual energy, and transcendence."

"You hear that, a mhuirnín?" Ciaran murmured as he leaned forward, his tongue tracing a slow line along the younger man's collarbone. "Do your best to hold back, now."

The fairy started as Noah swatted his cheek with the back of his hand. "No teasing."

Ciaran spared him a brief glare as the witch retreated half a step to give them some space, but he quickly returned his attention to Trent and began to kiss a slow line down his chest. The boy's fists were tight as they rested on his thighs, and Noah could see that his breath was unsteady. When Ciaran bent over him and drew his tongue slowly over the small ridge of his hip bone, Trent let out a tiny, shaky sound, but he wasn't responding where it mattered. He was too nervous. Noah watched Trent's face while Ciaran continued, waiting for the boy's tightly knit brow to relax. His jaw only set tighter when Ciaran took him into his mouth, and Trent turned his head away as if he could escape the situation by closing his eyes.

"Stop, stop," Noah spoke up, and he put a light hand on Trent's shoulder as Ciaran sat back on his knees. "You have to pay attention, Ciaran. It's your job to make him comfortable. Does he look comfortable to you?"

Ciaran hesitated, taking in the anxious frown on his lover's face and the way he flinched away even from Noah's gentle touch. He opened his mouth to speak, but something nudged the bedroom door, rattling it on its hinge. Noah let his hand drop as he sighed in frustration, and he strode across the room and flung open the door. Julien nearly came tumbling in on top of him, but the hunter caught himself on the door frame just before losing his balance.

"Are you kidding me with this?" Noah snapped. He put a hand on

Julien's chest and shut his eyes, taking a deep breath to swallow his irritation. When he looked up into the hunter's face, he paused. "Actually—you can help." He looked over his shoulder at Trent and Ciaran. "If you'll let him."

"Not with..." Ciaran trailed off, gesturing to himself and Trent with one finger. "Is he qualified?"

"To lead by example," Noah said. He pulled Julien into the room and shut the door behind him. The hunter did his best to avert his eye as he was guided a bit closer to the bed. Noah knew this was more of the fairy than Julien had ever hoped to see, but allowing Trent to think that the focus of the room wasn't just on him could be the difference between success and a waste of incense.

Noah positioned Julien so that he wasn't looking at the men on the bed, and he let his hands rest on the hunter's stomach as he looked around him at Trent and Ciaran. "It's not about the sex at all, really. It's about the difference between physical pleasure and spiritual acceptance. A practiced Tantrika can perform Maithuna with only a touch."

Noah kept his eyes on Julien's uncertain face as he lowered himself to his knees, his hands following the hard lines of the hunter's body through his clothing. He could feel the other man's muscles tensing, so he flattened his palms against his thighs and pressed a warm, slow kiss to the cotton covering his stomach.

"Just look at me," he whispered. He looked up into Julien's eye and heard the slow breath he took as he relaxed under the witch's touch. Noah drifted his hands up to his lover's belt, and he barely dipped his fingers beneath Julien's shirt to touch his skin directly. He let a scant line of tanned skin show and drew close enough for Julien to feel his breath but didn't allow his lips to touch him.

"Let him feel the things you want to show him," Noah said, just loud enough for Ciaran and Trent to hear him. "Remember that this is *worship.*" Noah slid his hands fully under the blond's shirt and savored the slight tension in his skin and the hitch in his breath. He ran his fingertips along every dip in Julien's muscled stomach, slowly, as if he was memorizing them. When Julien lifted a hand and ran it tenderly through the witch's hair, Noah met his gaze with a soft sigh in his throat.

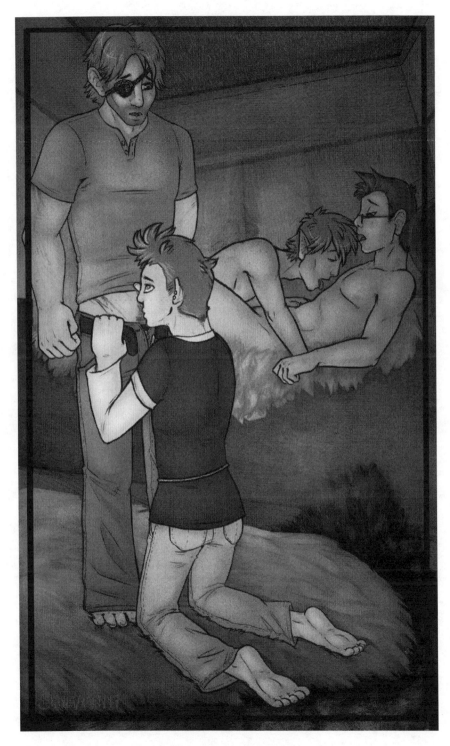

"I love you," he mouthed, finally placing a soft kiss just above the blond's belt buckle.

He heard a faint gasp through teeth from behind Julien and tilted just enough to catch sight of the bed beyond the hunter's hips. On the bed, Trent had fallen back onto his elbows, and his eyes were on the fairy leaning over him, lips parted and glasses slipped low on his nose as Ciaran lapped slowly at the soft skin just below his nipple. He was definitely responsive now. Noah pulled away from Julien just enough to put a quieting finger to his lips. He kept his place on the floor, hands resting lightly around the backs of Julien's knees, and watched the tension fade from Trent's face with every passing moment. The boy's back bowed as Ciaran's hand grazed his erection, and his eyes fluttered closed at the touch of his lover's lips on his stomach.

Noah pulled himself to his feet as quietly as he could, and he took light steps over to the bed. He kept an eye on Trent's face and touched the back of Ciaran's shoulder with just his fingertips to avoid startling him, but Ciaran didn't seem to mind the faint caress. Noah bent close to him, his cheek barely brushing the fairy's ear as he whispered, "Move up where he can reach you."

He moved back to let Ciaran do as he was told, and the fairy shifted on the bed, leaning over Trent and catching his lips in a slow, deep kiss. The boy's hand moved automatically to touch his lover, fingertips running along his stomach and through the dark nest of curls at the base of his cock. Noah smiled at the sighing groan Ciaran gave and crept backwards to Julien's side again. The hunter was staring at him, half disbelieving and half impressed, but Noah only shrugged one shoulder and put a finger to his lips again. He crouched by the fire and threw in the remaining batch of herbs, glancing upwards to make sure the smoke would reach the men on the bed, then he returned to the center of the room.

Julien was doing his best not to look at the scene so close to them, but Noah watched Trent's face as the boy's arm slipped around Ciaran's neck. He couldn't hear the words the fairy whispered into his lover's ear, but his heart throbbed pleasantly at the way the boy smiled against Ciaran's shoulder. He almost stepped close again to tell Ciaran that it was time to move forward, but he stopped when he saw the fairy's hand dip underneath Trent and heard the sudden gasp the younger man let out. It seemed Ciaran didn't need to be told to progress. Noah waited, keeping one hand against Julien to stop him from fidgeting, and when Trent began to shudder and grip his lover tighter, he moved to the bed to lightly touch Ciaran's shoulder again.

The fairy broke his attention from the flushed, panting boy beneath him, and Noah gestured quickly at himself and Julien. He pulled the hunter onto the floor with him and urged him to sit cross-legged, then the witch climbed into his lap with his legs around his waist and his arms around his shoulders, face to face with him and chest to chest. Ciaran took the hint and lifted Trent gently up with him as he rose. He settled the younger man in his lap, copying Noah's position, and he pulled him down for a kiss to muffle his lover's whimpering cry as he sank deep into him.

Noah's eyes followed the line of Trent's arched back as Ciaran supported him with strong hands on his waist. Neither of them moved for a few long moments, and Noah finally looked away once Trent began to roll his hips, fingers tangled in the fairy's dark hair and parted lips close enough to feel his lover's breath. He shut his eyes and whispered the incantation from his book, but the spell was mostly in Trent and Ciaran's hands now. Either it would work, and they would be joined as intended, or it wouldn't, and they would start back at square one. Either way, at least they would know that they'd tried literally everything.

Noah settled into Julien's lap with his arms resting lightly on the other man's shoulders, but he paused when he felt a familiar firm pressure against him. He shifted his hips a little, experimentally, and stopped when Julien's hands clamped tightly onto his waist. The hunter was looking up at him in the flickering orange light of the fire, but even in the darkness, Noah could tell that his face was red. The witch let his fingers slip through the soft hair at the back of Julien's neck as he leaned in close to his ear.

"This is a very serious ritual," he whispered, his voice barely a breath against the hunter's skin. "How am I supposed to be professional with your dick twitching like that?"

He smiled and chewed one of the piercings in his lip as he felt Julien's fingers digging into his sides. He rolled his hips just once and had to hold in his own silent gasp at the wave of expectation that washed through his belly. He knew it wasn't right to tease him. He knew that Julien was private about this sort of thing, and that he wouldn't take kindly to Noah's advances just now—even if the low, panting sounds of lovemaking two feet away from them were admittedly distracting. Noah was there to supervise and to guide, not to be a voyeur. But a little teasing couldn't hurt. If he was lucky, he could work the hunter up enough to make him willing to risk Lugh walking in on them in the other room.

It had been a long trip—even in the hotel room, when they had laid together and listened to Trent try to pretend he wasn't getting a handjob, Julien had brushed aside Noah's teasing hand and glared at him with a flustered frown. On the boat, Noah had more than once woken up with Julien hard against his ass, but every time the witch had tried to surreptitiously reach behind him, Julien had held his wrist and whispered to him to stop. Their tryst behind the longhouse had been satisfying, but it had only whet Noah's appetite for more. It was cute that Julien was so proper—frustrating too, but mostly cute. And Noah could have lived off of the way his single eye focused on him when the hunter wanted him but thought he couldn't have him. The way it did now.

Noah trailed his fingers along the blond's stubbled jaw and down his chest, scraping his fingernails in his shirt until he reached the thick leather of his belt. He felt the man's stomach tense under his touch and bit his lip at the pulse Julien's erection gave against him. Noah tugged at his belt, easing the leather through the buckle and peering down into the sharp hazel eye locked onto him. He couldn't tell if the glare was a warning or not, but he knew that even the stoic hunter wasn't immune to the gasping moans of the men on the bed. If Noah teased him just enough, maybe he could get another fevered loss of control out of him once they were alone.

He leaned forward and gave Julien's chin a soft bite that led into a kiss to the corner of his mouth, and once Julien's belt buckle was loose, Noah let his fingertips stroke the soft skin at the head of his cock, peeking out above the waistband of his underwear. He could tell that his name was on the hunter's tongue, held back only by the fear of being heard. Noah kissed his way back to Julien's ear and let out a warm sigh.

"Do you want to touch me, Julien?"

Noah jumped as the hunter suddenly snapped him tight against his chest, catching him in a kiss and sliding both hands smoothly down his hips and into the back of his jeans. The witch melted instantly, bracing himself on Julien's shoulders to better grind back against him. So much for professional.

He could smell the burning incense and the heated sweat of the bodies moving together on the bed, and the sound of Julien's rapid breathing mixed with Trent's soft moans in his ears, overwhelming his sense of responsibility. He kept one steadying arm around his hunter's neck and reached down to free him from his buttoned pants, barely holding back the groan in his own throat as he finally let his fingers wrap fully around Julien's cock. He fought Julien's tongue for dominance of their kiss, but when the blond's finger pressed firmly against his opening, Noah was forced to break the kiss to hide his gasp in the other man's neck. He reached back with a hastily-whispered spell to help Julien slick his fingers and returned to his work, squeezing the hunter and stroking him at a demanding pace.

When Julien slid the first finger into him, Noah bit his shoulder to keep from making a sound. He peeked up at the men on the bed behind Julien, telling himself that he was just checking on their progress, but he couldn't keep his eyes from following the path of Ciaran's hands on Trent's back, the way he held his lover so securely and so gently. He watched the soft bob of Trent's Adam's apple as he swallowed, Ciaran's tongue tracing the skin just below his jaw, and when he looked up into Trent's flushed face, he found that the boy's black eyes were on him, too.

18

Trent held onto his lover with both arms around his neck and his fingers in the other man's hair. Ciaran's body was hot against him, and Trent shuddered with every slow thrust the fairy made into him, glad for the other man's grip supporting him. He didn't think he had the strength anymore. Every time he thought he was about to finish, every time he clung to Ciaran's shoulders and whispered desperately in his ear, the fairy had slowed down again. When he had broken away to try to catch his ragged breath and seen Noah clutched tightly to Julien's shoulders, an unexpected jolt ran down his spine. The witch's cheeks were pink, his brow knit in pleasure as he bit the hunter's shirt to stifle a moan. Noah lifted his gaze, and for just a moment, their eyes met. Trent could see the want in the witch's face, willing and unashamed as his fingers tightened into the back of Julien's shirt. He was eager and wanton, and Trent watched his lips move as he whispered something soft into his lover's ear. There wasn't a hint of embarrassment on his face—none of the hesitation or shyness that Trent always felt when Ciaran first touched him. He wanted to be like that. He felt, warm in Ciaran's embrace and shuddering under his touch, that maybe he could be.

Trent turned his head at Ciaran's light touch to his cheek, drawing his attention back to his lover, and he opened his mouth to his kiss.

He didn't know if the heat in his chest was from the incense, or the spell, or from the slow caress of Ciaran's tongue against his, but it was at the same time perfect and torturous. He wanted more of Ciaran— he wanted all of him—but the more he tried to push down against him, the more the fairy eased him back, keeping him from falling over that edge. It didn't help that Noah's increasingly impatient pants began to reach his ears, punctuated by the hunter's half-restrained groans.

With every stroke, Ciaran expertly brushed the bundle of nerves inside him, sending lightning under his skin. He gripped the fairy's waist with his legs, trying to urge him faster, deeper, and he bit his lover's bottom lip in an attempt to demand slightly rougher treatment, but Ciaran only responded by fastening his hand in Trent's hair and locking a hot kiss onto the skin below his ear. Trent's cock was seeping against his stomach, hard and aching and desperate for climax. He wanted to ask Ciaran to touch him; he was prepared to beg for it, but his throat was too dry, his mind too fogged to find the right words.

When Noah let out a soft cry from the floor, Trent turned his eyes toward him again and shuddered at the way the witch writhed against Julien, his forehead on the hunter's shoulder and his arm hooked around his neck. He could practically feel the tension about to snap in Noah's arched back, and he saw the witch's arm tighten around Julien, hand clawing with need at his back as he shuddered and rolled his hips back into the other man's hand. He heard his tight-jawed moan of release and almost sobbed with envy.

"Please," Trent whispered into Ciaran's ear. He tugged him closer and ground his hips to draw him deeper, and Ciaran finally seemed to respond. He lifted Trent effortlessly and pulled him down again, quickening his pace and driving himself into the younger man so hard that Trent felt the fairy's hipbones crash almost painfully against him. He wrapped his hand around Trent's erection and caused a helpless cry from him, but as soon as Trent began to buck against him, climax coiling in his belly, Ciaran stopped completely and held the boy still. He stayed buried deep inside him, but he didn't let Trent move despite the boy's grasping at his shoulders.

He pulled the boy close to him and growled into his ear, "You think I'm going to let you come while you're looking at someone else?"

Trent couldn't make his brain work. Desperate whispers tumbled out of him, apologies and begging, and he tried to buck his hips, but the fairy's grip kept him motionless. He took Ciaran's face in both hands and looked him in the eyes, knowing his face was red and hearing himself panting like an animal. He didn't care.

"Please," he said again. Just when he thought his heart might actually give out, Ciaran started to move. He held Trent steady while he pushed up into him, keeping a demanding pace that drew a long string of mewling, pleading cries from the younger man. Ciaran stroked him in time with his thrusts, but it only took a few moments before Trent's head fell back, his orgasm arching his back and pulling a ragged moan from his throat. He felt the heat of his own semen on his stomach and gave one more shuddering sigh as Ciaran finished inside him with a final deep thrust.

Neither of them moved for what felt like an eternity. They held each other, panting, Ciaran's fingers gently stroking the younger man's hair. Trent didn't even have the strength to keep upright; he laid his head on Ciaran's shoulder and let his lover caress him. When he did finally manage to turn his head enough to look out at the room, it was empty. He hadn't even noticed Noah and Julien leaving.

Trent waited, hoping there might be a banner, or confetti, or anything to let him know for sure that the spell had worked. He felt warm, and Ciaran's heartbeat against his chest was steady and close, but he didn't know if anything was actually different.

"How do you feel, a mhuirnín?" Ciaran asked, his voice a soft rumble under Trent's cheek.

"Tired," he admitted. He didn't know what else to say. He didn't know what it felt like to be soul-joined to another person. He hoped Noah would know.

Ciaran gave a soft laugh. He helped ease the boy out of his lap and laid down beside him on the bed, neither of them minding the mess they would leave on the blankets. Trent settled in the crook of the fairy's shoulder, Ciaran's thumb lightly brushing the back of his arm, and he let his eyes drift closed as exhaustion overtook him.

When he woke up, Ciaran was sitting up on the bed beside him, still naked, but chewing on a bit of bread from the tray balanced on his crossed legs. Trent sat up and reached over to take a handful of berries from the plate, then dropped back onto the bed and dropped one into his mouth. He chewed slowly while he stared at the ceiling, waiting for any tingle or sign that they hadn't just shared an exceptionally close-quarters sexual experience with their two companions for absolutely no reason. But one didn't come.

He pushed himself up again and tugged one of the furs over his lap as a knock sounded on the door. Ciaran didn't bother—apparently the tray covered enough of him to satisfy his sense of modesty. Noah poked his head inside at Ciaran's answer and glanced between the pair of them.

"Anything?" he asked, slipping inside to shut the door behind him.

"Not that I can tell," Ciaran shrugged. He looked hopefully over at Trent, but the boy only shook his head.

"Should I feel different?"

Noah approached them and held out a hand over Trent's forehead, the same gesture he'd made to test him after every attempt. He paused for a moment, but then he let his hand drop and gave a low sigh, his shoulders slumping in disappointment. "I'm sorry," he said. "A spell like this—who knows if it could ever work at all? But I'll keep looking," he assured them. "We'll solve this problem somehow."

Trent didn't feel as depressed as he thought he would. Noah had said from the start that it was a spell he'd never completed before. And if his time with Ciaran the night before hadn't been enough to bind them this way, then maybe the spell was just a dud. They would find another way.

"Thanks," he said, and Noah looked slightly startled to hear it. "For trying."

A faint smile touched the witch's lips. "Of course." He turned to Ciaran with raised eyebrows. "Anyway, it's day three, right? Are we packing up?"

Ciaran's expression darkened. "Aye. I'll need to talk to everyone before we go."

"Then I'll let you finish your breakfast. I have some reading to do, anyway."

Noah excused himself, and Ciaran leaned back on his hands to look over at the boy beside him.

"He's remarkably nonchalant, considering the evening we all had."

Trent grimaced. "We don't actually have to talk about this, do we? The polite thing to do would be to pretend it didn't happen. That's my plan."

"That's fine for you; you didn't have to see your lover gazing affectionately into the eyes of another man while you were inside of him."

"I wasn't—there was no gazing," Trent snapped. "I was not gazing."

"The lady doth protest too much," Ciaran chuckled, but when he saw the frown on the younger man's lips, he paused. "I'm just teasing, a mhuirnín."

"I was—jealous."

"Jealous? Of what, that hulking creature Noah brings everywhere?"

"What? No. I mean...I was embarrassed, but we were at least supposed to be doing this sacred sex ritual, or whatever. They were just...you know." He gestured vaguely at the spot on the floor where the two men had been the night before. "And they didn't even care. I'm just...I'm sick of feeling so ashamed." Ciaran set aside the tray of food and edged closer to him on the bed, but Trent didn't look up at him. "I know it's ridiculous. But I spent *so* long telling myself that I wasn't allowed to be attracted to men. Hearing that it was a perversion, or a disease, or that I was hurting everyone by being this way, and I—" He pressed the ball of his hand against the headache forming between his eyes. "Maybe it's my fault this hasn't worked. I felt so confident. I love you, and I want to be with you, but even last night, there was just this...this knot in my chest, like I couldn't relax. And not just because Noah was in here with us. When I saw them, and Noah was just...he looked like he'd never been embarrassed about anything in his life. And I...don't know what that self-assurance feels like."

Ciaran put a hand on Trent's hair and pulled him close, tucking the boy's head under his chin. For a few moments, neither of them spoke, and Ciaran just lightly rubbed his thumb over his lover's hair. Trent shut his eyes and leaned against the fairy, letting himself absorb the other man's warmth. Then Ciaran gave a soft sigh and leaned away to look Trent in the face.

"Mo ghrá geal," he said as he cupped the boy's cheek, "I know you've had a rough go with all of this. But you are bright, and handsome, and stronger of stomach than you give yourself credit for—ocean voyages notwithstanding," he added, smiling at Trent's falsely sour look. "We're going to find a way, and we're going to have a thousand years together, and even if it takes you a thousand years to see what I see in you, I'll be there to hold you up until you do."

Trent hesitated, watching the gentle smile in the other man's green eyes, and then he leaned forward and hugged him around the neck. He didn't say anything, and Ciaran didn't push him. The fairy just held him, warm hands stroking his back, until the boy pulled back and scooted a polite distance away from him. Trent nodded, hoping Ciaran would understand that he wanted to drop the matter. His stomach felt too fluttery for him to trust his voice not to waver.

"Let's get with the others," Ciaran said after a few moments had passed. "We'll need to load the ship and be on our way."

"Without the staff?"

Ciaran got to the edge of the bed and paused. "Aye. I'll explain once everyone is together."

They cleaned themselves up and dressed in another set of borrowed clothes, and when they entered the common room, Noah, Julien, and Lugh were already waiting for them. Gunvard sat at his place at the head of the table, and Trent caught sight of Rathgeirr at the far end—probably purposely positioned there by his father to keep him from interrupting.

"I have taken the liberty of having supplies carried to your ship," Gunvard said as Ciaran approached. "You should have more than enough to carry you safely back to Írland. But have you decided what to do once you get there?"

"I have," Ciaran said. "Mostly." He looked around at his companions and gestured to the long benches with a sigh. He didn't care if Gunvard wanted humans at his table or not. When they were all seated, he leaned his elbows on the smooth wood. He told them all what he had learned about the brothers' plot, their plans for overthrowing the king, and what the supposed consequences of that might be for the world above, but he still left out what the seeress had told him concerning the weight of his personal decision. He wouldn't have been able to bear the look on Trent's face.

"I can't just do nothing," he said when he had finished, and they all stared at him in pensive silence. "Letting them hurt Airmed is not an option. I have to go back. Once I'm there...I think the best option is to make the High Kings aware of what I know. I can't bring Gaibhne what he asked for, and he wasn't interested in simply being paid. Maybe with the kings' help, I can sort things out before it all gets out of hand. It will mean letting everyone know that I'm alive," he added with a glance at Lugh. "And what the result of that will be, I can't possibly guess."

"They will ask for proof," Lugh said simply. "You cannot simply accuse the Trí Dé Dána of treason and conspiracy and expect that the Ard Rí will accept the word of a man who faked his own death to avoid his responsibilities."

"I know that," Ciaran answered, his voice curt. "But I'll have to think of something, won't I?"

"You've had two days to think of something."

"If I can prove that I was here at all," Ciaran sighed, "they would have to at least listen to the rest. My word won't even be enough to prove that. But even if I brought a souvenir, what can I take to them that Gaibhne can't claim I've fabricated? Anything I show them, he'll just claim I've enchanted it somehow."

A heavy quiet fell over the table. Then, from the far end of the bench, Rathgeirr spoke up.

"Take me," he said. All eyes turned to him, and a faint frown pulled his lips as he watched Ciaran's face. "Take me with you."

"Absolutely not," Gunvard snapped, perhaps a bit louder than was necessary. "Out of the question."

"Father, I—"

"An Alfar has not left this island in almost four thousand years," the older man cut him off. "And one will certainly not leave today in order to meddle in the affairs of Ævintýri." He sat up a little straighter in his seat and glanced at Ciaran as if he knew he'd said something rude. Ciaran didn't have the energy to be offended at the slur the Alfar had used for his people—it wasn't any worse than being called a fairy, really. More inaccurate than insulting.

"Cian," Gunvard went on, "your father was a friend to me, and I believe I have been more than welcoming during your time here. Ask of me anything that you think will help prove your cause to your Kings, but my son is not up for negotiation."

"I don't intend to intrude upon your hospitality as far as that, old friend. I won't take him against your wishes."

Gunvard seemed to relax, but he kept a wary eye on his son.

"We still have to get back to Tír na nÓg," Ciaran went on. "We have time to come up with a plan, but I suspect the right path won't show itself until I see how the High Kings react."

No one at the table seemed particularly pleased with this overly-positive outlook, but it was the best that Ciaran had. He couldn't tell them that it wasn't nearly as optimistic as it seemed—not when the best-case scenario involved him losing the thing most dear to him. He knew that he would have to tell Trent soon. But he didn't want to burden the boy before he had to.

Gunvard bid Ciaran and Lugh a fond goodbye as they loaded themselves up with their belongings, though by the time Ciaran and Trent returned from their rooms, Rathgeirr had vanished. Gunvard paid no attention to the human portion of their group, of course, but Ciaran expected that. He was grateful that the alfar had been gracious enough to let them stay in the house—right or wrong, he'd have been within his rights to treat them like slaves. The alfar passed him a carved stone as they stood in the doorway to say farewell.

"This may not be enough to convince your kings of everything," he said, "but let it serve as proof that you were a welcome guest of the Alfar. It is only a token, but leave it above the entry to your home, and it will safeguard those within from malicious magic."

Ciaran turned the stone in his hand, brushing his thumb over the carved runes. As he did, wisps of black smoke poured heavily from the lines, curling toward the floor and dissipating before they could pool onto the wood. It certainly looked like Lochlannan magic to Ciaran— but the others might be harder to satisfy.

"Thank you, Gunvard. For everything."

"I'm only doing what a friend should. Take care on your journey home, Cian." The alfar let a faint smile show on his face as he shook the fairy's hand one last time.

A small group of scouts escorted them from the compound and away from the city. Ciaran tried to take in the scent of the island before he left it again—this time forever, he knew. For all its troubles and the gruffness of its people, this place had once been his home. It was more his home than Tír na nÓg was, in many ways. No matter what had brought them here, he was glad to be able to see it again. He was glad that Trent had been able to see it. He could teach him how to ride a horse when they had put all of this behind them.

The scouts regarded them with silent, piercing eyes staring out from under dark hoods as they packed the waiting ship. Ciaran paused as he stepped onto the boat. He felt something strange, like someone he couldn't see was watching him. He took a brief look over the coastline with one hand on the side of the ship. There would be other scouts watching them, even if they were hidden. They weren't going to take any chances that the visitors overstayed their welcome. Julien clearly sensed it, too; he saw the hunter open his mouth to speak and get silenced by Lugh's firm hand on his shoulder. The scouts in the open waited until everyone was aboard and Lugh had pushed them away from the shore before they disappeared into the rocky cliffs again.

Once he had helped Lugh prepare the sails and get them moving, Ciaran dropped down on the bench closest to the front of the ship and watched the water breaking against the bow. He made an honest attempt to brood and think on the task that lay ahead of him, but before he could get too involved in the process, Julien's voice broke the silence.

"Are we not going to address this?"

Ciaran looked over his shoulder in confusion. The hunter was standing near the back of the ship, staring up at Lugh as he steered the ship away from the misty island.

"Peace, an duine," Lugh muttered, but Julien snorted and gestured to the empty space behind the fairy.

"I may only have one eye, but I can still see. You can't hide things from me. What is he doing here?"

"He?" Ciaran spoke up. He got to his feet and approached the rear of the ship. Trent and Noah turned to watch the exchange as he passed them.

Lugh let out a soft sigh through his nose. "No point anymore regardless," he said, and with a quiet word, a faint shimmer shook the air beside him. Rathgeirr looked up from his spot on the floor of the ship, where he sat between a small trunk and a roughly-sewn bag. He stood when he realized that everyone was actually looking at him and offered a timid smile.

Ciaran narrowed his eyes as he looked between the alfar and his own son. "What is he doing here?"

"He wanted to come," Lugh answered simply. "I helped him."

"Gunvard expressly forbid it!"

Lugh's eyes leveled on Ciaran. "And where would the world be if we all followed the example of our fathers?"

"Ach, as ucht Dé," Ciaran growled. "Gunvard kept us from being killed, and this is how you repay his hospitality? By kidnapping his son?"

"You wanted to be able to prove your story to the Ard Rí. This is the simplest way. Rathgeirr is not a child; if he wants to leave, it's his choice. Or are you the only one allowed to break ties and disappear?"

"Woah, woah," Noah spoke up, stepping over a bench to place himself between the two fairies. "Let's not start a family argument, here. Rathgeirr is here now, isn't he? We can't exactly take him back. If he's here willingly, and he wants to help, then we should let him."

"I do want to help," Rathgeirr said. "If you take me to Tír na nÓg, I will tell your kings everything they need to know."

"See?" Noah leaned over to catch Ciaran's eye and smile at him. "It's all for the best."

Ciaran frowned up at Lugh, but he knew that he was right. He resented being deceived more than anything else. But, if he was honest, he was a little relieved that his task had been made that much easier by Lugh's defiance. He may have given them a chance.

19

The journey back to Ireland was much faster than the way to Lochlann. There were no magical obstacles to keep them from leaving the hidden island, and Lugh's ship sailed faster than any built by human hands. Even the Hafgufa seemed to have relocated itself during their stay. They spent a single day sailing southward, listening to Noah and Rathgeirr chatter about anything they could think of. The alfar had apparently been so grateful for the opportunity to leave that all it had taken was a brief suggestion from Lugh that the witch might appreciate some reading material, and he had snuck into the library in Falias and made off with as many ancient spellbooks as he could carry. Noah had almost been moved to tears, but he had wasted no time in settling down with the alfar and listening to his translations. Apparently, Rathgeirr had never been skilled with magic despite his father's prominent status and reputation, and so he had been relegated to guard duty at an early age. Still, he was happy to share what he knew with Noah. They seemed to feed off of each other's curiosity until their topic of conversation had drifted from magic to archery to Coca-Cola and *RWBY*. Rathgeirr truly did want to know everything, and Noah was doing his best to oblige.

Ciaran spent the night steering the ship with Trent curled up in his sleeping bag nearby, and by the time the sun was rising, he spotted the coast they had departed from almost two weeks before. He didn't know what he could expect by returning to Tír na nÓg, but he knew that whatever came, he would die himself before he let Gaibhne lay a hand on either Airmed or Trent.

The others had stirred by the time he was pulling the ship to the shore. Even though it had been a significantly shorter trip, they were all still glad to see the ship disappear back under the surface of the water at Lugh's silent command. They stood on the rocks below the boardwalk with their bags at their feet and watched the last bubbles in the waves with great relief. Then Ciaran paused, and he glanced around him with a frown.

"Where is Rathgeirr?"

They turned to search for their missing companion, and Noah tapped Ciaran's arm as he spotted the alfar at the top of the tall boardwalk wall, clinging to the iron railing like a monkey and peering through the bars at the street beyond.

"Oi!" the fairy called. "Get down, ye muppet! You'll be seen!"

Rathgeirr didn't seem to hear him, but when Ciaran shouted again, he jumped, momentarily scrambling to keep his grip on the bars. He offered the others an appeasing smile and dropped back to the rocks as easily as taking a step.

"My apologies," he said, though he didn't seem much like he meant it.

"You'll draw a fair bit of attention on the street, I'll wager," Ciaran muttered. "Tar anseo." He waved the alfar closer to him and placed his palm against his forehead. "Bronntanas ceochán," he murmured, and a thin film seemed to pass over the other man, enclosing him in a faint mist that faded in a few seconds. Ciaran removed his hand and stepped back while Rathgeirr stared at him. "The Féth Fíada. The mist. It will keep the humans from seeing you. But you can still make trouble, so hands to yourself, you understand?"

"We don't have to go straight away, do we? There's so much I want to look at before we—"

"We're leaving now," Ciaran cut him off. "It may not mean much to you, but they still have my sister. Once we're done, you'll have the rest of eternity to look at human things."

Rathgeirr actually looked a little taken aback. "Of course," he said.

"I'm sorry. I came to help, Cian. Lead the way." Ciaran frowned a little at being addressed by his proper name, but he supposed he had better get used to hearing it again if he planned to show himself to the court of the Tuath Dé.

They made their way up the boardwalk and through the town with Noah frequently snatching Rathgeirr by the back of his dark cloak to keep him from drifting away from the group whenever they passed something that caught his interest. He didn't seem to mind taking on the burden of babysitting; he explained things as they went and looked over his shoulder to share amused smiles with Julien. The hunter wasn't sure in the slightest that they had made the right decision by bringing Rathgeirr along—he didn't trust anyone who seemed so eager to lend a hand. At least they were returning now, and he could see Airmed safe and take Noah far away from all of it. Hunting basilisks in Leverich Park seemed vastly safer compared to what they'd been through since they met Ciaran.

Julien assumed they would return the way they had come, by bus and by train, but as they approached the edge of town, Lugh clicked his tongue at his father to get his attention.

"I have a better way." He led them down the road away from the slow traffic of the village and put his fingers in his mouth to give a sharp whistle. At his call, the pounding of hooves sounded in the distance, and Julien recognized the mottled grey coat of the Enbarr as it galloped into a halt in front of them. Lugh approached it to stroke its nose and murmured, "Cuir glaoch ar do dheirfiúracha." The horse reared away from him with a sharp whinny, and a moment later, a pair of horses appeared at its flank—both of them a splotched black and white mirror of the other. Lugh reached for their bridles and guided them toward his waiting companions.

"Gainne and Rea," the fairy said. "They are not the Enbarr, but they should carry you more swiftly than a bus can. I will ride ahead and speak to the Ard Rí."

"*Now* he has spare horses," Trent muttered.

"There are five of us," Julien pointed out. "How are we supposed to ride two horses?"

Lugh paused, seeming to consider for a moment. "I will carry Noah with me."

The hunter bristled but tried to keep from snapping. "Wouldn't it make more sense to take the proof we brought all the way here?" he asked, lifting his hand to indicate Rathgeirr.

"It would be ill-advised to enter Tír na nÓg with an uninvited Lochlannan before anyone has a chance to speak with the Ard Rí. I will brief him on the situation before you arrive." Julien opened his mouth to argue, but Lugh cut him off. "You will not be far behind, an duine. Take care of our guest."

"I'll be fine," Noah assured him. He touched Julien's arm as he passed, and he let Lugh take the trunk of books Rathgeirr had given him and magic it into the Enbarr's saddlebag. "It's a much quicker trip from Vancouver, at least," the witch laughed.

Julien watched, helpless, as Lugh lifted his lover effortlessly by the waist and settled him on the horse's back, then mounted behind him, the reins in one hand and the other wrapped around the smaller man in front of him. He had seen the flush on Noah's face the first time he and Lugh had ridden together. Now that they knew each other better, and now that they would be alone—Julien set his jaw as the horse shifted under Lugh's weight. He had to trust Noah. He had to try.

"Be good to my horses," Lugh said with stern finality, and at his gentle kick, the Enbarr took off across the grass so fast that it soon faded out of sight.

Julien swore under his breath and took one of the horses by the reins. Ciaran had already mounted the other and helped Trent up behind him, but Julien paused and exchanged an awkward glance with Rathgeirr. Neither of them seemed keen to give up the reins to the other.

"Flip a coin," Ciaran called to them, his horse circling impatiently. "We need to be off."

"You seem more anxious to get there," Rathgeirr said in a quiet voice, his black eyes glancing briefly at the hill where Lugh and Noah had disappeared. "I am the stranger here, after all." He gave a quick nod, and Julien accepted his offer, lifting himself into the saddle and reaching back to give the alfar a hand up behind him.

The horses galloped side by side as though they were of one mind, their hooves keeping a steady rhythm in the grass as they sped toward the entrance to Tír na nÓg. Julien couldn't say he was thrilled to be returning—but Airmed had been too kind to him for him to leave now, even if Noah hadn't just ridden off with Lugh.

They passed hills, highways, villages, and cities as they rode, but no one seemed to pay them any attention. Julien wondered if the magic keeping fairies from being seen applied to the horses as well, and if anyone who cared to notice them would see Trent and himself, bouncing along on invisible horses and racing across the countryside.

When they reached the stone tomb hiding the entrance to the city underground and dropped from the horses, the animals snorted at them as though glad to have their work finished, then darted away through the thin crowd lining the path. Lugh's attitude had apparently been passed to his pets.

Ciaran led the way into the depths of the monument, weaving between the people who had stopped to inspect the carvings along the narrow tunnel. Rathgeirr stopped more than once to touch the wall and trace the lines there or to put his hands on his knees and bend down to peer into the face of a marveling tourist, tilting his head as he noticed the Bluetooth device perched on the woman's ear. Trent barely managed to grab hold of the alfar's sleeve before he actually touched her, but they successfully turned the corner of the tunnel without incident.

"I still can't believe it," Rathgeirr said with a faint laugh. "Humans, the dominant race. Of the entire world?"

"Yeah, we're crafty that way," Trent muttered. He glanced to the side as a man noticed him talking to himself, but he pressed forward with a frown.

"It's no wonder people like my father want to keep us separate from them," the alfar went on, not seeming to notice Trent's irritation. "If everyone at home knew, we'd have a revolt on our hands, surely."

"We wouldn't want that," the boy answered with bitterness in his voice. He stopped walking when Ciaran stopped ahead of him in the round central chamber.

Rathgeirr frowned as he stepped around Trent to look him in the face. "Do you think I'm like my father?" he asked. "That all of us are? I have never kept a slave. From the time I was young, I could see that humans were thinking, feeling creatures, just as we are. Their lack of magic is cause for sadness, even care—not enslavement."

Trent seemed mildly taken aback at the solemn affirmation, but he still moved back when the alfar got too close to him. "I didn't ask you," he grumbled.

"Ciúnas," Ciaran interrupted, holding up a hand to quiet them.

He stepped forward and touched the carvings on the standing stone at the center of the room, illuminating the swirling suns and knots with streaks of bright blue. The people milling around them didn't seem to notice the black portal that snapped open behind the stone, but Julien still tried to subtly keep the tourists away from the entrance while the others stepped through. The hunter went last, prodding Rathgeirr in the back to urge him forward when he stopped to try to touch the pulsating edge of the portal.

The walk down the black stone staircase to the distant city seemed longer with Rathgeirr constantly stopping to inspect the glowing mushrooms on the edge of the steps or reaching down to try to touch the luminescent water below, but with both Trent and Julien reminding him that they were in a hurry, they were able to reach the towering gates of the city without too much delay.

"What now?" Trent asked when Ciaran hesitated at the entrance. "You can't just walk in, right? Since you're dead?"

Ciaran let out a short sigh through his nose and looked up at the stone archway separating them from the streets of Tír na nÓg. Before he could make a decision, a carriage that had been barreling down the street lurched to a stop just a few feet from the gate. The iridescent beetle lashed to the front gave a soft chitter, and a man in a simple tunic leaned over the edge of the driver's seat. He seemed slightly out of breath, as though he'd been rushed.

"My Lady Ethniu sent me to fetch you, my lord," he said. "The Ard Rí is requesting your presence and that of your—" The fairy cut himself off as his gaze landed on Rathgeirr. "Companion," he added softly, his brow lifted in disbelieving awe. Julien was mildly surprised that he was able to understand him, but he supposed the spell the alfar had used to make them capable of communicating was still in effect. It would be ridiculously helpful if it was permanent.

"The woman does think of everything," Ciaran said with a chuckle. He let the servant drop down and open the carriage door for him, and the four of them piled into the back.

Ciaran allowed Rathgeirr to peek through the thick curtains of the carriage as they rode through the streets, and Julien could see the alfar's wide black eyes trying to take in every detail of the buildings and people they passed. Julien watched the city go by in the thin slit of open curtain, the sight of so many pointed-eared, magic-using immortals making his stomach churn. Here, and in Lochlann too, he had seen entire civilizations of magic creatures that went about their lives unknown to the world. There were humans here, according to Airmed, and he had seen the human slaves the alfar kept. These weren't harmless cultures. How many more were there, hidden away, silently snatching innocent people and forcing them into servitude? When this was over, Julien fully intended on making contact with his brothers. They needed to know what he had learned over the past few weeks—even if the idea of storming a city of this size was beyond their abilities. Even if it meant them finding out about Noah. That thought wasn't a pleasant one. His brothers might taunt him for being in a relationship with a man, but they wouldn't disapprove—he didn't think. As far as he knew, there was no prophecy about the seventh son of a seventh son of a seventh son. Unless that would count as the seventh son of a seventh son the same as he did, and the gifts he had inherited would be passed along indefinitely as long as his family line continued to consist of unbroken lines of seven boys. Maybe he wouldn't have anything to pass on at all after the deal he'd made with the presence in the well. Maybe he could tell them he had a long-lost daughter from a one night stand in his youth, and the whole idea was a bust anyway.

He pressed his lips together and tried to keep his sigh inside. There was too much at stake just dealing with Ciaran's debt. Julien could worry about his father's expectations later.

The carriage stopped at the edge of a seemingly endless lane lined with gnarled, twisting trees, and in the distance, Julien could see the dark stone facade of a sprawling castle. The walk to the castle took almost as long as the carriage ride, but he supposed it was meant to give you time to appreciate the importance of the person you were about to see. The stones under their feet were carved with angled knots and animals made of such flowing lines that they seemed to be moving. As they drew near the building, Julien saw that even the walls were covered in deeply carved filigree and knotwork, and the massive wooden doors were decorated with shining silver fixtures.

The doors seemed to open on their own as they approached, but when they stepped inside, Julien spotted the bowing servants who had hauled them open. A man in a long robe waited for them in the echoing hall, and he lowered his head in a subtle bow as Ciaran stopped in front of him.

"The Ard Rí awaits you, my lord," the stranger said, and he gestured toward the heavy doors behind him.

Ciaran moved to step forward and then paused. "Who is it?" he asked with a glance back at the robed servant. "I've lost track of the years."

"His Majesty Mac Cuill serves as High King, my lord."

"Oh, good," Ciaran muttered with mock enthusiasm. "The gentle one. Helpful." He took a quick, deep breath, then stepped forward and pushed on the doors with both hands, shoving them open in one creaking movement.

Julien leaned forward to look around the fairy's shoulders. The hall inside was draped with heavy tapestries depicting lush green fields and stone castles bathed in sunlight—the opposite of the gloomy caves these people now lived in. It must have been a memory of what they'd lost. Stone pews lined either side of a broad aisle leading to the back of the room, where three thrones stood on a raised platform. The center seat was larger and more ornately carved, and the man seated in it leaned forward with his elbows on the arms of his throne. He was flanked by two other men with similar features—brothers, if Julien had to guess. All three of them had hard faces and oiled dark brown hair hanging to their shoulders, and each wore tunics in shades of green and brooches of polished silver. Lugh stood to one side of them with folded arms and a thin frown, his dark cloak heavy on his shoulders, and the three brothers who had sent them on their journey faced him on the king's opposite side.

The seats on either side of the hall were full of waiting faces, but Julien scanned the rows in search of one in particular. He couldn't see Noah. Airmed was there, and he guessed the others with her were Ciaran's family, based on the quiet worry on their faces as they turned to watch him stride down the aisle.

When Julien tried to move forward, the robed servant put a warning hand on his chest and shook his head. He wouldn't let Trent pass, either—no humans allowed, he guessed. Still, they were permitted to watch from the doorway. Rathgeirr hesitated behind them, unsure as to whether or not he should approach unbidden.

Ciaran gave a low bow when he reached the end of the aisle. "Majesties," he said without lifting his head.

"There is a ghost in my hall," the man on the largest throne answered. "And he brings trouble with him, as usual."

Ciaran straightened with his chin held high. "It's rarely my intention."

"Rarely," the king said with a faint rumble of a chuckle in his throat. "But not never, hm? Lugh tells me that you have bad tidings for me. I would hear it in your own voice, Cian."

"Majesty, I was sent by the Trí Dé Dána on a quest to settle my debt. They requested I retrieve an item called the Gambenteinn, attainable only on the isle of Lochlann."

"And you actually went?" Mac Cuill asked, edging forward in his seat almost imperceptibly. "You honestly brought one of them back with you?"

Ciaran lowered his eyes in a polite nod. He turned back to the doorway and held out his hand, beckoning Rathgeirr forward. "Majesties, I present Rathgeirr Gunvardsen, Skaut-Vorðr of the isle of Laithlind."

Rathgeirr stepped in from the outer hall and made his way down the aisle to stand at Ciaran's side. Every pair of eyes in the room followed him with eager curiosity. He bowed before the kings, who now showed no restraint in leaning closer to look at him. They stared at him as though he was an exotic animal, unfamiliar and dangerous. Julien could admit that the alfar looked intimidating—his slate grey skin and empty black eyes would have been enough even without the wild-looking hairstyle and the well-used bow strung across his chest. But the kings hadn't spent the last two days listening to him chatter about the wonders of sodas and drive-through fast food.

"I am honored to be before you," Rathgeirr said with more poise than Julien had heard from him since they'd met. "And I stand ready to speak on Cian mac Cainte's behalf."

"We are humbled to have a warrior of the Lochlannan in our court," Mac Cuill answered. "We believed your people to be all but extinct."

"Perhaps as far as the world is concerned, we are."

"Ard Rí," Ciaran went on, "I believe that the Trí Dé Dána are planning to take the throne from you and I believe that they will use force if they must."

"Ridiculous!" Gaibhne spat, but Mac Cuill raised a hand to silence him.

"That is a grave accusation, Cian. I trust you have some proof?"

Ciaran hesitated. He swallowed once before continuing. "In Lochlann, while searching for the Gambanteinn, I found out that it is not for purifying magic, as Gaibhne led me to believe. It is a staff imbued with the ability to control the minds of men."

"Majesty," Gaibhne spoke up as he took a half step forward, "I only told what I had heard in stories. How was I to know the true nature of such a thing?"

"Further," Ciaran said, raising his voice just enough to speak over the other man, "a seeress of the Lochlannan showed me the intentions of the Trí Dé Dána. Violent intentions."

"A vision is not evidence," Gaibhne countered.

"If you had honest intentions, why keep my secret for me, when you could have told this court that I was alive? Why threaten my sister? Why refuse to be paid, to settle the debt in a civilized way?"

"As a favor to a distinguished family," Gaibhne said. His smile was placating and false, and Ciaran's jaw tightened in disgust. "Besides, your son sent our brothers on such a mission as recompense; why shouldn't we respond in kind?"

Mac Cuill leaned back in his seat and laced his fingers in front of him, regarding the two men with a pensive frown. He glanced either side of him to catch the eyes of his brothers, but none of them spoke. "It is circumstantial, Cian," Mac Cuill said at last. "The Tuath Dé have lived in peace for centuries; what reason could the Trí Dé Dána have to disrupt that peace now?"

"I—I can't say, Ard Rí. I only know that I've seen the future they would have come to pass."

"Without proof, I'm afraid the only matter for our consideration is that of the debt."

Ciaran's hands tightened into fists at his sides. If Mac Gréine had been High King, he would have had Gaibhne chained at the first whiff of rebellion. But it had long ago been agreed that the three brothers would rotate power year by year—and Ciaran didn't think he could put this issue off until the more proactive brother took the throne. No matter how flimsy his proof, no matter how slippery Gaibhne's words could be, he knew in his gut that he was right. He knew that the future the seeress had warned him of would come true if he didn't act. If he didn't fight.

He paused, the tension falling from his shoulders as realization washed over him. He had to fight.

"Ard Rí," he said suddenly, interrupting before Gaibhne could reiterate the preposterousness of Ciaran's accusations. "I must speak with my companion. I beg a moment, and then I will accept the court's judgment."

Mac Cuill seemed skeptical, but he raised his hand slightly in a gesture of acceptance. Ciaran strode past his questioning relatives all the way to the back of the room, leaving Rathgeirr to stand awkwardly in front of the remaining fairies. Ciaran took Trent by the hand and led him around the corner into the hall. Julien and the waiting servant were polite enough to give them some space while Ciaran pressed his lover gently against the stone wall behind the door.

"Tell me to leave," the fairy whispered, his hands on Trent's shoulders.

"What? What are you talking about?"

"The seeress," Ciaran said. "I...didn't know how to tell you. But what she saw—she said that I would lose something very dear to me if I did what I'm about to do. The thing that binds me to this world. That's you, a mhuirnín." He sighed, and his fingers tightened into the boy's shirt. "I don't know what that means. I don't know if it means you'll be killed, or if I'll end up doing something that makes you despise me. The seeress said that if I don't fight, it will mean war with the world above. It will mean my people taking up arms against each other, and against mankind. But I don't care—not if it means I lose you."

Trent's expression softened, and he reached up to grip Ciaran's sleeve. "Ciaran, this is—"

"Insane," the fairy finished for him. "I know. But I promised you no more secrets. I'm sorry it took me so long to tell you this one when you're the one at risk." He let one hand slip to the side of Trent's neck, cradling his jaw and brushing his fingers over the tender skin behind his ear. "If you tell me to, I'll choose you. If you ask it of me, I'll take you far from this place, and I'll keep you safe from whatever comes."

"At the expense of the rest of the world?"

"The rest of the world doesn't matter to me."

Trent couldn't help the little flutter his stomach gave. He leaned into Ciaran's touch and twisted his fingers in the fabric of his sleeve. "If I made you choose me over the entire world, I could never forgive myself." He lifted his free hand and pressed it to the other man's chest. "But thanks for offering," he added with a faint smile.

Ciaran moved in close to him, covering Trent's mouth with his in a fierce kiss. He allowed himself to feel the boy's warmth and burn the memory of his breathless sigh into his brain. Then he broke away, and with one more caress of his thumb over Trent's cheek, he turned the corner into the hall again and walked without looking back, his eyes facing forward all the way to the waiting king.

"I move that we let the goddess decide the truth," Ciaran said.

The room went still in the silence after his words, and for a few tense moments, no one spoke. Mac Cuill turned to look at each of his brothers in turn, and Ciaran saw the subtle nods they gave.

"The goddess will decide," Mac Cuill agreed. He sat up straighter on his throne and leveled an even gaze on Ciaran and Gaibhne. "In accordance with custom, the accuser and the accused may, upon mutual agreement, present themselves before the goddess and prove the truth of their cause through combat. The Trí Dé Dána may choose among themselves who will face Cian mac Cainte in the trial."

The three brothers tensed and exchanged anxious glances. One of them pulled on Gaibhne's shoulder and hissed something into his ear, but the eldest brushed him aside and returned his attention to Ciaran and the king. "I deny the challenge," he said.

"Gaibhne, by denying—"

"My family is not satisfied with the life the Ard Rí have given us. There are many Tuath Dé families behind us, and we demand more than this. We have spent thousands of years cowering underground when we were meant to rule this island. You sons of Cermait would have us grovel and hide from the Milesians until the end of time, as if we are not superior to them in every way. We rot underground while they die up above in the time it takes to blink, and we are made to watch them ruin our island because these kings are too soft-hearted to take it back. These men above are not the Milesians who defeated us so long ago—they are pale and simpering and soft. We could take our lands back in an instant, if only we be allowed to try."

"The world above has left us behind, Gaibhne," Ciaran snapped back over the sudden rumbling of the crowd. "There's no place for the Tuath Dé in man's world."

"Then we will carve one ourselves," the larger man growled. He looked up at Mac Cuill, who seemed more than a little unprepared to deal with this turn of events. His hands had curled painfully tight around the arms of his throne. "I demand that the sons of Cermait meet us as equals and allow us the opportunity to prove our right to rule."

Mac Cuill stammered softly in the face of the growing murmur from the assembled crowd, and Ciaran grit his teeth. This was exactly the submissive attitude that had led to them going underground in the first place. At this rate, the Ard Rí would hand over the crown to simply avoid bloodshed, and even his more aggressive brothers would be powerless to stop it. But Ciaran had no real say. As "distinguished" as his family was, they could only sit in their rows and listen for the High King's judgment.

"The kingship of the Tuath Dé is not a baton waiting to be passed to the next open hand," Lugh spoke up, his rough voice echoing through the hall and silencing the competing voices. "The Trí Dé Dána should have brought their grievances before the Ard Rí and requested that they be heard and addressed—not used underhanded methods to attempt to steal the throne."

Gaibhne's voice dropped to a more polite volume now that Lugh's eyes were on him, but he didn't back down. "It is my right to be met on the field if I have the support—"

"It is your *right*," Lugh cut him off, "to submit to your king and to the agreement laid out centuries past regarding what lands the Tuath Dé may rule."

"Forgive my plain speaking, Majesty, but I hardly think that a man who gave up the throne and vanished for a thousand years should have any say in the way the kingdom is handled today."

When Lugh took a single step forward, Gaibhne tried not to let anyone notice his subtle retreat. The larger man stared down at him with a stoic distance in his eyes, and though his voice was softer, it somehow seemed even more dangerous.

"I am Ollamh Érenn of the Tuatha Dé Danann," he said. "It is my duty to protect Tír na nÓg from all threats both within and without, and if it suits this court, I will gladly lead her armies against a shameless upstart grasping beyond his station."

The hall waited in tense silence as all eyes fell on Mac Cuill. The king glanced between the men before him and seemed to be wavering, but when he opened his mouth to speak, his voice was steady. "If the Trí Dé Dána wish to attempt to force my brothers and I from the throne, they are welcome to try. They will find I am not so easily removed."

Ciaran almost laughed, he was so relieved, but he set his jaw and kept quiet. The High King agreeing to fight was the beginning of the bloodshed—not the end.

20

The parties agreed to meet on Mag Dúshlán, a flat expanse deep within the tall caves of Tír na nÓg, at dawn of the second day following the challenge. A day wasn't long to get an entire army together, but with Lugh barking at them, Ciaran suspected that the soldiers would hurry.

When they were dismissed from the king's presence, Ciaran had to move quickly to avoid being mobbed by curious and angry nobles. His brothers did an effective job at shielding him as they made their way through the hall toward the exit, but it was Ethniu's single pointed clearing of her throat that finally parted the throng. At the gate, she offered to let Ciaran and his guests stay with her, but Trent was glad to hear Ciaran refuse her.

"It would be in poor taste, I think," he said. He hadn't released Trent's hand since they'd met outside the main hall, and now he gave it a gentle squeeze.

Ethniu didn't miss the movement. She snorted as her driver opened the door to her carriage. "I wasn't particularly eager for company in any case," she answered dryly. She flicked her orange eyes to Dian Cecht and offered him a small nod. "I return my husband to your care, my lord."

"Just when I thought I was finally rid of one," the older man said. He tilted his head toward his own waiting carriage, though his gaze lingered on Trent and Ciaran's locked hands with distaste apparent on his features.

Airmed inched closer to Julien and wrapped both of her arms around one of his, looking up at him with an affectionate smile. "You'll stay with me, won't you? Lugh already dropped Noah off earlier."

The hunter tried to hide his smile, but he could tell from the pleased glint in Airmed's eyes that she had noticed it. "I will," he said. "Thank you."

She tugged him down the side of the street away from the others. She was apparently the only person in the family without a private carriage. People on the path watched them with suspicious eyes as they made their way toward Airmed's home, but Julien stared right back at them. He didn't care what they thought—he only cared about getting back to Noah and preparing to argue with him about not getting involved in a fairy war. He could hear the witch's arguments already. Honestly, Julien was just glad that Rathgeirr had been part of the group staying with Ciaran's father—if he had had to listen to Noah explaining *Gilmore Girls* again, he might have strangled himself with a bedsheet.

Airmed opened the door to her modest home and was immediately greeted by Lenora, the slight-figured blonde woman that Julien recognized as her sole servant.

"My lady," the girl said breathlessly, her cheeks reddened, "thank the goddess you've returned. I was preparing supper, and I heard a strange noise from upstairs, and when I went into the guest bedroom, he—our guest, the witch, he—"

Julien brushed by the women without a word, taking the steps two at a time and rushing down the hall to the bedroom. Noah was on his side on the floor with an open book near his slack hands and thin streams of smoke trailing upwards from a smoldering hole in his shirt. He looked as though Lenora had shifted him and been interrupted before she could move him to the bed. Julien dropped to the floor in a panic, turning Noah by the shoulder and lifting him into his lap to check the injury. He was breathing, at least, but he was unresponsive. Julien tore the witch's shirt in his haste to get at the wound, and his stomach knotted at the sight of the angry welt staining Noah's skin. A thick line of red ran from Noah's shoulder down to his hip, curving across his spine and splitting into steadily smaller and smaller branches that marked almost the entirety of his back.

"Mon râleur, quelle bêtise as-tu faite la?" he whispered. He turned his head when Airmed appeared beside him, and together they lifted the witch to the bed and laid him down on his stomach.

"What in the world happened to him?" the fairy asked. "These marks look like they're from a lightning strike. I've only seen it once before."

Before they could speculate further, Noah coughed into the pillow and let out a low, pained groan. He tried to move and winced, and Airmed stroked his hair and shushed him.

"Lie still," she said gently. "I'll fetch you some medicine." She flitted out the door in a hurry and left Julien to kneel beside the bed, his hands tightly gripping Noah's.

"I'm not dead," Noah assured him, muffled by the pillow. He peeked up at Julien with a smile in his dark eyes, but the hunter couldn't return it.

"What did you do?" he pressed.

"Just a test. It was a success, in a way."

"A test?"

"You saw the storm we passed on the way to Lochlann. I wanted to know how they made it."

"The storm? Crisse, Noah, what—" Julien shut his mouth as Airmed returned with a small bowl in her hands, and he released Noah's hand to allow her better access to him. She urged Noah to shift enough to let her push his shirt up and over his head and scooped some of the paste from her bowl onto his welt. She ran gentle fingers over the red mark while Julien chewed the inside of his cheek to keep from raising his voice. Airmed must have sensed the tension in the air—as soon as she finished rubbing the ground herbs into the skin, she smiled at them and told them to call her if they needed anything, and then she excused herself and shut the door.

Noah sat up slowly, flinching as he tried rolling his shoulder. He smiled at the scowl on the hunter's face. "I'm all right, Julien. Really."

"You tried to make a storm. In the house. Airmed said it looked like you'd been struck by lightning. *In the house.*"

"I think I was," the witch laughed. He craned his neck to try to

TO KEEP YOU NEAR

look at the marks on his back. "Does it look cool? Your phone doesn't have any charge left, does it? I'd like to take a picture before the Lichtenberg figures fade."

"C'est t'assez!" Julien snapped. He didn't notice Noah's slight jump. "Do you hear yourself? What if we hadn't come back when we did? What if something worse happened to you?"

Noah crossed his legs on the bed and laced his fingers together in his lap. He still smiled, but it looked a little forced now. "Do you know you get French-er when you're mad?"

"I'm not playing games, Noah. How can I trust you if every time I turn my back, you're doing something dangerous?"

"I'm sorry; isn't doing stupid and dangerous things literally your job? I was trying out new magic—sometimes it backfires. That's just the way it is. This is how I get better. You can't tell me to stop doing magic, Julien."

"I'm not telling you to—" The hunter stopped and snorted out a sigh of frustration. "You can't do stupid magic."

"I *can't?*" Noah pushed himself up from the bed. He winced slightly but slapped Julien's hand away when he reached to help him. "You don't get to tell me what I *can't* do."

"I want to keep you safe. How can I do that if you don't care about your own safety?"

"Keeping me safe doesn't mean treating me like glass! We're equals, remember? Partners."

"I can't trust a partner who's constantly trying to get himself killed! Sometimes you need to just do as I say, Noah!" Julien knew that he was too loud, too close, too harsh. He knew he'd gone too far when he saw the witch shrink away from him. He tucked his hands under his arms and held them close to his chest. He took a few slow breaths, but they seemed timid and unsteady.

"You don't...you don't get to be like this," he whispered.

Julien knew that he was shouting. He saw the flinch in the younger man and struggled to lower his voice, but the sight of the witch motionless on the floor had been too much for him. "I'm trying to protect you! Don't you understand that? After everything that's happened, after all I've done, can you really not see that I'm trying to do what's best for you?"

"Stop it!" Noah cried out suddenly. He took another step back as Julien moved toward him, and when he held out a hand to keep the hunter at bay, Julien finally noticed the tremble in his fingers. "You can't be this! You can't be him! You don't—you can't tell me what to do, and you can't—you can't *shout* at me like this, like I'm some child, or like a...like a possession," he finished, a soft hiccup in his voice. "I don't belong to you. You can't use what you did for me against me. It isn't—it isn't fair."

Suddenly Noah seemed very small, and Julien felt like a bully. How many times had he raised his voice at the witch without noticing how frightened he seemed? More importantly, how terrible had he been that Noah could feel frightened of him at all? Julien raked a hand through his hair and let it rest at the back of his neck. He was going about this all wrong. He'd been going about it wrong for days.

"Noah," he tried again, sure to keep his voice soft. The witch stared at the floor rather than at him, and he returned his warning hand to its safe place hugging his own side, so Julien didn't try to move closer to him. He needed to be honest—truly. "You died," he said.

"I remember," the younger man replied in a harsh voice.

"No, you—you don't understand." Julien sighed. "On that island, I went through miserable trials. I did whatever that man asked of me, and more than once, I thought I might die doing it. I did it for you."

"Julien, that doesn't give you the right to—"

"No," the hunter cut him off, as gently as he could. "That isn't what I mean. I'm telling you this because I want you to know that no matter what I'd been made to do, no matter how afraid I was or how frustrated or how tired—when I got back, and I saw you lying there on that table, all I could think about was that I'd failed you. And that I would have fought through those tests a hundred thousand times if it would have brought you back. Seeing you there, Noah, I...you were so pale. So still. There was nothing left in you that was any of the things I'd fallen in love with. Your teasing, your focus, your wit, your kindness, your laughter—all vanished. Gone forever. Because of me. Because I'd pushed you, and because I'd been too slow to save you. When I saw you there, I suddenly knew what it meant to lose everything."

Noah slowly peeked up at him with wet lines on his cheeks. Julien stepped closer, hesitantly, waiting to see if Noah would push him away again. When he didn't, the hunter cupped his face in both hands and stroked away the tears with the pads of his thumbs.

"Even the thought of something like that happening again...I wouldn't survive it, Noah. If I seem overprotective—maybe I am. But it isn't because I don't trust you. It's because I'm afraid. I'm afraid that unless I keep you right beside me, right where I can see you, that I'll...that I'll fail you again. That I'll go away from you thinking everything will be fine, and then I'll come home to see you lying on that table again."

The witch sighed Julien's name and lifted his hand to gently grasp his lover's wrist. His shoulders had relaxed a little, and his hands didn't shake anymore. "I'm sorry," he said. He moved in closer and slid his arms around the hunter's waist, hiding his face in his shirt. Julien wanted to hold him tight enough to keep him there forever, but he didn't want to hurt the burn on his back, so he just touched his hair and let his free hand rest on Noah's waist with as light a touch as he could manage. He promised himself he would be gentler. He never wanted to see that flinching look on Noah's face again.

"It doesn't excuse the way I've treated you," Julien said. "But it's...hard to talk about. I hope you can understand. I never meant to frighten you."

"No," he answered, shaking his head without lifting it from Julien's chest. "I probably—I know I overreact sometimes."

Julien brushed his fingertips through the soft hair at the back of Noah's neck. "Because of the 'him' I can't be like?"

Noah tensed a little in his arms. "I guess I keep things from you, too. Travis was...I don't want to talk about him. But we dated for a while, if you could call it that, and he...was rough with me. So I get a little—you know, anxious. With the yelling."

The hunter's heart broke. He pulled Noah down onto the bed with him and settled the smaller man in his lap, holding his face in both hands to meet his dark eyes. "Je suis tellement désolé, Noah. If I'd known—" He sighed and pressed his forehead to the younger man's. "No. It doesn't matter. I never should have treated you this way to begin with. I can do better," he added softly. "I will do better."

Noah's fingers curled into the fabric at the back of Julien's shirt, and he closed the space between them to kiss him. "I believe you," he murmured. He kissed him again, clinging to his warmth and the tenderness of his touch, and he barely felt the sting in his back as the blond lowered him onto the blanket. He needed the other man's weight against him, needed to taste him and touch his skin. He tugged at his lover's shirt and sighed at the heat of Julien's chest under his palms.

They undressed each other, pausing frequently to kiss or caress, their movements eager yet slow. It couldn't be heavy and heated like outside the longhouse, or furtive and hasty like during the ritual. He wanted to feel every inch of Julien's skin, to kiss him slowly and rock against him. He panted into the hunter's shoulder, touching his lips to every scar, and when he leaned back to look up at him, he gently pushed the leather eyepatch from his face. Julien hesitated and reached up to stop him, but Noah stroked his thumb over the reddened skin where the strap had been and pulled the other man down to press a kiss to the mark.

"You don't have to hide anything from me," he whispered into the other man's ear.

Julien kissed him again, holding him just a little too tightly, but Noah didn't mind. They moved together, the witch trembling every time Julien's tongue ran over the silver rings in his lips. His body felt like it was on fire, and even the ache of the burn on his back seemed perfect and sweet. His fingernails scratched into Julien's back as their pace quickened, his legs wrapped securely around his lover's waist, both of them beginning to pant and bite. Noah hid his shaky moan in the crook of Julien's neck as the other man's heat spilled inside of him, his own orgasm arching his back away from the mattress. They took tired, lazy kisses from each other's lips until finally Julien retreated enough to lie beside him. He kept Noah close to him, one arm under the witch's head and the other draped over his waist. Noah tilted his head up to kiss him one more time.

"I love you," he said, and he felt Julien's warm smile against his lips.

"I love you, too. I'm sorry I've been so awful at showing it."

"I guess I should have expected the gruff, overworked monster hunter to have difficulty expressing his emotions," Noah chuckled.

"Thank you for putting all your cards on the table. I want you to know everything about me, too."

Julien seemed to hesitate, and Noah quirked an eyebrow at him.

"Those are all your cards, aren't they, Julien?"

The hunter sighed. "It's only jealousy," he admitted. "I know it's irrational."

"Jealousy? Who could you possibly be jealous of?"

Julien frowned and lowered his gaze, but it did nothing to hide the flush of embarrassment on his cheeks. "I don't know much about—dating," he muttered. "I know it's unreasonable to expect that you'll never find another man attractive, but when that other man also seems to be flirting with you, I just—"

"Wait, wait wait wait," Noah interrupted. He rolled onto his stomach and leaned up on his elbows to look the blond in the face. "Who's been flirting with me?"

Julien sighed. "Lugh."

A short burst of laughter sputtered from Noah's lips, and he ducked his head to cover his mouth and put a hand on Julien's chest in apology when he saw the offended frown on the hunter's face. He took a breath to compose himself before looking up again. "I'm sorry. But are you serious?"

"You really haven't noticed how he is with you? He's always—touching you, and he talks to you more than anyone else, and I've seen the way he looks at you—"

"Julien," Noah cut him off. "Believe me. You have absolutely nothing to worry about on that front."

"But when we were in Falias, when we—argued. I saw the two of you talking, and I just thought...that you have more in common with him than you do with me."

"I have more in common with an immortal half-giant fairy warrior hero than I do with a guy from Montreal. Quebeckers are weird, Julien, but you're not that weird."

"But the way he's so gentle with you, and everyone else we've met is so intimidated by him, but you seemed to get along with him so well—"

"Because I literally inherited all of his father's memories and emotions for a solid week. It's hard to be sexually into someone when your gut is basically telling you that they're your son. Is that why you've been acting so crazy whenever he's around? You've been afraid I'm going to cheat because—what, because he's taller than you? Are you kidding?"

"I told you it's irrational," he answered, knowing it sounded pathetic.

"And you've just been letting it eat at you instead of saying something. Of course. We really need to do something about this emotional constipation of yours."

Julien frowned and let out a small, childish huff. "I'm sorry," he said. "I'm trying."

He looked so flustered that Noah couldn't help smiling. He leaned forward on his elbows and pressed a lingering kiss to the blond's lips.

"Just tell me next time."

"I will," Julien promised. He reached out to cup Noah's cheek, his thumb brushing the piercing in his lip. "I really am trying, you know."

"I know. Me too." He settled against the other man's chest, smiling at the soft blond hair under his cheek, and then popped up again. "Oh! What happened with the whole fairy revolution thing? Nobody died, right? You would have told me if anybody died."

"We'll know the day after tomorrow. It seems like there's going to be a war."

Noah sat up too quickly, wincing at the sudden movement of his back, and Julien could tell by the look in the witch's eyes that he was about to have exactly the argument he'd imagined.

21

In the morning, Airmed treated them to a warm breakfast and took her payment in the form of endless questions about their trip. The revelation that it had been her life on the line had they failed didn't seem to concern her; she only lamented that Rathgeirr had been carried away to her father's house before she could speak to him.

"I was born *here*, you see," she said as she reached across the table for a second helping of sweet bread. "By the time I was born, we were already in Tír na nÓg. I'd heard stories about the vicious Lochlannan, but I've never actually seen an—Alfar, was it? He was very beautiful." She stopped with the bread halfway to her mouth as she realized what she'd said. "I mean, objectively, of course."

"Of course," Noah laughed.

"Well I don't recommend the trip we took," Julien said. "And I don't like the idea of more of him being out and about, either, so maybe it's better they stay hidden." He put down his cup and looked across the table at her. "Have you heard any news from your brother? About tomorrow?"

The fairy picked tiny pieces from her bread and tucked them into her mouth to give herself more time to answer, but Julien was patient.

"I suspect they'll be very busy today," she said when the silence grew awkward. "Those on the side of the Ard Rí will be at a disadvantage."

"Why's that?"

"The Trí Dé Dána—Gaibhne and his brothers—are called so because they are the three best craftsmen of the Tuatha Dé Danann. For ages, they've made all of our weapons, our armor, even our jewelry. Well, them and their journeymen. I can only imagine that they will have been holding out the best of their newest supplies in preparation for this. I hope that what arms we still have are sturdy."

"At a disadvantage, Julien," Noah said with a pointed glance in the hunter's direction. "Sounds like they need help, Julien."

Julien let out a long sigh through his nose. This was precisely what they'd spent the night discussing, and in the end, they'd still come to an impasse. Julien had agreed that they had a vested interest in the outcome of the battle despite being human—if Gaibhne and his brothers won, they had already promised that their next target would be mankind. But that didn't mean that either of them—or more specifically, Noah—was equipped to be of any help at all.

"What do you think you're going to do?" Julien asked him, not for the first time. "I know that you're capable of powerful magic, but this is an entirely different scale than what you're used to."

"Well it sure would be handy if we had someone who has literally spent his whole life fighting magic things, *Julien*."

"I never said I wasn't going to fight."

The witch leaned away from him as though offended. "You think you're going to go off to battle and leave me here? Are you stupid?"

"Not to intrude," Airmed piped up, both hands worrying the remnants of her bread roll, "but it is worth noting that long ago, it was the Milesian sorcerers who drove the Tuath Dé underground. If not for the humans' magic, we likely would have won the battle at Tailtiu and remained the rulers of this island. And human magic is the very last thing that the Trí Dé Dána and their allies would expect to see on the battlefield tomorrow."

Noah leaned his elbow on the table and opened his hand toward the woman to indicate the obvious sense of her argument.

Julien shook his head. There wasn't any point in trying to convince Noah once he'd set his mind to something—especially something this serious. And he honestly did want to make more of an attempt to stop telling the witch what to do.

"In the end," he said, "you don't need my permission."

Noah softened, as though he wasn't expecting this response. He reached out to put a hand over Julien's and gave his fingers a light squeeze. "I'll be careful," he promised.

"I know you will."

Airmed chewed her bottom lip as she watched them, barely holding in her smile. "When you're finished eating, I'll take you to where my nephew will be preparing. I'm sure he'll be glad for your help."

"I'm sure," Julien agreed, not feeling very sure at all.

The armory of the Tuatha Dé Danann was an impressive sight. It was a long hall with high ceilings and rows upon rows of weapon racks and armor stands, going so far back that Julien couldn't even see the far wall. On every side, people bustled by with their arms full, calling to each other and dropping supplies where they were needed. Sparks flew from spinning sharpening stones, scattering tiny scraps of light across the floor. Julien turned to take in the crowd around him as they walked, his bag slung over one shoulder. He tried to do a quick estimate in his head, but there were too many rushing bodies. He guessed at least a few hundred here, and who knew how many men elsewhere? This wasn't going to be a skirmish.

Airmed led them on a weaving path through the hurrying men, and when they reached the rear of the building, Julien spotted a long, sturdy table atop a raised platform. Lugh stood at the center with the three kings on either side of him, all four of them bent over a large document spread out over the surface. He stopped and looked up when Airmed arrived at the top of the steps.

"I've brought you a pair of volunteers, Lugh," the woman said brightly. She lifted her hands to present Julien and Noah as if they were prizes on a gameshow.

Lugh's face didn't change, but his eyes scanned the two humans before him. "Even though it isn't your fight, an duine?"

"I'm trying to keep it from becoming my fight," Julien clarified.

The fairy gave a soft snort and pulled away from the table, excusing himself as he rounded the table to face the outsiders.

"We can help, Lugh," Noah insisted. "Airmed said that human magic turned the tide against you once before. I can give you mine now."

Lugh seemed to consider for a moment, and Julien couldn't help feeling as if the larger man was tallying up their past actions to calculate their usefulness. He snapped his fingers at a servant waiting near the end of the table and tilted his head toward Julien and Noah once he had the boy's attention. "Outfit them," he said simply. "Tend to the Asarlaí with care."

The servant offered a quick bow and started down the steps, trusting them to follow. Airmed promised to wait for them, so they let the man lead them through the hall to a massive collection of waiting weapons and armor. Julien didn't like the idea of wearing doubtless enchanted armor crafted by fairies, but as the alternative was to show up to a medieval battle in nothing but jeans and a long-sleeved shirt in desperate need of washing, he allowed himself to be fitted with a simple leather chestpiece. The stitching was thick and the buckles were brass, the straps at his sides cinched closely around his waist. The leather was warm and well-oiled, and it moved easily as Julien experimentally twisted. There was no denying the craftsmanship; he actually felt a bit silly to be wearing it over a shirt he'd bought at the Salvation Army.

"Oh my god, Julien, look!" Noah called from nearby. He held his arms out at his sides as though waiting to be admired. His singed shirt had been replaced with a long-sleeved grey tunic, and over the top, he'd been dressed in a light vest of black leather with a high-backed collar and polished silver buckles down the chest. The bottom stitching hit his thighs, a poor match for his faded jeans and scuffed shoes, but he seemed pleased nonetheless.

"Look at me!" he said. "Look what they put me in! I look like a fucking wizard!"

Julien laughed softly. "Aren't you really a wizard?"

"No," Noah scoffed. "Wizards have to have their spells inscribed on tomes or scrolls to use them. Sorcerers possess magic innately."

"According to what?"

"Edition 3.5."

"What?"

"Never mind."

Noah looked down at himself and touched the leather against his chest, clearly proud of himself, but Julien wasn't very comforted by how un-armor-like the ensemble looked. He tapped the arm of the servant near him, causing the fairy to glance down at his sleeve as though expecting it to be stained.

He nodded toward Noah. "Why wasn't he given real armor?"

The servant seemed surprised at the question. "He is an Asarlaí. They do not enter direct combat."

"Lugh used that word too. What does it mean? I thought your word for 'witch' was something else."

The man started at hearing his master addressed so informally, but he let it pass with only an offended frown. "Cailleach. It is a woman—a healer, or a hermit. He should not be called this in polite conversation."

"Everyone's been calling him that."

"Perhaps the Ollamh Érenn is more respectful than some others you have met thus far," the servant said with an air of restrained superiority. "The Tuath Dé perform admirable magic, but admittedly, it is not on the scale of what is possible from an Asarlaí—a human magus. Additionally, it is considered poor form to use one's magic against a foe on the field of battle, but these rules apply only to the Tuath Dé themselves. I can't speak for my master, but I suspect he must be glad to have an Asarlaí to support his line. So much so that he allows human strangers to partake of our armory," the fairy added under his breath as he moved away to check the fit of Noah's vest.

Julien frowned after him, but he softened when he caught the smiling look on Noah's face. At least he knew they didn't plan on sending him into the thick of battle.

"You should have this too," he said. He waved Noah over and crouched down by his bag. After a bit of digging, he retrieved the sleek fur cloak made of the hide of the dobhar-chú he'd killed. He wrapped it around Noah's shoulders, and the servant passed him a silver cloak pin to fasten it with. "Manandán said it guards against magic. It might not be much help against swords, but...just don't get close to anyone with a sword."

Noah smiled and put a hand on the soft fur. "I'll be careful, Julien.

Thanks."

The servant offered to allow Julien to choose a sword, but he decided on using his own weapons when he could barely lift the first broadsword from its rack. He had spent so much time around Ciaran, who frequently acted like an idiot, that he had forgotten how strong these creatures were. He wouldn't forget it again—not with the fight that was coming tomorrow.

The servant led them back to the platform where Airmed waited for them, and Lugh broke away from his conversation again to approach them. He tilted his head just slightly to inspect Julien's chestpiece, but when his eyes turned to Noah, he reached out and touched him, slipping his fingers under the vest to check the snugness at the witch's shoulder.

"The fit is good," he decided. He moved his hand up to the side of Noah's neck to draw his gaze up to him. "I will put you with the archers," he said, his voice slightly quiet, "and I expect you'll stay there. The battlefield is no place for you."

"Don't worry about me," Noah said with a smile, apparently unconcerned with the fairy's thumb on his jaw.

"They won't be expecting your magic. So hit them with everything you have," Lugh said.

"I mean, I'm not going to actually try to…you know, kill anyone. But I'm a real pro at incapacitating," he added brightly.

"Of course," Lugh answered, and Julien swore he saw that faint wrinkle of a smile at the corners of his eyes. He wanted to shake Noah and ask him how he hadn't noticed that Lugh had been flirting with him for days. He bit the inside of his cheek in irritation, but then he frowned as the tension suddenly left him. Noah hadn't noticed because he honestly didn't see Lugh that way. Just like he had said. Julien had been building up Noah's interest in his head the entire time. But just because Noah didn't see it, that didn't mean it wasn't happening.

Julien stepped forward as Lugh finally removed his hand from Noah's cheek and turned to go back to his planning. "I need a word," he said, and the fairy's eyebrows lifted slightly as he looked down.

"I'm very busy, an duine."

"Make time."

Lugh seemed to hesitate at the firmness in Julien's voice. He glanced back at the men discussing among themselves while they waited for him, then nodded and lifted a hand to guide the hunter away from the platform. Airmed watched them with an anxious frown, looking as though she wanted to advise Julien against whatever hard words he was about to have with the man leading the army of the Tuatha Dé Danann, but she kept her peace and instead distracted Noah by complimenting how dashing he looked in his new equipment.

Lugh led Julien to a quiet hall outside the bustle of the main armory. They could still hear the distant voices of the soldiers and the sounds of metal rasping on stone sharpeners, but here the noise was dull and muffled. Lugh stood near the wall with his arms folded, and he tilted his head to invite Julien to speak.

"I need you to leave Noah alone," the hunter said simply.

"Again, an duine? I thought we'd had this conversation. I don't have the time to have it again."

"I know what you're doing," Julien went on. "You think if you don't admit it, I'll get in my own head and think I'm imagining it. But I see the way you look at him, the way you touch him and treat him gently. And I'm telling you that you're wasting your time. Noah doesn't think of you that way. He never will. If you keep acting like this, there are going to be problems between us—and despite everything, you've...been a friend. So." Julien frowned as he looked up into the fairy's slightly narrowed green eyes. "If you have feelings for him, I'm sorry—but he's chosen me."

Lugh watched him for a few beats, so long that Julien almost thought the larger man might hit him, but then a sudden unexpected sound fell from the fairy's lips, his deep voice rough and loud as it echoed through the stone hallway. He was laughing.

Julien wasn't quite sure what to do with laughing. He just stood and watched the fairy quake with his laughter, and when the sound died and Lugh reached out to put a hand on the hunter's shoulder, he had the first genuine smile on his face that Julien had ever seen.

"That's more like it," he said, giving the blond's shoulder a single solid shake. "I was hoping you would come to your senses before tomorrow."

"What? What are you talking about?"

"I've been fucking with you, an duine."

Julien stared up at him with confusion on his face, but no words made it out of his mouth.

"I saw the mess you'd become after we returned to Tír na nÓg. The focused and determined man I'd taken to Emain Ablach had been replaced by a fearful, jealous one. I don't fault you—not many men have done what you have, and love makes every man an idiot. But you needed to learn to trust that witch of yours as well as care for him."

"And…you thought the best way to teach me that lesson was to make me think you wanted to sleep with him?"

"Well," Lugh chuckled, "I had to have a bit of fun."

Julien let out a short sigh. He couldn't be angry—Lugh was right. He had been too afraid to trust Noah completely, and it had kept him anxious and short-tempered for two weeks. He looked up when the fairy squeezed his shoulder again.

"You were going to fight me for him, Julien. *Me*," he emphasized, bending slightly to look the hunter in the eye. "You're going to do just fine by him."

Julien felt a faint flush of embarrassment in his cheeks that he hoped didn't show. "I know."

Lugh gave a small nod and released him, straightening to his full height. "You're a tough one, sealgaire. Keep that fire in your belly when you meet our enemies on the field tomorrow." He tilted his head toward the end of the hall to indicate that their conversation was over. The fleeting kindness was gone from his face; he was Lugh Lámfada again, stoic and stern-mouthed. "Now go and get a good night's rest. I'll expect you and your witch at Mag Dúshlán."

Julien nodded. He hesitated for a moment, but there was nothing else to say. "Thank you," he said simply, and he left the hall, greeting Airmed and Noah with a faint smile.

22

Trent hadn't expected to find himself back in Ciaran's father's house so soon. Or ever, really. But there he stood, in the same bedroom he'd been in when Ciaran had finally lost his mind and forgotten him. It wasn't exactly the best memory he had of their time together. He and Ciaran had been shown to the room, but they had only been alone for a moment before Cu had stuck his head through the door and called his brother to plan for the coming battle. Now Trent sat on the bed in the quiet room and tried not to think about the ramifications of the decision Ciaran had made. He could hear the men talking when he'd poked his head into the hall, but they were discussing numbers and the difficulties of outfitting an army in a day—not anything that Trent had a hope of contributing to. Even when he'd given up and gone to sleep, he could still hear their muffled voices downstairs.

He didn't sleep well. He felt Ciaran climb into the bed with him sometime late in the night, but the fairy only curled up behind him and nuzzled the back of his neck without speaking. It took him a long time to finally doze off, and when he woke up, the space beside him was empty again.

Ciaran spent the next day with his brothers, and Trent hid from the servants who came to check on him. Through the bedroom window, he could see that the streets outside were deserted. Even from inside, he could sense the tension in the air. He'd never been somewhere that was about to break out into a war, but this feeling seemed about right.

Trent waited. He wished that he could help, but he knew that he was useless. He didn't know anything about fighting or battle strategies. Soon enough, Ciaran would come into the bedroom with a weary look on his face and make Trent promise to stay far, far away from the field tomorrow. He would have to agree—if there was any truth at all to what the seeress had said, then Trent was in danger because of Ciaran's decision, and he wasn't especially keen on dying. He would just have to worry alone, locked away in this house where he wasn't really welcome.

When Ciaran did return to the bedroom hours later, he didn't have the tired expression Trent expected. He was quiet, but as he sat at the foot of the bed and tugged off his boots, he seemed focused and withdrawn. He undressed and washed himself in the basin on the dresser while Trent waited in silence from under the thick blankets. Ciaran had never seemed particularly delicate, but now as Trent watched his shoulders move the muscles in his back as he washed, he realized how strong he looked. Those shoulders belonged to a man who knew how to lift a sword, and who was prepared to do it again for the sake of a home he'd tried to abandon.

Ciaran gave his face one last scrub with a dry cloth and climbed into bed beside Trent without a word. Trent had expected jokes, or pleas for promises, or maybe even desperate I-might-die-tomorrow sex, but Ciaran just laid next to him with his arm around the younger man, holding him close to his chest and breathing softly into his hair. He was in a deep sleep before Trent could even settle properly. Trent tucked his head against the fairy's shoulder and listened to his slow, steady heartbeat.

How many times had Ciaran performed this exact ritual— planning, bathing, and a good night's sleep before a fight? Trent's instinct was to be offended that Ciaran hadn't bothered to say a word to him when tomorrow was so uncertain, but as he felt the weight of the other man's arm around his waist and heard the sound of his quiet breath slipping through his lips, he knew that Ciaran was doing what he thought would best keep Trent safe. Trent may not have known much about fairy battles, but he knew it must be dangerous to show up to one distracted. Those three brothers would have their sights on Ciaran tomorrow, he was sure—so the best way to stay alive was to rest and focus.

Trent curled his fingers against Ciaran's back and shut his eyes. At least one of them would be sleeping.

When the fairy rose, Trent felt the loss of his warmth immediately. He dressed himself quickly in a set of borrowed clothes and tried to keep quiet while Ciaran prepared. The flat line of his lover's mouth and the faint pensive crease in his brow were unchanging as he slid on his boots, tapping the heel on the floor to test the fit, and settled his worn chestpiece over his shoulders. The leather was dark, with grey fur lining at the shoulders and neck, and two silver brooches carved with the same knot as his pendant kept the armor secure at the shoulders. On his chest, two fearsome boar's heads had been etched into the leather above the rows of flat sections leading down his stomach. He tightened the buckles at his waist and fastened his belt around his hips, sliding the silver knife his brother had given him into its narrow sheath.

"You know what I'm going to say, a mhuirnín," Ciaran murmured, breaking the tense silence in the room. He didn't look up, but Trent could still see the hint of a frown on his lips.

"Stay here?"

"Stay safe," he corrected. He took a step toward Trent and put a gentle hand on the back of his lover's neck. "Come to Mag Dúshlán or don't come—Airmed will go regardless. Go with her if you like. But don't let me worry for you. Promise me you'll be careful, or I won't be able to concentrate."

"I promise," Trent answered without hesitation. "No risks today. I'll be right here when you come back."

"Thank you," the fairy breathed, the relief obvious in his voice. He bent to touch his forehead to Trent's for a moment, then pressed a soft kiss to the boy's lips. "When this is done, I'll take you far away from here. We'll go wherever you like—and you won't ever suffer for my sake again."

"That seems unlikely," Trent teased. He was grateful for the twitch of a smile the fairy gave. "But I'm looking forward to it."

Ciaran pulled away from him, but he let his thumb run down Trent's jaw before he released him. They walked together down the stairs and into the common room, where Ciaran's brothers and father already waited. All three of them were dressed in armor similar to Ciaran's, with heavy silver swords at their hips. Rathgeirr stood at the edge of the room in his grey tunic and cloak, his sword on his belt and his bow and quiver strapped across his chest. He had stained his jaw with black from his bottom lip down to his neck, and black kohl was smeared across both of his eyes and over the bridge of his nose, making the empty orbs look even deeper. He seemed somehow much darker than the chatty boy he'd been on the boat. He held the bowstring at his chest with both hands and lifted his eyes when Trent and Ciaran entered, but he didn't speak. Now that they were downstairs, Trent could hear the rumbling of footsteps outside, broken by the clatter of weapons and shouts of commands.

Ethniu stepped into the room with a long cloth-wrapped parcel in her hands, and she touched Ciaran's shoulder to draw his attention. She pulled the dark cloth away to reveal a heavy cane of wood with a thick knot at one end and scattered blunt thorns running down the length. The narrow end had been worn smooth near the thick leather strap, and the entire surface was covered in haphazard notches and scratches. Ciaran took the weapon from her, slipping the strap around his wrist and testing the weight of the wood in his grip.

"You kept it?" he asked, ticking his eyebrow as he looked up at her.

The woman folded the empty cloth over her arm with a delicate snort. "I would hardly be blamed for throwing away the prized weapon of Cian mac Cainte, should he ever deign to return for it."

"Thank you, Ethniu."

She didn't quite let a smile touch her lips, but Trent thought he saw a trace of one in her eyes. "It has served you will 'til now," she said. "I trust it will do so today." Ciaran reached for her hand and gave it a quick squeeze, but she scoffed and swatted him away. "Away with you," she scolded. "Our son will be waiting."

Ciaran glanced over his shoulder at the men in his family, and without a word exchanged between them, they all moved through the room, opening the door into the courtyard and letting the noise of the outside into the house. They scooped up the round shields that sat leaned against the wall in the corridor and settled them on their arms. Each was decorated with animals made of long, swirling and knotted lines—Cethen's shield bore horses, Cu's dogs, and Ciaran's had the same snarling boars that were etched into his armor. Ciaran hesitated at the door and let his father and brothers out ahead of him, and he turned back to Trent and held out his hand. Trent took it, allowing himself to be drawn close, and he pressed a palm against the firm leather covering the fairy's chest as Ciaran leaned in to kiss him.

"I'm going to take you away from here," he promised, as if he could make it more certain by repeating it. Trent nodded, keeping hold of Ciaran's hand as he retreated until they were forced to separate. He watched him walk with his brothers and join the ranks of men passing by on the street beyond the courtyard, and he leaned against the door frame with a hand over his churning stomach. Everything was going to be fine.

Airmed appeared at the end of the courtyard a moment after Ciaran passed out of sight, and she waved Trent over, easily taking him by the hand as soon as he was within reach. Julien and Noah were with her, the hunter's worn duffel bag in his hand and both of them dressed for a fight. Julien was fairly intimidating, being half a head taller than most of the men passing by, though Noah looked a bit less battle-ready in his long vest and thick fur cloak fastened at the shoulder.

"You two are fighting?" Trent asked, sure his surprise was showing on his face.

"We can help," Noah said simply.

"Come along," Airmed urged them, pulling Trent forward by the hand. He followed obediently behind her, but he felt sick. Everyone was doing their part, and he was staying behind with the baby sister. He didn't know if it was really better to go with her and watch the battle than it would be to stay inside and wait for news. At least locked inside there was no chance of seeing anything he'd wish he hadn't.

They walked for ages, but there were no carriages on the streets today—just armed men moving in a wave away from the outskirts of the city, shouting and chanting and singing with progressively louder enthusiasm as they drew closer to the chosen field. Women and servants stood in doorways to watch them march, some of them handing off tokens to men who kissed their hands in thanks as they passed. When they reached the end of the curving passage leading to the place called Mag Dúshlán, the stone ceiling opened up above them, the ever-present luminescent moss and fungus almost giving the impression of a distant sky. Stalactites covered in sparkling water droplets hung down from the ceiling, and a cool wind even blew as air rushed across the stretching plain of dark stone.

The crowd had already started to fill a far edge of the massive cave, the men forming themselves into rows and companies. Blocks of archers aligned themselves at the rear of the warriors and tested their bows as servants propped up full quivers of arrows at their feet. Another army had amassed at the opposite end, and both groups moved like water as they made up their ranks. At the front of the group they were headed toward, Trent spotted Lugh, the sole mounted soldier, in his thick plates of etched leather and a heavy, fur-lined cloak hung over one shoulder. His split tunic fell long over his legs, secured around his waist by a wide belt with an intricate knot of polished silver in place of a buckle. He held the reins of his horse with one hand and the shaft of his spear in the other, the tip burning with bright orange flame. He rode back and forth in front of the growing army, shouting at the men at the front and pausing to coordinate with the three ornately-armored kings who stood just behind him. Even his horse looked fearsome—its face was covered by a silver mask with large curling horns, and it snorted and shook its head as though tired of waiting.

"How the hell did he get a horse all the way down here?" Trent asked, and Airmed smiled up at him.

"The Enbarr is not a horse," she answered, as if that explained everything. She parted from Julien and Noah after giving them both earnest kisses on the cheek, and she led Trent away from the flow of men and up to a tall outcropping of rock. From there, they could see the entire field, though it was difficult to make out individuals in the crowd. He supposed that was better; he would only make himself sick with worry if he could have picked Ciaran out and watched him the whole time.

The whole thing was like a scene out of an epic historical movie, and Trent stared out at the mass of people in disbelief.

"First, Lugh and the Ard Rí will go to accept the challenge," Airmed began. Trent forgot that she was holding his hand until she gave it a gentle, comforting squeeze, but he didn't try to pull away. Not right now. "They will agree to terms, and then the battle will begin. The archers first," she said. Even Trent could hear the tinge of worry in her voice. He had a lover down there, but Airmed had brothers, a father, a nephew, and who knew how many friends. He didn't mind if she wanted to hold his hand.

Trent's heart sank as he noticed the crowd parting far below them, and he recognized the sway of Rathgeirr's ashen cloak as the men around him rushed to move out of his way. He made his way toward the front of the army with three men following in his wake—one of whom carried a shillelagh on his shoulder. So much for not picking him out of the crowd. Trent's eyes were locked on Ciaran from that moment on. He watched him follow Rathgeirr to the head of the army, where the alfar briefly locked hands with Lugh. If Ciaran exchanged any words with his son, Trent didn't have a chance of hearing them, but he saw him line up with his brothers beside the horse's broad flank while they waited. Trent found himself squeezing Airmed's hand to try to slow the rapid pounding of his heart, but his chest was so tight he could scarcely find the room to breathe. Then Lugh began to move forward, the three kings at his side as they went to meet the brothers who approached them.

23

Ciaran's weapon felt heavy as he watched Lugh and the Ard Rí head toward the center of the field. He let out a long breath through his mouth and let the weight settle on his shoulder. Gaibhne had more men than he'd anticipated, and the families willing to join him had been of the warrior class—eager for change and blood and the chance for glory. The Ard Rí had the greater numbers, but the men standing behind Ciaran were mostly artisans. It was an army of poets, physicians, craftsmen, and nobles. But they were all Tuatha Dé Danann—and even the softest of them wouldn't be easily overcome. Ciaran would just have to trust that they hadn't forgotten how to fight. He had to trust that he hadn't, either, to be honest. But he could already sense the electricity in the air that always came before the clash, the shifting mass of bodies ready to rush. He could smell the sweat and the leather. He would never forget this feeling.

He glanced beside him and noticed Rathgeirr worrying his bow string between his fingers as he stared across the field. He was focused and quiet, but the anxious movement of his hand gave him away.

"Ever been in a real battle before, lad?" Ciaran asked, politely pretending he didn't notice the way the boy jumped when he spoke.

"Training," Rathgeirr answered without looking at him. "Lots of training."

"Right now, Lugh and the Ard Rí are discussing terms," the fairy explained. "Gaibhne will demand the capitulation of the sons of Cermait as leaders of the Tuath Dé and the recognition of himself as Ard Rí. Mac Cuill will likely suggest that Gaibhne be imprisoned if his people lose the battle today, but Lugh will demand his execution. As is appropriate—this is treason, after all. When they're finished talking, they'll come back. Then, on Lugh's signal, we charge. I'm sure you'll be able to figure it out from there."

"I'm not sure how I'm to know the difference between you," the alfar admitted. "Everyone looks the same."

"You rest assured that those on our side know we've a fearsome Lochlannan among us," Ciaran chuckled. "Just worry about whoever comes after you first."

Rathgeirr nodded, his fingers tightening around his bowstring in an attempt to keep them still. Ciaran could see the set of his blackened jaw and the grim frown on his lips, and he knew even a young border scout of the Alfar would be a force to be reckoned with—if he could overcome his own nerves.

"Just stay near to me," Ciaran added in a softer voice. "You'll be fine, lad."

The alfar finally looked over, and he didn't quite smile, but his hands relaxed just slightly.

In the distance, Lugh turned his horse, and the leaders on each side retreated toward their waiting armies. The kings took their places at the heads of their companies while Lugh rode a last quick patrol up and down the line.

"The Trí Dé Dána and their allies will take no prisoners and give no quarter," he shouted, his booming voice easily reaching the ears of every waiting soldier. "So take none and give none in return. The Tuath Dé will not submit to one man's greed. Músclaígí do lanna!"

The voices of the soldiers cried out as one, "Farrah! Farrah!" as they pounded their shields. The words tore from Ciaran's throat on reflex, fire igniting in his blood at the sound of the cries around him. Lugh gave the call, the Enbarr reared back with a shrill whinny, and at once, it was Cian mac Cainte who rushed forward, not Ciaran. The men moved with one mind, rough yells and stomping boots rattling the sprawling cave. He heard the whistle of arrows above him as the archers fired past them into the center of the opposing force, and when he glanced up and saw the shining points of the enemy arrows flying toward him, he skidded to a stop beside his brothers and ducked low to the ground beneath his shield.

He waited for the thunk of arrows falling around him, but it didn't come. When he looked around his shield, he saw a cloud of black arrow shafts hanging still in the air, and a moment later, the hundreds of projectiles clattered harmlessly to the ground around him, littering the field with wasted effort. Ciaran caught Cu's eyes and felt a slow smirk pull at his lips. Human magic. With another forceful shout, the men rose and pushed forward, finally clashing with the warriors running toward them.

From then on, Ciaran moved on instinct. He raised his shield and swung his weapon, and everything around him was noise, and sweat, and blood. Bones shattered under the weight of the sturdy wood in his hand, jaws snapped, and skulls crumpled. His arm throbbed at the impact of greatswords against his shield, but he held firm and lashed out in return with vicious precision. Everywhere his enemy expected him, he was somewhere else; everywhere they looked for him, he was not. Men fell under his strikes without even knowing what had killed them, and their black blood on his hands was the only warmth in the cool stone cave.

Ciaran kept an eye out for Rathgeirr, but the alfar hardly seemed to need it—he almost danced around his enemy's strikes, his sword finding every opening in their armor. Even when a blow threatened to land, a pale silver shimmer formed around him, rippling out from the point of impact. Training on the island of Lochlann was likely more intensive than any fight these men had been in for a thousand years.

Ciaran was forced to turn his attention from the alfar when he felt a searing heat near his arm, and he spun in time to see the burning tip of Lugh's spear bury itself in the torso of a man who would have landed a blow against him a second later. Lugh jerked the bloodstained blade free of the fallen body and spared his father a scant nod before his horse galloped forward again.

Shouts of pain and fury sounded all around them as men fell on both sides. Ciaran didn't try to count how many he put down; he charged and swung and stumbled when he was hit, but the wounds that seeped black ichor down his arms and temple only fueled him. He turned to face the next foe and saw him jerked toward the ceiling before he could strike, suspended by thin vines that bound his limbs and covered his mouth. He was lifted high and dangled head down over the battlefield, swaying slightly as he struggled. When Ciaran looked up, he noticed at least a dozen hanging men above the field, strung up with crawling vines and left to hang like insects waiting for the spider. The gentle-hearted witch had found a way to help, after all.

Men fell on both sides. Ciaran and his brothers did their share, and Rathgeirr stuck close to the fairy's side. Ciaran even spotted Julien in the thick of the fight, heaving men from their feet on his shoulders and leaving them thrashing on the ground after a well-placed wound from his poisonous iron blade. He looked like he had lost a fair bit of blood for his trouble, but he seemed to be holding his own. All the while, men continued to be snatched away by Noah's reaching tendrils, their shouts of alarm fading as they were hauled into the air.

Ciaran's muscles began to ache, and his weapon grew heavy in his grip, but he couldn't afford to slow down. The battle was turning in their favor, but any falter could change the outcome in an instant. So he pressed on, waiting for Lugh to call out either victory or surrender. Until he did, Ciaran had no choice but to fight. When a space finally opened up in front of him, the clearing ahead littered with bodies, he heard a cry of rage and locked eyes with Gaibhne.

The larger man ran at Ciaran without hesitation, leading with his shield and raising his sword for a lethal blow. Ciaran took the hit on his shield and had to plant his feet to hold his ground against the ringing strike. He exchanged hits with the man who had started all of his troubles, cracking him in the bicep with the weighted end of his shillelagh and wincing as Gaibhne's silver blade caught his thigh. He managed to knock the other man to his knees, but as he lifted his weapon to finish the fight, he heard Cethen's warning shout and felt the cold silver of Gaibhne's blade sink under his ribs.

The noise around him went dull, and his grip failed, the weight of his shillelagh jerking his arm downward by the strap around his wrist. He saw his brothers in his periphery, rushing forward as his knees buckled. The blade slid out of him as he fell, letting his blood pour from the wound and stain the ground underneath him. He gasped for breath, black bubbling from his lips as the dark fluid seeped into his lungs. Rathgeirr was at his side immediately with his hands over the wound. A glistening silver light sparked under his palms as he pressed them to the open skin, but Ciaran was too numb with shock to tell if it was helping. He heard Lugh's rough voice muffled above him, and then he was lifted under the arms as his vision blurred.

"A mhuirnín," he heard himself say. He felt his hand clutching at the tunic of whoever was carrying him. Not like this. Not when he was so close to being free. Not without seeing Trent's face again.

24

Trent's lungs burned as he ran down the cliffside toward the battlefield with Airmed on his heels. He'd kept his eyes on Ciaran since the start as well as he could, clutching the hand of the woman beside him, but when they'd seen him fall, both of them had taken off at a sprint. Trent could hear cheering shouts around them, and he saw Lugh's horse rearing as he raised his fiery spear, so he assumed that their side had won—but it didn't matter. None of it would matter if Ciaran died. He forced his way through the crowd while Airmed shouted for the men to clear the way, and when she spotted her brothers, she grabbed Trent's hand and pulled him along with her.

Ciaran lay on a cloak that had been spread on the ground, his brothers and father kneeling around him and Rathgeirr standing beside them. Ciaran's armor had been removed, and his whole body seemed stained black with blood from various wounds, but his chest still shakily rose and fell. His father hummed a calm tune and ran his hand over the wound in his son's belly, but when Ciaran gave a rough cough that spattered blood from his mouth, Dian Cecht leaned back.

"It is too grave," he said. "There are others who will live that need my aid." He pushed himself to his feet, sparing Ciaran a look of regret if not affection, and then he moved away to tend to other wounded, writhing bodies.

"Cian," Airmed sobbed, but she dropped to her knees and immediately began to pull herbs and tonics from the bag at her waist. She brushed tears from her face with her sleeve and set her lips into a determined line as she began to hum.

Trent couldn't breathe. He couldn't make himself walk forward. Ciaran was dying. His mouth and cheeks were covered in blood that oozed from the edges of his lips, and his lidded eyes seemed cloudy. It was only the sound of the fairy's voice softly begging "a mhuirnín" that made him finally move. He knelt beside Ciaran's head and touched his hair with a trembling hand.

"I'm here," he said through a tight throat, the words barely audible under the clamoring around them. "I'm right here."

The crowd nearby stumbled apart as Noah burst through them with Julien right behind him. The witch fell beside Airmed and helped her peel Ciaran's tunic away from the wound in his abdomen. Noah looked pale, and sweat dripped from his chin, but he stayed focused even though he must have been exhausted.

Trent doubled over on the ground with his forehead pressed against Ciaran's. He couldn't contain the sob that shook him as the fairy's bloodstained hand reached unsteadily up for him and slowly caressed his cheek.

"I'm sorry," Ciaran whispered, his voice weak and gurgling through the fluid in his chest. Even those two words sent another slow gush of blood from his mouth.

"Shut up," Trent insisted. His fingers tightened in his lover's hair. "Airmed and Noah are here. They're going to help you."

The fairy's thumb brushed his cheek, and a faint, distant smile touched his lips. "No," he said.

"Yes they are!" Trent argued. He turned his head to look at the pair tending to Ciaran's wound. "Help him!"

Noah sat back on his heels while Airmed continued to hum with her hands over the bleeding injury. He didn't seem to want to reply. Then his eyes snapped up to Julien. The hunter seemed to recognize what he wanted without a word, and he dashed away, returning a moment later with his bag in his hand. After a few tense seconds of digging, he produced a small bundle of cloth and unfolded it to reveal a polished silver apple.

"Oh, goddess be praised," Airmed gasped. She took the fruit when Julien offered it and carefully sliced it with the small knife from her belt. She edged Noah out of the way, not letting even a single drop of the precious juice drip from her hands, and she tilted Ciaran's chin up and urged small bites into his mouth. "Try to swallow, Cian," she urged softly.

Trent watched with his heart in his throat as Ciaran struggled to chew. He paused to cough, and Trent wiped the blood from his lover's mouth with his sleeve. Ciaran managed to get half of the apple down before he jerked in pain. The wound in his gut spilled more blood down his side before the skin knit itself together again, leaving an angry red scar on his belly. Airmed stopped to check it, faint hope written on her face, but Ciaran's every breath still sounded labored, and new blood still spilled from his lips. He was drowning, and there was no way to help him. A soft hiccup escaped her as she placed her hand on her brother's skin.

"It might really be too much," she whispered. "The blade went all the way through him. Even Manandán's apples can't perform miracles."

Trent bent close to Ciaran again, his hands fisting in his lover's soaked shirt. The fairy's breathing was slower now, and more strained. This couldn't be the end. Not after everything they'd been through. Ciaran couldn't die here, stabbed and beaten to death in a dark cave in a fight over a place he didn't even want. He should be on horseback, laughing and racing across the grass with the wind in his hair and the sun on his face. He couldn't die here.

Noah took a firm hold of the boy's shoulder and bent low to speak into his ear. "There might be one other way," he said, and Trent looked up at him without even attempting to clean the tears from his face. "I found a spell in the library in Falias, and I thought it might help you two, but it—it isn't the same as the joining we tried. It's more like…giving, instead of sharing. I think. I thought that if Ciaran could do it, it would solve your problem, but like this—"

"What are you talking about?"

"It's like giving him a part of you, and binding you together that way, but sort of…unequal, or like entrusting, to link your fates but as a host—"

"You're not making sense, Noah!"

The witch sighed in frustration. "Like a horcrux, okay? It's like a...backwards horcrux. You give him a piece of you, and as long as you live, he lives. Right?" He looked up at Rathgeirr, who seemed startled at being addressed.

"I—I don't know what a horcrux is. But if you mean the ílát spell we discussed, then...yes, it's like that. But with the Alfar it's more of a symbolic gesture. Between an immortal and a human, I don't know what—"

"But it'll save him," Trent cut in, searching Noah's face for any sign of hope. "You can do it, and it'll save him."

"There is a risk to you," Noah said. "But I think so."

"Then do it," Trent answered immediately. "Don't let him die like this. Please."

Noah nodded at him and reached up toward the waiting alfar. "Rathgeirr, will you help me?"

"Y-Yes," he answered. Airmed made room for him to take his place beside Noah, who took his hand.

"Correct me if I say it wrong," the witch muttered. He touched Trent's back to urge him closer to Ciaran.

At the witch's guidance, Trent bent over the fairy, their foreheads gently touching and Trent's hands cupping the other man's face. He could smell the thick blood on Ciaran's lips and feel the weakness of his breath. The fairy's eyes were still open, but Trent wasn't sure his lover could see him anymore.

"Stay with me," he whispered. Ciaran didn't reply.

Noah moved his hand to rest lightly on the back of Trent's head, keeping him in place. "Focus on him," he said. "Breathe deeply, and give him what he needs. Trust him."

Trent tried to do as he was told. He shut his eyes and fought to slow his anxious breathing as Noah began to chant. For a long while, nothing seemed to happen. Trent felt the heat in Ciaran's skin slipping away, and he clutched him tighter, silently begging the fairy to live. He'd come so close to losing him so many times since they'd met. If giving him part of himself was the way to keep him, then that's what Trent would do. He wasn't afraid of being with a man, or being with a fairy, a Tuatha Dé Danann, or with Cian mac Cainte, who was as old as rocks. It was just Ciaran. It was the man who smiled at him and saw through his prickly exterior, who held him and kissed away his tears and told him he was worthwhile. Whatever Ciaran needed, Trent would give it to him.

He felt a chill run up his spine, a tingling sensation that seemed to coil under Noah's hand in his hair. It seeped into his skull and settled in his mouth, and the next time he parted his lips to exhale, the icy air flowed from him and into Ciaran's weakly struggling lungs. Trent shuddered, feeling as though something inside of him had been removed—a sensation of emptiness and nausea, as though he'd thrown up everything he had and couldn't stop retching. But Ciaran's breathing had grown steadier. The flow of blood from his mouth slowed to a stop, and his fingers curled against Trent's sleeve just slightly. When Trent leaned back, the fairy's eyes were closed in the calmness of sleep.

Airmed let out a sob of relief and threw her arms around Rathgeirr's neck, almost knocking the alfar to the ground. He froze and looked over at Noah for guidance, but the witch was checking Trent's eyes and Ciaran's breathing, so he awkwardly patted the clinging woman on the back.

"Did it work?" Trent asked.

"Well, he seems stabilized," Noah answered. "We'll know more when he wakes up."

When Noah tried to move away, Trent took him by the sleeve, but he hesitated when the witch looked back at him. "Thank you," he said after a moment.

Noah managed a tired smile. "Thank me when we know what I've done." He tried to push to his feet, but his legs gave out under him, and he had to grab onto Julien's waiting arm to stay standing.

Trent leaned close to Ciaran again, swallowing down the bile rising in him and squeezing the last tears of relief from his eyes. He clung to his lover's tunic and laid his head on his shoulder, and as soon as he'd whispered his soft "I love you," the nausea and exhaustion pulled him into a heavy sleep.

When Trent woke up, he was in a warm bed, but he felt like death. He didn't know how long he'd been unconscious. His skin was chilled even under the furs and blankets, and his pillow was stained with sweat. But when he saw Ciaran in the bed beside him, clean of blood and sleeping soundly, he forced himself up onto one elbow to look at him despite the wave of nausea and dizziness the movement caused. The fairy had a cloth bandage over a wound where his neck met his shoulder and a deep cut on his temple that looked as though it had been dressed with some kind of oil. Trent lifted the blanket and gingerly pulled at his tunic to check the wound in his stomach, but all that remained was the thick red scar just under his ribs.

"I'll need a bit more rest before you get affectionate, a mhuirnín," the fairy mumbled. He peered up at Trent with a sleepy smile.

Trent didn't even snap at him. He hugged Ciaran around the middle and hid his face in his chest. The fairy wrapped an arm around the boy's shoulders and held him close, pressing a warm kiss to the top of his head. Neither of them said anything. They were too tired; too relieved. Warm in his lover's gentle grip, Trent fell back into an easy sleep with Ciaran's thumb brushing softly over his arm.

The next time he opened his eyes, Ciaran was missing, but Trent spotted him in a deep chair by the fireplace. He had his golden pendant in his hand, the leather straps hanging freely from his palm. Trent sat up and let the blankets pool around his waist. His head swam a little at the movement and his stomach lurched, but he swallowed his nausea and found his voice.

"Something wrong?"

Ciaran looked up with the faint crease of a frown in his brow. "It's cracked," he said. He moved to the bed in a limp, favoring his right leg, and sat down beside Trent to show him the pendant. A thick fracture spread from the center of the knotted cross, seemingly made by an ashen black stain that crept over the surface of the gold. "I didn't know they could crack," he murmured. "And I feel...heavy. What exactly happened while I was out?" He reached up to touch Trent's cheek. "And why do you look ill? Have you caught something?"

"I think I gave something," Trent corrected. "I think you're a horcrux now. Or I am. I'm not sure."

"A what?"

Trent explained the spell Noah had cast as best he could, Ciaran's expression softening the longer he spoke. When he finished and looked up at Ciaran with the blankets twisted in his fingers, the fairy leaned close to him and kissed him so fervently that Trent's breath left him. He felt himself pushed back onto the bed and heard the pendant clatter to the floor as Ciaran climbed over him, his tongue sliding into the younger man's mouth and his hand fastening on his hip. Trent shuddered at the sudden affection. He couldn't keep in his faint groan as Ciaran's fingers tightened on him, but when the fairy shifted above him, Ciaran suddenly hissed and pulled away. Trent's hands moved automatically to Ciaran's chest as though checking him for injury, and the fairy arched his back like a cat to look down at himself. Black blood had begun to seep through the fabric of his trousers on his right thigh.

Ciaran let out a soft swear and eased himself off of Trent, settling for leaning against the headboard beside him. "Maybe just a bit more rest is in order," he admitted with a smile.

"If you die of gangrene or something after I literally puked half my soul into you, I swear to God—"

"But I can't," Ciaran cut him off. He reached up to stroke Trent's jaw with the pad of his thumb. "I'm bound to you. A chuid den tsaol. My share of life," he murmured.

"Do you think that's why the pendant broke? Because you're...I don't know, bonded or whatever. With a human. Rathgeirr said it might make a difference. And isn't the pendant a gift from your goddess?"

Ciaran paused. "That may be. That's probably a poor omen, isn't it?"

"And you said you feel heavy—what does that mean?"

Ciaran shifted on the bed. "It's a bit like before. When I was ill, I mean. I thought I might simply be tired, but—" He stopped and tilted his head at Trent, then slid his arms underneath the younger man at the shoulders and knees. Trent grabbed on automatically as Ciaran hefted him closer and dropped him down again with a pensive grunt. "Hm. You're definitely heavier."

"What? Heavier than when?"

"Than yesterday. To me, I mean." He sat back and looked down at his hands, flexing his fingers and frowning as though they'd betrayed him. "Weaker, and heavier, with a cracked token," he mused. "And snatched from the jaws of death by the gift of a human soul. Let me try something," he added as he turned to face Trent more directly. "Don't be alarmed. If it works, I'll undo it straight away."

"If what works?" Trent asked in a concerned voice, but Ciaran's hand was already gently covering his eyes.

"Déan dall," he said, and he paused a moment before removing his hand. Nothing had happened.

Trent stared up at him in confusion. "What was that?"

"It was...nothing," Ciaran muttered. "Nothing at all. I can't use magic." He let out a quiet laugh, but it sounded a little hollow. "I think you've made me mortal."

Trent's throat closed up so tight that he could barely squeeze out the word, "What?"

"I'll have to test it more," he went on, "but I suppose it makes sense. Perhaps the goddess isn't pleased with me for letting myself be sullied with something like a human soul," he chuckled. "Is this what the seeress meant? Losing that which binds me to this world." Ciaran looked up into Trent's face with a faint frown. "I assumed it was you I'd lose, but...you're fine, aren't you?"

"Except for feeling like I've got the flu, yeah."

"And you aren't...planning to leave me, are you?"

"No," Trent said without hesitation. "I'm not."

"Then I suppose I have my answer."

Trent stared at him. "So, what you're saying is, the seeress proved that the thing most dear to you isn't me, but you."

"Well, to be fair, I have known me for far longer."

"You're such a prick." Trent swatted at the fairy's arm, but Ciaran snatched up his hand and held it tight, brushing a warm kiss over the boy's knuckles.

"It's a small price to pay," he murmured, "to see you in good spirits. And now I can take you away. Just like I promised. We can go to Greece."

Trent softened slightly but tried not to let it show on his face. "I feel like you ought to be more concerned than you are. It doesn't worry you that you're only going to live another few decades, like I am?"

"Why? Aren't I going to live them with you?"

Trent opened his mouth, but his sarcastic reply died on his lips. He found himself smiling and tried to hide it in Ciaran's shoulder. The fairy laughed softly and held him close with a warm hand in his hair.

"You saved my life, a mhuirnín," he whispered against the boy's temple. He touched Trent's cheek to draw his eyes up and kissed him, more gently this time. "Whatever's left of it is yours. Everything I have is yours."

Trent jumped at a knock on the door, snatching the blankets closer around him on reflex as Cu poked his head through the door without waiting for a response.

"Ah, I thought I heard voices," he said. He pushed the door further open and leaned against the frame. "Feeling better, Cian? Not quite dead yet?"

"Not for lack of trying."

"Aye, you surely did your best. And how's your other half? Still feverish, lad?"

"A little," Trent answered.

"Well, you both still have time to rest, so use it while you can. The Ard Rí has called for Cian at his next audience."

"What about Gaibhne?" Ciaran asked. "Was there a trial?"

"Right," Cu chuckled, "you were dying for that bit. There was no need for a trial. Lugh ran him through on the spot as soon as you fell. Still avenging his father's injuries at his age," he added with a tutting click of his tongue. "Either way, his brothers called surrender without Gaibhne to lead them, and the rest of the families backed down and swore fealty before the battlefield was even clear. The crown will be accepting their reparations for ages to come."

Trent saw the relief on Ciaran's face as he sighed. "At least it's finished now."

Cu pushed away from the door frame. "I'll tell Airmed you're awake. Get that leg tended to. She didn't want to fuss with you too much until you woke up on your own." He gave his brother a smile as he eased the door shut behind him.

"Gaibhne's brothers will accept a payment for my debt," Ciaran said. He let out a quiet chuckle. "And hopefully Ethniu will pay it for me. She'll say it would have been cheaper to make her a widow." He paused and looked over as though he expected the boy to flinch at the sound of his wife's name, but Trent was faintly smiling. Ethniu didn't bother him now. He was glad that Ciaran had someone he could call a friend.

"What do you think the king wants to see you for?"

"We'll see, won't we?" He touched a kiss to the corner of the younger man's mouth. "Now kiss me until my sister comes. I've lost time to make up for."

"Ciaran—" Trent tried to object, cut off by the firm press of the fairy's lips. He pushed him by the shoulder as he was forced back into the blankets again. "Wait—"

"For what, a mhuirnín?" the fairy whispered, sending a shiver down Trent's spine.

"For us to actually be alone for more than five minutes," he grumbled. "What if she comes and I'm—you know. These pants they let me borrow don't exactly hide anything."

Ciaran's eyebrows lifted in understanding, and he smiled and placed a light, tender kiss to Trent's mouth before releasing him. "You're a tease. But I'll punish you when you're over your fever."

"Great," Trent sighed, but he couldn't deny the tiny tremor of anticipation that sparked in his stomach.

25

After Airmed had hummed her magic over Ciaran's remaining wounds, she encouraged him to test his movement. Ciaran flexed his leg and rolled his shoulder, and as soon as he gave her his approval, she smacked him in the chest and made him apologize for scaring her half to death. He didn't tell her his suspicions about his lost magic, but he held her and patted her head until she was satisfied. He still looked the same physically, and the blood Airmed cleaned from his wound was still black, so clearly not everything about him had changed. It would take some experimentation to find out his limits.

He and Trent dressed in the clothes the servant laid out for them, and when they went downstairs, the entire entourage was filling the common room—his father, his brothers, Airmed, Julien and Noah, Rathgeirr, and even Lugh.

Ciaran chuckled as he looked up at his son. "Come to make sure I didn't die after all, mo mhac?"

"To make sure you don't leave again without abiding by the Ard Rí's wishes," Lugh clarified. "You are expected."

"Aye, sure," Ciaran sighed. "For what, I can't imagine. Mac Cuill needs an audience for telling me to pay my debts?"

"You come when he calls," Lugh said simply. "So I've come to collect you."

Ciaran exchanged a look with Trent and his brothers, and the whole lot of them followed Lugh out of the estate—Ciaran's father only out of a feeling of obligation, he was sure. It took more than one carriage to fit them all, but they made it to the sprawling castle without fuss, and Lugh led his father through the long courtyard and into the great hall. The rows of seats were just as full as the last time, and Trent, Julien, and Noah were still kept outside, but the atmosphere inside was significantly cheerier. The High King sat tall in his seat, and a faint smile touched his lips as Ciaran approached and gave a deep bow.

"Cian mac Cainte," the king said. Ciaran lifted his head upon being addressed. "This court owes you a debt. Because of your loyalty, we were able to face our enemy head on, instead of being attacked from the shadows."

Ciaran paused. This wasn't quite the audience he had expected. He glanced back at the front row of benches and saw Credne and Luchtaine looking rather morose without their most boisterous brother there to speak for them.

"In light of the circumstances," the king went on, snapping Ciaran's attention back to him, "the remaining sons of Tuirenn have agreed to forfeit any price you may have owed them in exchange for mercy from this court for their sniveling treachery."

Ciaran's eyebrows lifted at the aggressive language, but he supposed even the gentlest of kings drew the line at attempted revolution. He remembered himself and gave another small bow. "Thank you, Ard Rí."

"This court thanks you and your family for your service. We will hold a ball," he announced in a slightly louder voice, "to celebrate our victory over treason." Mac Cuill tilted his chin toward the open door at the far end of the aisle and offered Ciaran a small, private smile. "And your guests are welcome, of course."

"His Majesty is gracious," Ciaran answered, and when the king dismissed him, he returned to his waiting companions so that they could excuse themselves from the hall. Lugh and Dian Cecht stayed behind, as they were much more important than Ciaran and his siblings and so obligated to remain for the rest of the day's business.

"Better than a scolding and a notice of fines," Cu chuckled once they were out of earshot, clapping his brother on the back as they went.

"Did I hear him right?" Noah asked. "We get to go to this ball too?"

"Only if you have an escort of suitable status," Cu answered. He leaned down close to Noah's cheek with a sly smile. "And I just so happen to have an empty arm."

Noah gave him a playful shove. "He didn't say that. I already have an arm to take, anyway," he added as he slid his fingers through Julien's, and the hunter's lips twitched into a poorly-hidden smile. Noah leaned forward to catch Ciaran's eye. "So you're feeling okay? You look pretty good for almost dying yesterday."

"Well enough," Ciaran answered.

"No side effects?"

"None that matter."

"Well that's evasive. If there's something going on, maybe I can—"

"You've done enough, lad. Just enjoy the party."

Noah didn't seem convinced, but he allowed himself to be distracted by Airmed's enthusiastic insistence that he and Julien be fitted for something appropriate immediately. She practically dragged the pair away once they reached the street, and the rest of them headed for their waiting carriage. Cu put a friendly hand on Rathgeirr's shoulder, making him jump and pull his gaze away from the retreating group.

"We'll need to have something done for you as well, friend. A vicious Lochlannan will be all the rage at a gala like this. You'll have your choice of company, I'm sure."

"Company?"

"Aye. Even the Lochlannan like some warm company of an evening, don't they?"

Rathgeirr stopped with one foot on the carriage step. "Oh," he said. Ciaran couldn't tell if there was a blush in the alfar's slate skin, but the timid frown on his lips gave him away. "I'm not—concerned about that."

"Aye, as you say," Cu laughed. "We'll see how you change your tune when you're neck deep in noble ladies vying to be the first to have you." He urged the alfar ahead of him and climbed inside, letting Cethen shut the door and call to the driver. Rathgeirr seemed uncomfortably put out by the notion, but he didn't answer.

Back at the estate, Ciaran allowed himself to be measured, but Trent was reluctant to agree to attend at all.

"It's got nothing to do with me, does it?" he said when Ciaran had gently dismissed the servant trying to fit him. "And I'm not interested in listening to speeches and watching you bow to people all night."

"What do you think a ball is like?" Ciaran asked with a laugh. He stepped over to Trent and slid one arm around his waist, his hand flat on the small of his back as he slowly drew his fingers down the boy's arm. He lifted Trent's hand in his and pulled him close against him. "No speeches. Minimal bowing. Just music, and drink—" He leaned in to touch his cheek to Trent's. "And quiet spaces," he finished in a low murmur, gently swaying the boy on his feet.

"Are they going to fit me for a gown?" Trent grumped despite the tensing in his stomach at the promise in the fairy's words.

"If you like."

Trent shook his hand to free it from Ciaran's grip and pulled himself away from the embrace. He frowned at the floor for a moment before looking back up at him. "Do you want me to go? Really?"

"I want to see you relax, a mhuirnín. Soon we'll be gone from this place and all its troubles—before we go, you can see a few of the good things it has to offer."

Trent considered, watching the fairy's face, and then he sighed and nodded. "All right."

Ciaran leaned out the door to call for the servant again, and as soon as they were both measured and the servant scuttled off to prepare their clothes, Ciaran pushed his lover back toward the bed with one hand on his chest. "We'll be alone for more than five minutes," he purred, and Trent couldn't quite find the voice to argue.

He let Ciaran ease him back onto the bed, his hand trailing its way down Trent's stomach, and he felt his back arch instinctively under the touch. Trent was done being shy. How could he be? He'd almost lost Ciaran—for the second time in the span of a month—and now they were both alive, safe, and bound together the way they'd hoped to be. Even if things went bad again somehow, they had time to breathe tonight. Trent intended to use it.

He pulled the fairy down by his collar so hard he had to catch himself on the bed, and he kissed him with everything he'd been holding back since the day they met. All the anxiety, all the shame, the insecurities, the hangups about their differences, Trent's family, his desires—they all seemed so distant and unimportant now. Ciaran was here, real, solid and warm on top of him. Trent loved him. That was all that mattered.

A low chuckle rumbled in Ciaran's throat as Trent forced him down onto the bed and swung over his hips in one smooth motion. "Feeling spirited, a mhuirnín?"

"You're still recovering. You ought to take it easy."

Ciaran's lips curved into a sly, knowing smile as he slipped his hands under his lover's tunic, his thumbs making small circles over the other man's sharp hipbones. "Make sure you're gentle with me," he murmured, and Trent bent over him to give his bottom lip a soft bite.

"I won't wear you out before your big thank-you party; don't worry." He brushed Ciaran's hands aside so that he could urge him out of his tunic, tracing his fingertips over each bump of the fairy's ribs on his way. With the shirt discarded, Trent flattened his hands on his lover's chest, the skin hot under his palms. It felt firmer, somehow, than it had before. Trent found himself noticing all of the little nicks and gouges that scarred Ciaran's torso—some only just healed from the recent battle, others worn smooth and brown with age. Each one might have been a hundred or a thousand years older than Trent himself. But the one that mattered, the jagged deep red just under the ribs that marked the spot where Ciaran had almost been taken from him—that one was fresh, both on the fairy's skin and in Trent's mind. He'd wasted so much time feeling sorry for himself.

Trent edged down on the bed and touched his lips to every scar he could reach. He let Ciaran slip gentle fingers through his hair and smiled faintly against the fairy's stomach as he felt the soft catch in his breath. He couldn't pretend that his heart wasn't racing at the knowledge that Ciaran was at his mercy, waiting for him, back arching under his kisses. It reminded him of their first time, hasty and tense and Trent trembling with nerves. He was still inexperienced, and he still felt awkward taking the lead when normally Ciaran was more than willing to pin him down and have his way with him. He forced his hands to work the lacing at the fairy's hips and held his breath as he slid the soft fabric down his legs to the floor. His traitorous brain presented him with a hundred ways he might screw up, but when Trent settled himself across Ciaran's lap again and tilted his chin to taste the sharp dip at his collarbone, he heard that sudden, quiet gasp and felt just a little emboldened.

He may not have been the most experienced lover, but he knew the body of the man beneath him better than anyone.

Ciaran seemed to melt under his touch; he bucked as Trent's fingers curled around him and sighed into his lover's kiss as the younger man's tongue grazed the roof of his mouth. Trent knew every soft clench of Ciaran's fingers, every panting breath, every slow roll of his hips. When he sat back on his knees and looked down at him, tracing the subtle lines of muscle on the fairy's stomach, he knew the parted lips and hazy green eyes that stared up at him. It was Trent's. All of it was Trent's.

Ciaran let out a growl of anticipation as Trent leaned across him for the vial of oil from the bedside table, forced to reach blindly for it by the fairy's grasping fingers pulling him into a kiss by his hair.

"Easy," Trent whispered against the other man's lips. "I don't want you to hurt yourself."

"I'll hurt you in a minute," Ciaran muttered in response, but Trent only leaned back, tugging his own tunic over his head and dropping it to the floor. He could see Ciaran's eyes scanning his bare torso, the same wanting look in his eyes that Trent had shied away from in embarrassment so many times before. He didn't mind it now—he met Ciaran's gaze and felt his heart throb at the unapologetic admiration he saw there. He eased his lover's legs apart and let some of the oil spill onto his fingers.

"No you won't," he answered softly, a faint smile quirking his lips as Ciaran's hips jerked under the press of his touch. The fairy turned his head with eyes squeezed shut, clearly trying to keep his moans inside as Trent slid a slim finger into him. Trent shifted close to him, his lover's hips supported on his thighs, and he watched Ciaran tense and writhe under his attention. Whispered Gaelic fell from the fairy's lips the way it always did. Trent still didn't know what the words meant, exactly, but he had begun to understand what Ciaran wanted when he said them. These words were impatient.

He waited, slowly stroking his fingertips against the sensitive spot inside the other man until he heard the fairy whine through his teeth. When Ciaran finally bucked his hips and hissed out a noise that sounded suspiciously like begging, Trent withdrew his fingers and placed a steadying hand on his lover's stomach as he eased forward. Ciaran tried to help him, to push down and grind against him, but Trent tutted softly at him and retreated until he went still. He wasn't going to rush this. He wanted to see every twitch of taut muscle in the fairy's chest, savor the way his hands twisted in the blanket above his head, and watch the shallow breaths he took, each movement reminding Trent that he was still there—still alive, still close. His eyes fell to the vicious-looking scar below Ciaran's ribs, and he traced it lightly with his thumb. He'd been so frightened before of everything that Ciaran was. He'd been so overwhelmed, thinking of the fairy as immortal, magical, unknowable, and forgetting that he was also a person. He was caring, protective, and bold—the things that had made Trent love him in the first place. He wasn't going to forget again.

Ciaran sat up on one elbow and reached up to cup Trent's chin, drawing him gently out of his thoughts. "All right, a mhuirnín?"

Trent bent over him instead of answering, pressing a slow kiss to his lips and urging him back down onto the bed. He let himself enjoy the quiet sound Ciaran made, and then he broke the kiss to look down into his lover's curious eyes.

"I just love you," he murmured, and the smile that parted Ciaran's lips sent an almost painful throb of heat through the younger man's chest.

"I love you, too."

Trent kissed him again and shifted forward on his knees, drawing a sharp gasp from the man beneath him as he sank into him. He stopped when his hips met the splay of Ciaran's thighs, shuddering as the fairy tightened around him. Ciaran's fingernails bit into Trent's back when he began to move, and the soft sounds of the fairy's breath filled Trent's ears. He slid his arms under Ciaran's shoulders to hold him tight as he rocked slowly against him, the fairy's lips on his cheek, his ear, his mouth—anywhere they could reach.

Trent tried to keep his pace steady, allow himself to feel every tense shift of his lover's hips, but when the heat of Ciaran's tongue traced his upper lip and slid into his mouth, Trent couldn't hold back. He swallowed Ciaran's satisfied moan in his kiss as he began to move faster, the fairy's legs fastening securely around his waist to better twist against him. He wasn't embarrassed or nervous now—he just wanted Ciaran. He wanted Ciaran's hands in his hair, his kiss, the wanton cry that sounded in his throat as Trent's fingers wrapped around his neglected erection. He wanted all of him.

Trent knew how to shift his hips to hit the spot deep inside Ciaran that would reduce his growling moans to whimpers. He kept the fairy's back arched from the bed until Ciaran began to beg in heated whispers against the younger man's ear, pushed to near babbling by the steady thrust and practiced touch of his lover. He could feel Ciaran tightening around him and knew the urgent words panting against his cheek, urging him on faster and harder. Trent set his jaw, his grip tight around his lover's shoulders and his heart thumping in his chest. He caught Ciaran in another kiss and refused to let him go, both of them rocking together until Ciaran's release spilled between them, striping the fairy's stomach with glistening heat. Ciaran kept Trent close, holding his face in both hands and whispering breathless affirmations against his lover's lips while he rode out the final desperate thrusts before his orgasm.

Ciaran held him when Trent dropped his head against the fairy's shoulder, both of them gasping for breath but unwilling to move. They laid together until the stickiness and sweat forced Trent to shift onto his side.

"I'm...glad you didn't die," Trent murmured, settled with his face nuzzling the fairy's neck.

Ciaran chuckled, the sound low and gentle in his chest. He pressed a light kiss to the younger man's dark hair. "I am too."

26

However uncomfortable and awkward Trent felt as he walked beside Ciaran toward the entrance to the grand hall housing the gala, his embarrassment was worth it if it meant getting to look at the fairy in front of him.

Ciaran had been dressed in black pants, tall boots, and a white tunic that brushed above his knees, the chest and high collar decorated with intricate black and silver embroidery. His wide sleeves were cuffed at the wrist with delicate silver bracers, and a black robe lined with silver and cut to show his sleeves fell to his ankles. Trent would never have imagined that the medieval look would do it for him, but the leather belt carefully folded to trail from the buckle hung from Ciaran's hips so perfectly that he had to force himself to look away. His brothers looked just as impressive, and Rathgeirr had been fitted with clothing more in line with the style Trent had seen back on his home island—a long black tunic split at the front from the waist to the ankles and secured with a broad leather belt at his hips. The trimming along the edges and down his shoulders and arms was heavy and gold, and a warm cloak was pinned over one of his shoulders with a thick golden brooch.

Trent's own provided outfit was similar but simple, in a dark forest green and a thigh-length vest in place of Ciaran's more formal-looking robe. He felt ridiculous, but his mood lifted a little when they reached the doors and he saw the equal measure of awkwardness on Julien's face. He stood stiff and still, as though he'd never been anywhere so formal. He'd even been given a more fancy-looking eyepatch in deep brown silk to match the color of his outfit. Noah, on the other hand, seemed endlessly entertained by spinning in place and watching the ocean blue robe billow out around him as he moved.

"We get to keep these when we leave, right?" he asked.

"Classy, Noah," Julien sighed, but the witch just stared up at him. "What?"

"Oh, I'm so glad you all came," Airmed cut in, a bright smile on her face as she took her brothers' hands and kissed their cheeks in turn. Her gown was made of flowing silk that seemed to shift from green to gold depending on the light, with long, split sleeves that sat just off of her shoulders and hung in graceful lines almost to the floor. She squeezed Trent's hands and kissed his face affectionately before he could protest, but when she reached Rathgeirr, she seemed to hesitate.

"Good evening," she said in a more subdued voice, and she peeked up at him with her bottom lip caught in her teeth.

"Good evening," he answered. Neither of them seemed to know what to do from there, but before things could get too awkward, Ciaran cleared his throat with pointed volume and continued through the door.

The hall had been hung with colored silk and lit with flickering blue lanterns that curved away from the stone columns on arching silver sconces, and the sound of pipes, drums, and soft horns filled the air inside. Everywhere, people were talking, or dancing, or taking drinks from the countless servants who darted around the hall. Ciaran kept a gentle hold of Trent's hand as they moved through the crowd, occasionally pausing so that he could answer the greeting of someone Trent had never seen before and that Ciaran himself hardly seemed to remember. He was received by the Ard Rí and his brothers in his turn, and even Lugh acknowledged him with a polite nod. The delicate formal wear didn't suit the general, and he seemed to realize it, but the dark cape and heavy matching brooches were impressive, at least.

Trent could feel a hundred sets of eyes on him as they mingled, but as soon as the guests noticed Rathgeirr, the human Ciaran had brought with him seemed far less important. Trent almost felt a little sorry for the way the alfar was rushed and surrounded. But it meant that Ciaran could share a quiet smile with him and laugh when his face scrunched up at the powerful taste of cuirm, which Ciaran informed him was almost like beer—so he was prepared to throw Rathgeirr under that bus.

In a lot of ways, it was a similar sort of party to the kind Trent had been forced to attend whenever he was in Hong Kong with his father—quiet music playing, polite chatter over cups of alcohol, and forced smiles. He'd always been bored to tears at the charity events his father had dragged him to, and it seemed that fairy parties were no different. Noah seemed to be enjoying the atmosphere, at least, even if Julien looked only slightly less on his guard than he had the morning of the battle. He kept a wary eye on Cu and subtly moved closer to Noah every time the fairy got too friendly.

Ciaran and Trent sat at one of the low tables along the wall, drinking their beer and letting their knees touch underneath the table while the party continued around them. Beyond the wall of people in front of them, a space had opened up for dancing, and ornately-dressed men and women began to pair off with formal curtsies and politely distant embraces.

"This is really what it's like here, all the time?" Trent asked.

Ciaran smiled. "Aye, mostly. You see why I wanted to leave."

"Then why did you want to come tonight at all?"

"It's worth the wait," Ciaran answered with a chuckle, and he emptied his cup and waved over a passing servant to replace it.

"What is?"

They were interrupted by a tall figure approaching their table, and Trent lifted his head to see Ethniu staring down at them, dressed in an icy blue gown. Her dark hair was knotted at her nape and strung with delicate silver chain that glittered in the lantern light, and even her fire-colored eyes seemed cold.

"Are you not going to ask me to dance, Cian?" she asked in a voice that suggested there was definitely a correct answer to this question.

"Are you feeling neglected, treasure?"

"I have simply grown accustomed to your particular variety of ineptitude; learning to dodge another man's missteps would be a wasted effort at this stage of my life."

Ciaran glanced sidelong at Trent, who took his cup from him with a faint nod. He watched the fairy stand and offer his arm to the taller woman, and the two of them walked to the dance floor, Ciaran placing his hand at Ethniu's waist as though he'd done it a thousand times. He probably had, Trent realized. How many of these torturous parties had they been to together, sitting quietly off to the side just as Trent and Ciaran had been, talking in low voices and making fun of the people around them? Ciaran had a familiar smile on his face as they danced, and despite Ethniu's taunting, he moved more gracefully than Trent had expected. He guessed he'd had a lot of practice. Even a week ago, Trent might have been jealous at the casual way Ciaran's hand touched the small of Ethniu's back, but he didn't feel anything like that now. He didn't have anything to fear from her. He was content to watch the way Ciaran's cloak swirled around him as they turned and the strong line of his back in the sleek black.

He could see Noah and Julien across the floor, standing near Lugh. Cu had apparently gotten distracted, but Noah was occupied with accepting drinks and laughing with the fairies who were happy to chat with him. Trent saw him lean in to a stranger to listen more closely and then nod and hold out his hand, where a bright spark popped noisily into the air. Julien looked like he wanted to intervene, but Lugh leaned a friendly elbow on the hunter's shoulder and tapped their cups together to encourage him to drink.

A sudden bustling movement caught Trent's eye, and he leaned forward in his seat to see Rathgeirr retreating from a flock of women, led by Airmed's guiding hand on his arm.

"What did I tell you about that fever," Trent heard her say. "Oh, I'm so very sorry, ladies; I did tell him to be careful of illness since he's away from home. I must tend to my brother's guest—you understand," she insisted as she pulled the alfar away and into a more isolated corner. Trent couldn't hear the words they exchanged, but he saw the grateful look on Rathgeirr's face. He smiled at something Airmed said, and by the time Ciaran returned from his dance, the two of them had found a quiet place to sit. They sat not quite next to each other at the round table, both shyly peeking at the other and holding their cups of beer as they talked, but Trent could have sworn he saw Rathgeirr inch close enough to brush one knuckle down the back of her hand.

Ciaran followed the boy's gaze as he took his seat again, and his eyes narrowed along with his wary frown. "That's how it is, hm?" he murmured into his cup.

"Where's Ethniu?"

"She has more important people to talk to. Besides, she always prefers to be gone before the evening winds down."

"Winds down? You mean it's going to get more boring than this?"

"Drink up, a mhuirnín. The night is young."

Trent's lips pulled into a skeptical frown. At least the almost-beer became more palatable the more of it he drank. He watched Ciaran surveying the room, his eyes landing on the polished silver buckle on his belt bearing the same circle of boars made of smooth, curling lines.

"Why a boar?" he asked. He poked the buckle with one finger when Ciaran glanced at him with his eyebrows raised in a question. "Your armor had the same thing. Why does everybody have animals?"

The fairy chuckled. "Well, we have to decorate with something. It usually starts with a gift. Your father or your older brother might give you your first set of armor, and they'll have chosen something fitting for you, but sometimes people become known for things, so they might adopt a new sigil." He nodded across the room toward his brothers, who stood chatting with a small group of nobles. "Before my people came below, Cethen used to breed horses. They were known across Éire for being swift and good-tempered. Cu's name literally means hound, and it ended up suiting him, so it stuck. Even the knot that Lugh wears is meant to represent a storm. That one's a bit more metaphorical."

"Uh-huh," Trent nodded. He leaned forward with his elbows on the table. "And the boar?"

The fairy sighed through his nose, like he didn't really want to answer. "Mine used to be a stag. They're identified with being handsome. My father's way of telling me that my face was the only useful thing about me. But after we returned from Lochlann, when we had our first battle with the Fir Bolg, I...may have gotten a bit enthusiastic and charged at a man twice my size. I did knock him down, but I went down as well, of course. Almost got myself killed. So, afterwards, Cu presented me with a very fine set of armor, decorated with the boars you saw. I'm associated with a boar because of a joke from my younger brother that stuck around for two thousand years."

Trent snorted into his cup and earned himself a playful frown. "That's not as heroic as I expected."

Ciaran laughed. "Do I strike you as particularly heroic?"

The boy paused with the cup at his lips and peeked over the rim at Ciaran. "Not before this," he muttered, half hoping the other man wouldn't hear him.

"Were you admiring me, a mhuirnín?" Ciaran teased. He leaned closer to the boy with a smirk on his lips. "I didn't know you were attracted to the strapping warrior type."

"Nobody called you strapping."

"I'm a little strapping."

Trent sipped loudly from his cup and turned his attention away from the man beside him, but he let him lay a gentle hand on his arm, the fairy's thumb brushing his sleeve as they sat and watched the party go by.

People trickled out of the hall as the night wore on, but many stayed, downing more cups and talking a bit louder. Finally, the room seemed to tense with an air of anticipation, and Trent leaned forward to follow Ciaran's eyes as the large doors at the end of the hall opened to allow the three brother-kings to exit. People bowed as they passed and bid them good night along with the rest of the most ostentatious nobility. When the doors closed again, there were a few prolonged moments of quiet in the wake of the heavy thud, and then someone from across the room gave a piercing whoop. The music cut short and immediately started again, livelier and louder than before.

Ciaran pushed to his feet and emptied his cup, thumping it upside down on the table as he offered Trent his hand. "Now, a mhuirnín," he chuckled, "you'll get to see a real Tuath Dé celebration."

"What the hell just happened?" Trent asked, but he couldn't keep in his quiet laugh. His head had begun to swim from the alcohol, and the music filled his ears as Ciaran pulled him up. The fairy pulled the robe from his own shoulders and discarded it onto his seat, leaving him in only the embroidered tunic cinched so pleasantly at his hips.

Ciaran tugged Trent closer and touched a kiss to his cheek just in front of his ear. "Have you had enough to drink that you'll dance with me?"

"It's cute that you think I know how to dance."

"Aren't all rich sons made to learn?"

"Fuck off," Trent snorted, but Ciaran kept him from pulling away.

"Don't worry, a mhuirnín. I'll lead."

He pulled the boy with him into the crowd of dancers, none of whom could be called anything close to sober. Trent was awkward at first, but Ciaran caught him every time, and soon the not-quite-beer had caught up with him enough that he didn't care when he stumbled. He held on tightly to Ciaran's shoulder and let him guide him across the floor, both of them laughing as they bumped into other pairs of party-goers. Trent even caught sight of Rathgeirr, his cloak abandoned, with his arm around Airmed's waist as they spun carelessly to the music. The woman clung to him with her hair falling loose from its pins, her ringing laughter audible even in the crowded hall.

Trent and his lover stopped to down another cup of beer, and then Ciaran was somehow drawn into a drinking game with his brothers, the rules of which Trent couldn't hope to understand through his alcoholic haze. Noah seemed to catch on quickly enough, and he drew Julien and Lugh into the game. Before Trent could hope to focus enough to play, Cethen apparently won, and the others shouted in dismay and drained their cups. He didn't know what was going on, but he laughed at the honest frustration on Ciaran's face and didn't even fight when the fairy drew him into his lap.

Airmed broke away from her dance partner and leaned heavily on Julien's shoulder. When he looked up at her, she pointed between Noah and the hunter with a proud smile on her face.

"You boys are getting on, aren't you?" she asked. She leaned a little too close to Julien's face and only followed him when he moved back. "Getting on well?"

"Uh—yes?" Julien answered, and Noah smacked his arm.

"Why is it a question?"

"I know you are," Airmed answered herself, "because I hear you in my guest bedroom." Julien's cheeks flared red, and Noah laughed out an insincere apology. "Nonsense," the fairy went on, waving away with witch's words. "But I did expect a certain amount of affection at this party, and it has been notably lacking. One kiss in a dark dungeon is the best I get? As the one almost wholly responsible for this relationship, I demand to see the fruits of my labor!"

"I don't know about wholly responsible—" Julien started, but he was immediately cut off by a stranger across the table calling, "Kiss!"

"Kiss!" Airmed repeated with genuine enthusiasm. The demand was repeated by laughing voices all around them—even Ciaran's, though Trent tried unsuccessfully to cover the fairy's mouth with both hands.

Julien only managed to stammer out a single objection before Noah had him by the collar, pulling him down into a kiss clearly meant to end all curiosity about the nature of their relationship. The hunter gave in, one hand fastening in Noah's shirt at the back of his neck while Airmed clapped and bounced happily on the balls of her feet. When Noah finally released him, Julien sat back in his seat with an embarrassed frown on his lips, the red flush on his face only growing deeper as Noah touched a final peck to his jaw.

"You're awfully sheepish, hunter, for someone so happy to touch their lover in his most private places on the floor of another man's room," Ciaran said.

Julien's eye snapped to the fairy's smirking face as Airmed pressed her fingertips to her mouth to suppress the squeal of astonishment threatening to escape.

"Is that what you lot were doing in there?" Lugh asked over his cup. "Afraid your witch would ask me to join in, an duine?"

Julien scowled across the table at him, but Noah saw the look on his face and promptly clapped his hand against the table and called for another round of the game. Ciaran excused himself and Trent from the table rather than join in, and while Airmed was distracted with leaning her chin on the top of Julien's head to watch the game, he reached out to tap Rathgeirr's arm with the back of his hand.

"A moment, lad?" he said. Rathgeirr smiled a bit hazily at him, and Ciaran put an arm around the alfar's shoulders and urged him a few steps away from the table. Trent wasn't sure if he should follow, so he just stood by and waited, but Ciaran didn't actually lower his voice very much. "I see the way you're looking at her," he said with his head bent close to Rathgeirr's.

"At—at her?" the alfar stammered.

"Don't be coy," Ciaran scolded him. "I also see the way she's looking at you."

"You do?" The excited lift of Rathgeirr's eyebrows was a clear giveaway.

"I do," Ciaran confirmed. "So I wanted to have a word with you. As the eldest sibling." Trent saw the fairy's fingers tighten on Rathgeirr's shoulder so hard that the alfar gave a slight flinch. "My sister," Ciaran went on in a voice that was almost too friendly, "is a delicate, kind, and perfect flower, and if she's taken a liking to you and you hurt her, I will pull out your tongue through your asshole. Do we understand each other, lad?"

Rathgeirr nodded enthusiastically until Ciaran loosened his grip.

"Good." Ciaran slapped him on the back and shooed him away back to Airmed's side. He took Trent's hand again to lead him away, apparently satisfied with his threat. Trent almost protested against the idea of more dancing, as he was already drunk beyond the point of good sense and would definitely embarrass both of them, but the fairy pulled him along by the hand past the dance floor and into a nook near a back hallway door.

Trent's question died on his lips as Ciaran pushed him back against the wall, half devouring him in a kiss. The fairy's hands fastened on his waist for only a moment before one began to travel to the small of his back, the other sliding underneath his vest to caress his nipple through the fabric of his shirt. Trent couldn't voice a protest. Ciaran's tongue was too hot against his own, his hands too practiced at drawing moans from the younger man. He tangled his fingers in the fairy's hair and let him press his hips against him without a thought as so how close they might be to being discovered. Ciaran only broke the kiss to nip at Trent's ear and neck.

"I couldn't just look at you anymore," he whispered, his voice low and husky with drink. "I want you, a mhuirnín."

Trent's grip tensed, but it wasn't shyness that made his heart thump. He drew his hand down Ciaran's firm chest, tracing the silver embroidery with his fingertips, and tried to make his brain work enough to form an answer. He gave up when the fairy pulled him closer by the hand at his back and let him feel his arousal. Ciaran's lips were on Trent's neck the instant he nodded his agreement, his hand underneath the boy's tunic to touch his heated skin.

A shout from the main hall startled them, and Trent shoved Ciaran away from him on instinct. The fairy looked thoroughly offended, but the heavy scrape and clatter of wood on stone reverberated through the hall so loudly that they both leaned out of the corner to look for the source.

Julien was on his feet, his chair knocked to its side, and he had his eye on Lugh, who seemed to be talking very normally with Noah across the table but had a sly look on his face that suggested he'd earned the hunter's glare.

"Osti de tabarnak, c'est assez!" Julien snapped. He finished his cup and near slammed it back to the table with the growing pile of empty ones in front of him. "Attache ta tuque, colon. M'a te débabiner!"

Lugh frowned faintly and glanced back at Noah. "What did he say?"

The witch hesitated as though he had to let the alcohol work its way through the gears in his brain. "I think he said he's going to punch you in the face."

"Déguédine!" Julien called as he stepped back from the table, seeming to beckon Lugh forward while he shrugged off his confining overcoat. "Drette là, champion des épais!"

"Julien," Noah tried to intervene as Lugh got to his feet, "I really think we ought to have a talk about stupid decisions—"

"J'men calice de ce bâtard!"

Trent looked up at Ciaran as Lugh unfastened his cape, letting it pool on the floor behind him, and moved around the table to face the hunter. "Shouldn't you stop them? Julien's going to die."

"Nonsense. This is a bit of fun."

Julien didn't wait for Lugh to speak again. As soon as the fairy was in front of him, he swung, putting his full weight behind the hit. Lugh's chin snapped to one side, but in the next moment, he had Julien's head trapped in the crook of his arm and was forcing the other man to the floor. Julien struggled against him, his boots skidding on the smooth stone. The remaining crowd gathered around the pair in a broad circle and shouted for their chosen fighter with taunts and drunken cheers. Noah pushed his way to the front, and even Trent and Ciaran edged their way close enough to see.

"This doesn't look like a bit of fun," Trent said warily as Julien's arms pulled at Lugh's in vain.

"My son became champion of the Tuath Dé by picking up a flagstone that took eighty oxen to move and throwing it across the city," Ciaran answered. "Our hunter isn't dead already. So it's a bit of fun."

Julien wasn't going down quite as quickly as Trent would have imagined, but Ciaran was right—Lugh was clearly playing with him. They struggled against each other, both men gripping their opponent around the waist or the neck as the opportunity presented itself. Julien was almost on the floor, his knee bent close to the stone, but then with a sudden shout of rage, he surged upward with his shoulder planted firmly in Lugh's sternum. The fairy didn't quite fall, but Trent was certain he saw the larger man's boots move a centimeter from the floor as he lost his grip and stumbled backward.

A triumphant smirk pulled Julien's lips. "That's the problem with fairies," he taunted. "Airy as dandelions."

Lugh's nostrils flared in irritation, and in a single step he was on top of the hunter again with his arm dangerously tight around his throat. He flipped Julien from his feet in one fluid movement and sat down firmly on his back with the hunter's arm pinned in an unnatural twist behind him. Julien gave a pained grunt, but he didn't fight once he jerked and realized the precarious situation his arm bones were in. Lugh bent down close to his ear.

"Got it out of your system, an duine?"

Julien huffed with his cheek against the floor and glared sidelong up at the fairy. He frowned instead of nodding, but Lugh let him up anyway, pulling the hunter to his feet and clapping him on the shoulder. By the time Noah reached them, Julien was laughing, and he looked down at the witch with a smile on his face.

"I almost knocked him over," he said. He stumbled a little when Lugh shoved him in retaliation.

"Yes, sweetie, I saw," Noah answered with a chuckle. The crowd around them closed in, congratulating the human on standing his ground and shoving even more drinks into his hands, which he gladly accepted.

Trent looked over at Ciaran with confusion on his face, but the fairy just shrugged and laughed.

The hall slowly began to grow quiet as time passed by, and Trent suspected that if there had been a sun in Tír na nÓg, it would have been rising. The music had stopped some time ago. The people still drinking were nursing their cups instead of gulping them, and almost everyone had found a place to sit either at a table or on the floor along the wall. Trent sat in a circle that had formed near the dance floor, his head on Ciaran's shoulder. Noah was on his other side with his back on the floor and his legs in Julien's lap, and the rest of the circle was made up of Ciaran's brothers, Lugh, and Rathgeirr and Airmed, who were now definitely subtly lacing their fingers together between them.

"So the big adventure is done, huh?" Noah asked. He splayed his arms out at his sides and let his knuckles drum on the stone floor. "We survived the trip to the secret magic island, stopped a fairy coup d'etat, and even got you two soul-joined properly," he added, twisting his neck to look over at Ciaran and Trent. "Now I guess we'll go our separate ways, huh?"

"I imagine your hunter is eager to get back to work," Ciaran chuckled.

"My brothers will have been trying to contact me," Julien said, more to Noah than in answer to Ciaran.

The witch lifted his head from the floor enough to smile at him. "I've never been to Montreal."

Trent frowned faintly and tried to calculate how much money he still had left. With Ciaran unable to use his magic, any traveling they hoped to do would have to be paid for solely by the money he'd been able to take from his bank account. He refused to call his mother—when the money ran out, he would get a job somewhere until they could afford to move again. He wasn't going to be a burden to Ciaran now that they were finally on more even footing, but he couldn't exactly count on the fairy to maintain a grasp on their financial situation.

"Where do you want to go first, a mhuirnín?" Ciaran asked softly as he nuzzled the younger man's hair. "It's a long way to Greece."

"First, I want to get out of fairyland before another month goes by and I have to live it all at once when we leave," the boy answered. He couldn't say it, but now that he knew Ciaran's life was dependent on his, a month seemed like a much more precious length of time.

"Oh!" Noah shouted from across the way. He rolled on the floor and propped himself up on one elbow so that he could look over at Rathgeirr. "You're an important person's son, aren't you?"

The alfar paused before looking up, as though he wasn't expecting to be spoken to. "Yes? What?"

"Your dad," Noah said. "He was at the king's meeting or whatever when we got there. I kept meaning to ask you—there was a demon there. Do you know why?"

"Oh, Father mentioned," Rathgeirr murmured, "but he told me it wasn't any of my concern. He said there was no way I was going to be sent."

"Sent? Sent where?"

"To the outside. The demon asked for the aid of the Alfar in his war."

The circle went silent, and Noah pulled his legs from Julien's lap and sat up to properly face Rathgeirr. "What war?"

"His war with men," the alfar answered simply. "The demon means to send his forces against the humans, and he said that he needed warriors with 'more permanence' than the ones he had. I'm not sure what that means, and Father wouldn't explain."

"Rathgeirr," Noah said, his voice sounding slightly strained. "A demon lord came to your people and asked for their help fighting a war against humanity?"

"Yes."

The witch gaped at him, his mouth opening and closing a couple of times before he could make his voice work again. "And you didn't think this was important to mention?"

"Oh." The alfar's brow furrowed as he frowned. "I...suppose that would matter to you, wouldn't it?"

"Uh, yeah!"

Julien was on his feet already, and he snatched Rathgeirr up by the front of his tunic, drawing a startled protest from Airmed. "When?" he growled.

"Oh, I—I imagine very soon," the alfar said in a subdued voice. "I was already hearing about mobilization shortly before we left."

The group seemed suddenly sober now as Julien shoved Rathgeirr away from him in disgust. The hunter turned to Noah with a grim frown on his face.

"We need to go. Now."

Noah accepted his lover's hand up and turned to Rathgeirr, who seemed mildly confused but contrite. "Anything you can tell us will be helpful, Rathgeirr. A demon army is bad enough, but—oh!" He stopped, putting a hand on Julien's sleeve. "Sabin. The mass possession he said he encountered. I need to write to him right away."

"I—I'll go too," Rathgeirr spoke up. "Please. I want to help."

Julien's lip curled as he looked the alfar up and down. He seemed reluctant, but Noah shook his sleeve, so the hunter gave a short, irritated sigh. "Fine. But you do as I tell you, understand? And full disclosure from you—about everything."

"Yes," Rathgeirr answered promptly. "Of course. Yes."

Trent looked up at Ciaran, trying to gauge the look on his face. "What do we do?" he asked.

The fairy glanced down at him. "What do you want to do?"

"There's nothing we can do, right? Not against an army of demons and alfar." His fingers curled into the fabric of Ciaran's shirt. This couldn't be happening. They were finally free of Ciaran's past, and now there was going to be some sort of apocalypse? Where the hell had that come from? What had Trent done wrong in a past life? He let out a breath that sounded shakier than he liked. "There's nothing anyone will be able to do, is there?"

"We could," Cu cut in. He glanced between his brothers and Lugh, whose mouth was set in a thin line. "We could help them," he pressed with his eyes on his nephew. When Lugh didn't answer, Cu scooted closer to him. "The Tuatha Dé Danann have a responsibility to protect Inisfail. This army will not stop at our borders. If the Lochlannan get the upper hand, they'll have every human on the surface either enslaved or dead, and you know it. Where, then, will they turn their gaze?"

Lugh's deep voice was quiet, but it held the attention of the entire circle. "You suggest we join a war against the Lochlannan for the sake of maintaining the humans' status quo."

"Didn't we just get done having one amongst ourselves in any case? You don't want to go back to the way things were when magic was alive above us—the endless wars, the clawing for power, the destruction—you remember those times. And even if we could hide away down here and let the war rage above, you can't pretend no human has ever been dear to you. It's Deichtine's people you'd be condemning—"

Lugh gave a sharp warning hiss to quiet the other man, and Cu sighed as he looked to Ciaran.

"Talk sense to him," he said. "The Tuath Dé will not benefit from staying neutral in this conflict, and I say we take the side of the humans."

Ciaran hesitated, a pensive frown on his lips as he glanced down at Trent. "I'm biased," he admitted. He looked across the circle at his son. "But if it's a choice between a world as it is now and a world run by the Lochlannan and some upstart demons, then it's an easy one. Besides," he added, "it's hardly a fair fight, is it? Wouldn't it just gall you to have watched the humans finally scrape their way into moderately civilized behavior only to be knocked down by an enemy they had no way of anticipating?"

Lugh scowled at him, but he didn't deny it. After a few agonizing moments of consideration, he stood, and he moved to stand in front of Julien. "You are needed above. I will arrange for your passage home, and I will contact you in three days' time. Find out all you can. As soon as I have the Ard Rí's blessing," he said, "the Tuath Dé will go to war."

27

Trent stood half behind Ciaran while they waited inside a large ring of carefully piled stones that lay outside the city. They had walked a long path to get there, and now their small group stood near the edge of the ring while Lugh took his place at the center.

"What exactly are we doing?" Noah asked.

"He'll open the way for us to take a sídaige conar," Ciaran answered. "A fairy path, if you will."

"Which is what?"

"It's a path," the fairy answered dryly. "A way to get from one place to another in a hurry. They run between raths—forts, or remnants of them, like this one. We'll be able to get to Montreal in moments, rather than hours or days."

Noah stared up at him. "And we haven't used this until now—why, exactly? I had to ride a horse across the Atlantic Ocean and we took a bus to the coast when this sort of thing existed?"

"Well, they do tend to...cause a bit of trouble. The magic isn't harmless. We'll essentially be passing through anything in our way along a straight line from here to Montreal, and that sometimes shows itself in unpleasant ways for the things we pass. Or the people."

"Hold up," the witch said, "this is going to hurt people?"

"Not so much that it's cause for distress."

"What the hell does that mean?"

Ciaran sighed. "My kind have a reputation for being vindictive, but it's mostly exaggerated. The Irish above say that if you build a house along a fairy road, it's offensive to us, and people in your family may become ill, or your cattle might up and die. It's not because we're offended, so much as children and cattle aren't very used to having that kind of magic run through them."

Trent leaned around Ciaran to catch his eye. "You're saying that by taking this path, we might literally kill anyone who happens to be in the way."

"There are only five of us," the fairy answered with a careless shrug. "In those days, there were entire retinues running to and fro, armies sent this way and that, you know. That makes a difference. We do still tend to avoid using them nowadays, but our little band isn't likely to induce much more than nausea. Maybe a flu."

Julien's grip tightened on the strap of his bag, and Noah could see the disgust on his face without the hunter having to say a word. He wouldn't like the idea of putting the general public in danger, but with his weapon-filled duffel and Ciaran's complete lack of identification of any kind, their travel options were limited—and so was their time.

Ahead of them, a large circle snapped open in the air, just like the portal that allowed them to enter Tír na nÓg. The shimmer of blue that formed the ring moved in subtle waves around the empty space, but the inside was only black and endless.

"You know," Noah said, "I'm all for adventure and everything, but I kind of don't want to go in there."

"It is the fastest way," Lugh assured him. He shifted his eyes to Julien and tilted his head toward the portal as though urging him on. "Three days," he said.

"I'll figure out what's going on," Julien promised. "We'll be ready."

Lugh took a step back to clear the way between the group and the portal, and the hunter led the way through the glimmering circle with Noah right on his heels. Ciaran took hold of Trent's hand to guide him through, and Rathgeirr stepped across the barrier just before it snapped shut behind him. Everything around them was pitch black, but the ground under their feet seemed solid, so they walked forward as best they could. Julien kept a hand out in front of him to keep from running into any obstacles, and before even a minute had passed, he felt the chill of a cool wind on his fingertips. The next step he took landed him on a wooden floor with the morning sun glaring on his face, and he flinched as he lifted a hand to shield his eye. He heard the others exiting the black passage behind him and squinted as he tried to locate himself.

This was definitely Montreal—Julien could see the Biosphère and the Pont Jacques-Cartier bridge, which meant they were on Île Sainte-Hélène. This was the Tour de Lévis. It wasn't so much a fort as the last remaining tower of an old military compound, but he supposed it was close enough for fairy technicalities.

"Holy shit," Noah breathed from behind him. He moved to the metal railing and leaned out to look across the treetops surrounding them. "That really worked!"

"Bienvenue à Montréal," Julien said. Noah's bright smile cheered him, just a little.

"We'll need to find somewhere to get some clothes," Trent pointed out. They had all long since ruined any clothing they had that weren't leggings and fairy tunics, and they would surely get more attention than they wanted wandering the city dressed as they were. "I mean, unless you want to say we're going to a Renaissance Fair, or something."

Julien grunted in agreement and led them down the spiral steps to the ground. The tower was locked, but it only took a quick spell from Noah to open the door once they reached the bottom.

They managed to find a clothing store not too far from where they were, limiting the number of strange stares they received, but clothing everyone wasn't free, and Trent was the only one with any money to speak of. Maybe he would have to pawn one of his watches sooner than he'd expected. Julien, at least, promised to give him some money when they got to his house. Ciaran had temporarily solved the problem of his lack of invisibility with the hat they'd bought back when they first came to Ireland, which hid his ears effectively enough to keep him from drawing attention. And since Rathgeirr was still invisible, they didn't have to worry about clothing him—only keeping him from wandering off every other step.

"I didn't know you had a house," Noah said as he plucked the tag off of his new jeans. He walked with one hand clinging to the back of Rathgeirr's cloak, as though the alfar was a child prone to straying.

"It isn't mine," Julien answered. "Not really. It's the family home. My brothers and uncles and I stay there when we're in the city. My brothers had been telling me to come home before we left for Ireland, so I assume at least some of them will be there now. If nothing else, I'll be able to call Edouard."

"Are your brothers like you?" Rathgeirr asked. "You all hunt monsters?"

"Yes. And they're not going to be pleased at my bringing home any of you. I'm hoping they'll overlook it in light of the situation," he muttered, not seeming particularly convinced that was likely in the slightest. He glanced over at Rathgeirr without stopping. "Maybe don't show yourself until I've spoken to them."

The alfar nodded. "Whatever you think is best."

The house Julien led them to was at the top of a hill lined with square stone buildings that looked more like apartments than homes. Julien stopped in front of a squat-looking three story house made of red brick, the front wall dotted with neat rows of small windows. The bottom two windows beside the door had carved gargoyle faces above them, glaring down at the group on the sidewalk as though daring them to approach. Julien took the short set of steps two at a time and tilted one of the heavy stone vases flanking the door to fetch the key underneath. He shifted his bag on his shoulder as he unlocked the door and pushed it open.

The inside of the house was remarkably sterile. The tile of the entryway was well worn, and the wood floor beyond creaked under the hunter's steps, but there was nothing on the walls. No photos, no paintings, not even attractive wallpaper—nothing that made the place seem like a home. The only sign that anyone had ever lived there were the scuffs on the walls and the strip of worn-away paint on the center of the staircase across the room.

"Edouard!" Julien called a few steps into the front hall. "Joseph! Personne icitte?"

A set of double doors opened around the corner, and the group turned to face the sound. A grizzled man in his forties stood in the doorway with a heavy frown on his face. A set of clawmark scars ran across his left cheek, the puckered skin leaving the corner of his mouth in a permanent grimace. Behind him, five other men stood at a long table covered in papers, maps, and a pair of laptops, and every face turned to look through the door at the newcomer. Noah knew them right away—he saw Julien's tense shoulders, his thin frown, and dirty blond hair pushed out of hard faces just like his.

"Le septième fils revient," the man in the doorway said with mock admiration. "It's about fucking time."

TO KEEP YOU NEAR

ABOUT THE AUTHOR

T.S. Barnett is the author of The Beast of Birmingham werewolf thriller series, steampunk horror romance A Soul's Worth, dark urban fantasy series The Left-Hand Path, and a number of m/m paranormal romances.

T.S. likes to write about what makes people tick, whether that's deeply-rooted emotional issues, childhood trauma, or just plain hedonism. Throw in a heaping helping of action and violence, a sprinkling of steamy bits, and a whisper of wit (with alliteration optional but preferred), and you have her idea of a perfect novel. She believes in telling stories about real people who live in less-real worlds full of werewolves, witches, demons, vampires, and the occasional alien.

Born and bred in the South, T.S. started writing young, but began writing real novels while working full time as a legal secretary. When she's not writing, she reads other people's books, plays video games, watches movies, and spends time with her husband and daughter. She hopes her daughter grows into a woman who knows what she wants, grabs it, and gets into significantly less trouble than the women in her mother's novels.

www.hisprincelydelicates.com

Made in the USA
San Bernardino, CA
18 June 2017